ALIEN OVERNIGHT
ROBIN L. ROTHAM

ELLORA'S CAVE
ROMANTICA PUBLISHING

An Ellora's Cave Romantica Publication

www.ellorascave.com

Alien Overnight

ISBN 9781419956546
ALL RIGHTS RESERVED.
Alien Overnight Copyright © 2007 Robin L. Rotham
Edited by Heather Osborn & Mary Altman
Photography and cover art by Les Byerley

This book printed in the U.S.A. by Jasmine-Jade Enterprises, LLC.

Electronic book Publication May 2007
Trade paperback Publication June 2007

Content Advisory:

S – ENSUOUS
E – ROTIC
X – TREME

Ellora's Cave Publishing offers three levels of Romantica™ reading entertainment: S (S-ensuous), E (E-rotic), and X (X-treme).

The following material contains graphic sexual content meant for mature readers. This story has been rated E–rotic.

S-*ensuous* love scenes are explicit and leave nothing to the imagination.

E-*rotic* love scenes are explicit, leave nothing to the imagination, and are high in volume per the overall word count. E-rated titles might contain material that some readers find objectionable—in other words, almost anything goes, sexually. E-rated titles are the most graphic titles we carry in terms of both sexual language and descriptiveness in these works of literature.

X-*treme* titles differ from E-rated titles only in plot premise and storyline execution. Stories designated with the letter X tend to contain difficult or controversial subject matter not for the faint of heart.

About the Author

இ

A bookworm from the age of ten, Robin L. Rotham lived vicariously through daring, romantic heroines for nearly twenty years, dreaming all the while of one day writing her own romance novels, as well as her own happily ever after. When she finally found her real-life hero, he wasn't quite what--or where--she expected. Undaunted, she chased him over three states and four years before he finally swept her off her feet. He's been more than worth the effort.

The realities of home and family kept her from fulfilling her other dream for ten more years, but Robin finally succumbed to the writing bug in 2005 and cranked out her first novel on a used laptop from eBay in less than seven weeks. Alien Overnight is her second completed novel.

Robin welcomes comments from readers. You can find her website and email address on her author bio page at www.ellorascave.com.

Tell Us What You Think

We appreciate hearing reader opinions about our books. You can email us at Comments@EllorasCave.com.

ALIEN OVERNIGHT

∾

Trademarks Acknowledgement

Chapter One

෨

"Notice the slight emergence of the male's accessory sexual organ, or what the Garathani refer to as a breeding spur."

Kellen bit back a grin at Dr. Alvin Snow's play-by-play of the xenophysiology demonstration currently spotlighted in the dim theater-style classroom. His hushed delivery called to mind one of those fascinating televised nature programs, where the khaki-clad host hid in the bushes with a microphone while two wild animals went at it, oblivious to the watchful lens of his camera. Only *these* particular animals were both perfectly cognizant of their audience and could hear and understand every word the man said.

The female subject, a plump and greedy red-haired Terran whose pronounced facial grooves and silvery abdominal stretch marks proclaimed her well past the established age limit for reproductive service, grasped anxiously at Ensign Hastion's flexing buttocks and whimpered for more. He gave it, pounding her without reservation, knowing as they all did that this female had already accommodated another Garathani soldier with ease. Her shout of approval tightened Kellen's scrotum and he shallowed his breathing in an effort to relax it. The degree of exhibitionism this creature displayed was unheard-of among Garathani females, but he was disinclined to condemn it, in light of its service to his people—not to mention the vicarious pleasure it afforded him.

The appropriately white-haired Dr. Snow cleared his throat and continued, "Garathani texts place the time from penile penetration to full spur emergence at typically ten to fifteen minutes. However, because of the protracted nature of this male's enforced abstinence, today's interval will be somewhat shorter."

Now there was an understatement if he'd ever heard one. Already, Hastion's spur was beginning to ride up into the hollow where an intriguingly narrow strip of orange pubic hair met the female's denuded labia, and she was carrying on as if she were about to expire from the pleasure of it. And pleasure it was, though a few of the sixteen Terran females in the study group looked as if they had their doubts. Most of the males, on the other hand, were exhibiting signs of arousal, their faces flushed and respiration rapid. So much for their claims of clinical detachment. They had no more control than he and his men, some of whom had suffered in excess of eleven Terran years without mating.

Could they possibly have any concept of the delicious torture it was for a Garathani soldier to stand guard over such a demonstration? Obviously not. If they had, their female colleagues would be locked safely away in another part of the compound instead of sitting there among them, fragrant and tender and begging to be impaled without warning, much less consent.

The Powers take him if he wasn't having trouble resisting the call of their alien flesh himself. His head swam with the musk of aroused female, and not just the one onstage. Three others sat among the crowd, weeping from their feminine passages and no doubt imagining their succulent secrets were inviolate. In this case, ignorance was indeed bliss. Terran females were oddly defensive of their personal scents, and these three would probably drop dead from the shame of knowing that every Garathani nose in the room, followed closely by every Garathani cock, had homed in on their genitalia.

Cock. The word prompted an inward smile, conjuring images of unruly feathered heads straining to escape the confines of his officers' uniforms. Comprehensive download aside, English was an elusive and remarkably messy tongue in which Kellen found new idiosyncrasies to appreciate daily. In truth, no cerecom program could teach the more engaging subtleties of a language as well as a year or two spent among the natives.

Dr. Snow's renewed commentary interrupted his musings.

"The fully extended spur is designed to penetrate the Garathani female's complementary orifice or, loosely translated, her spur nook. We have no firsthand knowledge of this structure, since only Garathani males are included in our studies, but the delegation's physicians tell us that it houses their females' equivalent of a clitoris."

Kellen shifted his stance. The last thing he needed to think about was the welcoming quiver of a nook under his long-deprived spur. Glancing across the classroom at Shauss, who appeared to be suffering the agonies of the condemned, he finally gave in to the grin and accessed his cerecom.

Are you going to walk out of here with your dignity intact, Lieutenant?

Shauss returned the grin with a grimace as a bead of sweat trickled down his brow. *Hope springs eternal, Sir.*

Ah, I like that one. Pithy.

Yes, Commander, by all means, let us examine the complexities of the English language for the next three to five minutes. Perhaps that will bank the open fires currently roasting my chestnuts.

Kellen's chest shook with silent laughter. *Oh, now that one I like even better, my friend.*

Why are you not suffering as I am?

Rest assured, I'm emitting as fast and thick as the rest of you. It's probably a good thing there are no Garathani maidens in the room. Between the five of us, we'd have them under the table by now.

Under the table, Sir?

Drunk off their asses.

Ah.

Judging by his increasingly rough thrusts and the sweat condensing on his sleek musculature, Ensign Hastion was reaching critical mass. Unable to help himself, Kellen watched as Hastion pulled out and flipped the female onto her belly, yanking her to her knees and immediately driving his desperate length back into her glistening red vaginal opening, his spur coming closer to her puckered anal sphincter with every thrust.

That could be him soon, Kellen was a bit disturbed to realize, ramming himself into an unfamiliar backside with less sentiment than an animal. He'd never taken a female in such a position, would never have thought to introduce his spur into his mate's waste canal, not that she'd have permitted it. But considering the yawning span of years since he'd last spent his seed, the idea was far less unpalatable than it might once have been.

"The position of a Terran woman's anus relative to her vagina, and the sturdy thickness of the tissue separating vagina from rectum, make it possible for the Garathani's spur not only to penetrate, but to clamp down sufficiently for ejaculation to occur," the doctor continued. "Which is why Terran females are such ideal candidates for both copulative and reproductive services to the Garathani."

Hastion paused to adjust the positioning of his knees, grasping the female's fleshy hips tightly to perfect his angle for double penetration. He was just driving inward when Dr. Snow cleared his throat.

"Excuse me, Ensign—this might be a good time for the students to get a look at your spur."

Opening the link to Hastion, Shauss commiserated, *Oh, now* that's *brutal.*

But that's the agreement, Hastion sighed. Jaw clenched, eyes squeezed shut, he pulled out altogether and leaned back on his hands, arching his pelvis upward to display his jutting sexual organs. The smooth-skinned spur, broader and flatter than Kellen's own, showed no signs of flagging under the

Terrans' scrutiny. An abundance of natural female lubricant matted the dark hair at Hastion's groin, a single shimmering strand of it bridging the gap between the head of his penis and her swollen opening. How long could it hang there?

Only Kellen's acute Garathani hearing, picking up two barely audible whispers from the back of the room, saved him from the lustful abyss threatening to engulf him at the intimate sight.

"I wish I had binoculars."

"Binoculars, hell. I wish I had my camera."

Peserin's gown! He averted his eyes with a tight smile, tucking the mental image safely away before it brought him to his knees.

"You'll note that this male exhibits textbook erectile proportions, having a spur length of roughly one-half that of his penis," the doctor approved. "We're still uncertain why ejaculation can't be manually or artificially induced, but we'll continue to investigate all conceivable causes, including both physiological and psychological."

I beg your pardon? Shauss' eyes grew wide as he stiffened. *Did he just suggest the problem might be all in our* heads?

Stand down, Lieutenant, Kellen ordered. *Terrans tend to leave no stone, however futile, unturned. You should be used to it by now.*

"Thank you, Ensign. Please continue."

Needing no further encouragement, Hastion sprang forward and powered into the redhead. She let loose a throaty scream, twisting handfuls of the white hospital bedding beneath her forehead as his spur sank deep into her anal orifice, which had been carefully prepared prior to the demonstration. Or so Kellen had been told, although what it took to prepare her fell quite outside the scope of what he cared to know. Another glance around the dimmed room told him a few of the females were looking decidedly worried now, despite their foreknowledge of the subject's previous experience.

When her orgasmic cries threatened to completely undo him, Kellen turned his eyes to the wood-paneled wall ahead and mentally began reciting the elements of the periodic table—the complete one, not the pitifully inadequate Terran version—and their weights. He'd only gotten as far as helium when he heard the long, gurgling growl of a hungry stomach from very nearby.

His chin snapped down as he scanned the seats closest to him. When the rumbling sounded again, he zeroed in on a pair of Terran females. The tiny blonde had caught his notice earlier, simply because she insisted on looking everywhere but at the couple she was here to observe. The other one was leaning over her desk, arms wrapped across her stomach. At least he was fairly certain that one was female. He'd glimpsed her in the compound several times and wondered at her androgynous and deliberately bizarre look. The shells of her ears were lined with metal studs and rings, the opaque black of her hair, cut ruthlessly short, was obviously artificial, and her facial cosmetics appeared to have been applied with…some sort of gardening implement.

A *trowel*, that was it.

Mildly curious, he'd taken note of her, and upon hearing a colleague call her Dr. Gothchild, he'd looked up the name, only to find there was no such person listed on the compound's roster. A chance discussion among his men had enlightened him about the Goth subculture, thus explaining her appearance, and he'd promptly dismissed the odd female from his mind.

That might have been a mistake.

Her companion gaped in astonishment as the Goth female's stomach gurgled again.

Commander, are you hearing what I'm hearing?

Shauss' sharp gaze caught his.

"Jeez, Teague—try eating breakfast next time," one of the males leaned over and whispered.

"Had breakfast." The reply from the bent head was groggy, sounding urgent alarms in Kellen's head.

"Monica, are you okay?" asked her blonde friend.

In reply, the hunched-over Monica slurred, "Oh God, Shel, what are they cooking for lunch? It smells absolutely divine!"

Kellen's thoughts raced. Androgynous appearance, hunger response, olfactory excitement—

"Holy shit, are you drunk?" the male hissed.

And apparent intoxication in a room bursting with Garathani male pheromones...

Could she possibly be a Sparnite?

Kellen linked with the cerecom server.

Empran, research Monica Teague, current assignment Beaumont–Thayer Compound, he requested, his link with Shauss still open.

The computer replied almost instantly.

Beaumont–Thayer file incomplete. Searching alternate sources. Three seconds later, Empran continued, **Dr. Monica Sessienne Teague, female, aged thirty-two Terran years. Medical specialty, perinatology. Contracted for ten-year service on Garathan.**

Spell Sessienne.

His eyes narrowed as Empran complied. The name was too close for coincidence, and she was thirty-two, the perfect age...

Known developmental anomalies?

*Searching. Conflicting data, Commander. Only one of seven available pediatric charts cites incomplete development of reproductive organs. One gynecological examination at age fifteen, terminated prematurely for reasons unknown, notes delayed development of secondary sexual characteristics. Beaumont–Thayer

intake documents indicate sterility attributed to anovulation, no determination of pathology.*

With his heartbeat thrumming in his ears, Kellen ordered, *Empran, file an instant petition with the High Council on my behalf to claim full-spectrum mating privileges with Dr. Monica Teague, tentatively identified as a GaraTer hybrid. Request mass notification immediately upon approval, withholding the female's middle name, and restrict access to the petition.*

Shauss' eyes widened but he didn't comment.

Secondary claimant? Empran inquired.

Lieutenant Shauss.

I think I love you, Sir. Shauss grinned at him.

Kellen frowned. *Save it for the Sparnite.*

Tertiary claimant?

Reserve.

The next eighty-four seconds were the longest of his life. He and Shauss both stared at the female with an intensity that would probably have frightened her, had she raised her head and noticed them. The demonstration on stage was all but forgotten by the two officers as they watched her rock forward and back in her seat, taking deep breaths of the air so heavily saturated with their pheromones.

Petition filed, Council audience waived, unilateral approval by Minister Cecine. Mass notification pending.

At Empran's words, anticipation like he hadn't known in years hammered through Kellen and the smile that curved his lips must have been predatory indeed, because Shauss urged, *Careful, Commander. It could be months, even years before she matures enough for mating.* Then he had to go and add, *If she even survives.*

Kellen grimaced. It was nothing less than the truth—her death was not beyond the realm of possibility. Only a handful of Garathani females, fewer than two dozen in all of their recorded history, had ever experienced Sparna's Delay, and of those, six had not survived the violent maturation that commenced once they were exposed to male pheromones. There was no predicting what effect her Terran genes might have on the process. It seemed the odd but now infinitely precious Dr. Teague was about to make the history books on Garathan.

Unfortunately, he doubted she was going to enjoy the experience.

Critical notification, Empran announced over the cerecom system to every Garathani within range. Even Hastion paused mid-thrust to listen. *Effective immediately, Commander Kellen, third son Aizery, first house Menina, is awarded full-spectrum mating privileges with the GaraTer hybrid known as Dr. Monica Teague, current domicile Beaumont–Thayer Compound, Montana, United States, Planet Earth. The commander is seconded by Lieutenant Shauss, first son Frantere, third house Andagon, allegiance transfer pending. Tertiary claimant is in reserve. This award and all information related to it are classified under the seal of the Garathani High Council as authorized by Minister Cecine.*

Well, that bites, Hastion grimaced humorously over his shoulder as he resumed pounding his partner into erotic oblivion. *Here I am, taking one for the team —*

And we all feel so sorry for you, Shauss drawled.

While you two are busy snapping up one of the missing hybrids right — behind — my — back! Hastion exploded into the woman with a roar that provoked paper-shuffling and throat-clearing from one end of the classroom to the other.

Kellen just smiled.

* * * * *

"Cripes, Monica," Shelley muttered as the lights went up and doctors and nurses began shuffling out around them. "You picked a hell of a time to come in three sheets to the wind."

"I square to God, I haven't had a drop!" Monica leaned back in her seat, blinking at the sudden brightness.

"You *square*, huh?"

"Nice," Sean snorted. "You'd better pull your head out of your ass before Snow pulls the plug on your contract."

"Get lost, McKay," Shelley fired back. "I'll take care of Monica."

Monica sighed, her bleary eyes following the slightly squishy-looking butt of Dr. Sean McKay as he sauntered to the door. "God, Shel, I love you so much! Thank you for saving me from that creepin' cretin."

She giggled at her own creativity, giggled even louder when Shelley rolled her eyes.

"What is with you? Are you diabetic or something? Is your blood sugar bottoming out?"

"I don' know, but I'm absolutely staaaarving!" Monica bellowed, mystified yet pleased by the sensations that speaking so loudly sparked in her lower belly. "Take me to the catef-cafeteria and get me some o' whatever they're dishin' up today, 'cause, by God, it smells good enough to eat for a change!"

"Shhh!" Shelley looked around wildly before leaning over the side of her desk and muttering, "Sean wasn't kidding when he said Snow would have your butt in a sling if he thought you were drunk."

"Shhh-Sean, Shelley, Shnow. Shhh-Sean, Shelley, Shnow," Monica sang. "It's like a lil' tittie-twister, isn't it?"

"That's tongue-twister, you idiot! Now shut the fuck up before Dr. Snow comes over here!"

"May I be of assistance, ladies?"

Shelley's squeal of alarm made Monica laugh out loud. Then she caught sight of a bulging crotch covered in sublimely tight steel-gray synthetic and fell silent mid-guffaw. Her eyes traveled up, up, up, skimming over a granite belly, pecs that were sharply defined even in uniform and shoulders too wide to be real. She got hooked for a second on a set of sculpted lips and had to drag her eyes upward until they finally met the dark blue gaze of the formidable Commander Kellen.

Speaking of good enough to eat! The super-sized hot tamale looking down at her made half the female tongues in the compound drag the ground, and a few of the male ones, too. But not hers, though. Nuh-uh, no way, because God, he was so *fucking* far out of her orbit, he'd need the Hubble telescope to notice her. She'd be dumber than a bag of hammers to get all gooey over his lion-haired splendor.

"Ooooh, hi, Commander," she heard herself breathe anyway. God, when had she started talking like Marilyn Monroe? "Are you a gentle giant?"

Then she smacked herself on the forehead. *Duh!* Of course, he wasn't any such thing. He'd blasted Planet Narthan into a flaming charcoal briquette and roasted wienies over the smoldering embers. But what the hell. Nobody was perfect, and it wasn't like he didn't have cause, losing his wife and little girl that way.

Aw, the poor guy could probably use a hug.

The quirk of his lips as he crouched in front of her desk was inviting enough to make her breath catch in her throat. Okay, scratch the poor guy thing. And the hug. He was a hottie and he knew it, Conan the Barbarian with a James Bond accent. "When the occasion calls for it."

"And when it doesn't?" she dared. Shit, it almost sounded like she was flirting with him. *Flirting* with Kellen, the ass-kicking commander from outer space. And from Shelley's fish-eyed look, it sounded that way to her, too.

And hell if it wasn't giving Monica her first-ever tingle in panty territory. Okay, second-ever. Watching that other sweaty spaceman push his long hard self into Carrie's open charms had triggered the first-ever. Maybe this was only the beginning of a major tingle-fest south of her border. Wouldn't that be, like, the fucking greatest thing ever? She'd always secretly dreamed of tingling, especially whenever she passed the commander in the hall. He was hot enough to —

No! Monica tossed her spiky head back and forth, trying not to pout. Damn it, it just wasn't fair! She could flirt with the commander 'til the cows came home, but in the end, it would get her nowhere. Ever. Even if, in some freaky right turn into an alternate reality, she managed to catch this hunky alien's eye, the joke would be on the both of them, because the only two things he'd want from her, she had no way of supplying.

Sex and babies.

Damn it.

"Then I'm a different sort of giant altogether." The commander's reply to her sally was accompanied by a full-fledged grin that made her squirm with…something. Something sticky and warm and anxious. "But enough about me," he continued, lowering his tone. "I must apologize to you, Dr. Teague."

"Oh?"

Her little pity-party promptly forgotten, Monica followed his gaze as it flickered to Dr. Snow, who was now deep in conversation with — what was his name? Lieutenant…something. Shauss, that was it, Lieutenant Shauss. Now there was another primo piece of alien real estate. Why had she never noticed how yummy he was? Those thick streaks of pale blue in his otherwise black hair were just *inspired.* God, what she wouldn't give to trickle it through her —

"For your own safety," Kellen was saying, "I would advise you to keep what I'm about to tell you to yourselves." He paused and looked hard at Monica, probably making sure she was listening. To prove that she was, she forced her eyes as wide-open as they'd go, and he shook his head and sighed. "I believe that you, Dr. Teague, are experiencing pheromone intoxication."

"Excuse me?" she and Shelley said simultaneously.

"Jinx! You owe me a Coke!" Monica crowed.

"Congratulations, Doctor," Kellen said dryly. "As I was saying, you appear to have suffered an overexposure to Garathani pheromones. You must carry the twenty-second halethoid mutation, which renders Terrans' olfactory receptors more susceptible to their influence."

Monica gasped in outrage. "I do not!"

"It's nothing to be ashamed of, Doctor."

"I don't!"

"But you think it smells divine in here, don't you?" he challenged, glancing at Snow once more.

"Well, yeah, but that's just lunch."

Kellen looked at Shelley's BTC badge and asked, "So, S. Bonham, RN, have you noticed anything out of the ordinary? Does it smell to you like the kitchen is preparing something especially delicious?"

Shelley shook her head with a frown. "No, it smells like it always does in here, like new hospital and old jockstraps."

Monica struggled to her feet, anxiety suddenly taking hold of her. "I'm *not* a mutant. Now leave me alone."

When she turned to leave, the world swirled and she just about ended up on her ass. It was humiliating to be rescued by the commander, who swung her up in his incredibly hulky arms like the overgrown child she resembled. Thrilling, but humiliating.

"Let me help you to your quarters," he offered gently. "The effect should wear off within a half-hour of my departure."

Since her head was still spinning like she'd had one or six too many margaritas, Monica laid her head against his chest. *His mile-wide, rock-hard chest.* Her hand itched to slide over every pectoral hill and valley outlined by the satiny finish of his uniform, but she confined herself to a visual tour with a sigh of regret. Some behaviors were just too deeply ingrained to be overridden, even by the table-dancingest, lampshade-wearingest kind of intoxication.

Damn it.

"Lay on, MacDuff," she murmured, closing her eyes and basking in the novelty of being carried for the first time in her memory. That lovely, scrumptious scent drew her nose to his armpit, where she sucked in a lungful and held it before exhaling in a rapturous rush. "Oh my God, did anyone ever tell you that you smell good enough to eat?"

"Yes, but not recently," came the amused chuckle in her ear. "Thank you for saying so."

"Hey, why hasn't this ever happened to her before?" From the sound of her huffing and puffing, Shelley must be practically running to keep up with them. "She works with you guys every day."

Kellen's hesitation made Monica open her eyes and look at him. It was disconcerting to find him looking back. Such amazing eyes. Maybe if she stared into that velvety navy-blue long enough, she'd see stars.

"We only emit actively when we're excited. Sexually."

Sexually. Ooooh, that tantalizingly adult word, so rich and delicious as it dripped off his tongue, made her shudder. She was seeing stars, all right, and they were falling fast and landing hard, right in her achingly empty lap.

"So it was the guy doing the na—er, *performing* on stage who caused this?" Shelley asked.

Stopping in the middle of the hall, Kellen and his amazing eyes looked at her friend. "In a sense. To be perfectly truthful, the demonstration was arousing enough to the rest of us that our glands…went into overdrive, so to speak. It takes more than one emitting male to saturate a room that size."

Diverted by the play of muscles in his jaw as he spoke, it took a moment for Monica to assimilate what he'd said.

"You're horny!" she accused, wide-eyed, her heartbeat accelerating. Part of her was horrified, knew she ought to be blushing to the tips of her toes at both the idea and her own candor. Fortunately, that part of her brain currently in the driver's seat was deriving too much pleasure from the flurry of intriguing visuals to be concerned. "That's why you smell so good."

"Yeah, okay, Monica, we get the picture," Shelley hurried to head her off.

Although Kellen's gaze had focused on Monica once more, it was his tongue that distracted her now, snaking out to lick his lips before he answered as if Shelley hadn't spoken.

"Guilty as charged."

Uh-oh. Her heart stopped as his confession echoed in her head. Just stopped dead, right there in her chest. *Beat, damn it, beat*! Then her brain signaled that she wasn't getting any air, either. *And breathe, damn it, breathe*! What the hell was going on with her autonomic nervous system? Weren't these things supposed to take care of themselves?

Her pulse rebounded with a thump, her indrawn breath with a shudder. But then she noticed the saliva pooling under her tongue and had to swallow audibly. Oh God, the commander was horny, and he was holding her, and his lips were thick and shiny and they'd be close enough to suck on, if she just had the guts to grab his neck...

Like he'd want to kiss a freak like you, the ugly voice of sobriety sneered.

Monica squeezed her eyes shut tight and set her jaw, suddenly depressed and weary.

"Well, not to worry. You should be back to normal shortly," she choked with a bitter laugh, pressing her face into his chest for one last snuggle as he continued down the corridor. "Shelley's knocked up and I'm glandularly challenged, so there should be nothing here to turn you on."

His murmured reply was too low for her to catch and she was too tired to ask him to repeat it. By the time he laid her on the bed, she couldn't even manage to thank him properly and she was out like a light before he'd left the room.

* * * * *

Kellen strode down the corridor at a brisk pace, filled with purpose, energized by this morning's coup and the subsequent encounter with his new mate.

Don't bet on it, he'd told her. The unexpected and charmingly offbeat Dr. Teague may not be emitting pheromones of her own just yet, and her current form certainly made him doubt she would ever develop any measure of physical beauty, but the knowledge of her Garathani heritage and her all-but-irrevocable bond with him made his cock rise to rapt attention. Convincing it to stand down until she was ripe for mating would require heroic resolve. Or an entire vat of Malascan ale.

Convincing it to stand down *after* she was ripe for mating… His lips curled in a wicked smile. Here he'd been bracing himself for the occasional and hopefully brief coupling with a Terran female, and instead the Powers had seen fit to bless him with the object of his darkest fantasies—a Garathani female without rank or authority. Refusing to even consider that her Terran genes might have shown themselves between her legs, Kellen began counting the ways he would enjoy her and wondered if his cock would ever stand down again.

He had to stop outside the door and adjust himself before stepping into the diplomatic offices. A waiting page led him directly to Ambassador Pret.

"Congratulations, Commander," Pret told him. "I was dumbfounded to learn that a hybrid was hiding right under our noses."

"Thank you." Kellen sank into an oversized conference chair and took the proffered mug of lorba tea, though ale would have stood him in better stead. "No one was more surprised than I."

"And let me compliment you on your deft handling of the matter. Many others might have requested probabilities on hybridism or Sparnism before filing."

"Many others might have had their petitions preempted by some com-hacking opportunist," Kellen pointed out. "Since I'm more than capable of calculating probabilities for myself, I decided not to take the chance."

"A shrewd, if somewhat cynical decision on your part, Commander. You should consider a transfer to the diplomatic corps when this assignment ends. We could use an officer who thinks on his feet, as it were."

Not likely, Kellen thought, amused by the quandary of being too innately honest for diplomatic assignments but too diplomatic to say so. He took a sip of the tea and then reached to set the mug on a strategically positioned coaster on the ambassador's polished cherry desk.

"I was wondering if you could get Dr. Teague reassigned as my aide," he said casually as he leaned back and crossed his ankles.

Pret's brows rose. "With all due respect, Commander, I would have thought you'd remove her at once to the *Heptoral*."

"That would, of course, be my preference." In fact, only Nurse Bonham's watchful presence had prevented him from flaring the little doctor directly to his on-board quarters. His initial annoyance had given way to amusement and then a grudging respect for the way she protected her unconscious friend. Obviously frightened of him, she'd nonetheless stood there with her hand on the knob of the open door, inviting him without words to leave. After a lingering glance at the boneless figure on the bed, he'd bowed slightly and taken his leave.

His bow, once a deeply ingrained habit, a gesture of deference from a bygone era, had taken him by surprise. He hadn't bowed to a female since... Actually, he couldn't remember the last time he'd felt compelled to bow to a female out of genuine respect. He'd always bowed because it was customary and expected. And more importantly, because to not bow was to invite retribution.

"Unfortunately," he continued, his look daring Pret to object, "there are factors at work here besides my personal preferences."

The ambassador turned away at once, making a show of topping off Kellen's still-full mug from an ornate sterling teapot. The dainty Terran antique couldn't have looked more ridiculous in his long fingers.

"You, of course, must be the judge of that." He set the pot down with meticulous care, aligning the handle at a precise ninety-degree angle to the tray, then focused on Kellen once more. "Having the good doctor transferred to your service shouldn't present a problem. But I'm certain you'll agree with the necessity of keeping the truth of her parentage from the Terrans for as long as possible. I wouldn't put it past them to whisk her away for use as leverage against us."

"That would be quite unwise," Kellen said dryly. "We wouldn't even have to destroy them ourselves. Simply posting a habitat beacon on their solar system would attract every scavenger race from Aptorm to Zeccha."

"Wisdom and elected officials rarely walk hand in hand, Commander."

"It's not the elected officials who concern me."

"Ah—you're referring to TAIM?"

"Among others." Terrans Against Interspecies Mating, while certainly a nuisance, was only one of a dozen or more groups that had sprung up in opposition to the Alliance since its formal inception almost a year ago. Most of them were spawned in cyberspace, and for the most part only existed there, circulating fantastic propaganda in an effort to sway public opinion against the Garathani. TAIM, on the other hand, was a well-organized campaign with seemingly bottomless pockets, and their thinking man's approach to scare tactics had done much to foment Terran distrust of the Alliance. But Kellen wasn't convinced TAIM was the true threat. No, it was the nameless, faceless splinter groups that worried him.

"Put a protective detail on her, just in case," Pret cautioned.

"Already done. Bayan and Tarkan units are covering her now and three more have been called into the rotation."

"Good. Cecine would be quite displeased," the ambassador concluded with a speaking look, "were anything to happen to this one."

Kellen's jaw tightened. How had he found out so quickly?

Mentally consigning all diplomats to the oiliest corners of Peserin's hell, Kellen returned his look with a flat stare.

"Not nearly as displeased as I."

Chapter Two

ↀ

Monica squinted at the digital numbers glaring in the dark of her room and groaned. Three-thirty had never been her favorite time of the morning, but lately she was starting to flat-out hate it. Almost of their own volition, her legs shifted beneath the quilts she'd piled on in a futile attempt to ward off the brutal bone pain and cramps that had kept her awake the past few nights. The ibuprofen she'd taken before coming to bed at eleven had worn off and the ache in her legs now throbbed with a sharp intensity that made her want to scream. It felt like hundreds of tiny gremlins were gouging the marrow out of her femurs with ice picks, and now the bones in her calves and feet were getting in on the action, too.

Rolling to her stomach, she groaned again, as much in anxiety as in pain. Bone pain at her age was rarely a good thing, and if she let herself dwell on the possible causes, each more dire than the last, she could work herself into a hot lather in under two minutes.

Cursing, Monica threw back the quilts and stumbled into the adjoining bathroom. After using the toilet in the shadow of the night light, she pawed through the medicine cabinet in search of acetaminophen, knowing she was probably killing off more liver cells than she could afford by taking so much over-the-counter pain reliever. God, maybe she'd better see someone…

She squashed the thought before it could take root. If this was something that would kill her, she might as well let it, because she'd be too miserable to live if she got scrubbed from the mission now.

Three caplets and sixteen ounces of icy-cold Montana tap water later, she was snuggled under the quilts once more, thinking she'd have to order a heating pad or an electric blanket from the quartermaster in the morning. Drifting into a fitful sleep, she finally found relief in the heady otherworld of her dreams.

She always smelled him first, that deliciously spicy, savory yet sweet odor that no one but she seemed to notice. All the Garathani smelled yummy even when they weren't aroused, like towering homemade gingerbread men. *His* scent especially, which really reminded her more of mincemeat pie, made Monica's stomach growl with hunger. She took several deep breaths, coating her airways and saturating her senses with it, feeling her body relax and grow strangely alert at the same time.

Then the quilts were drawn away and the chill of sixty-degree air seeped through her thermals for just an instant before her back was covered once more, this time by an extraordinarily large and heavy male body.

Monica sighed with delight. Oh, now this was more like it. This was the kind of dream she'd always wanted to have. She groaned with pleasure at the steady breaths gusting warm and damp against the side of her neck, shivered with anticipation at the sheer size and hardness of the arms braced beside her shoulders. His spread thighs bracketing hers brought tears of relief to her eyes, their incredible heat making her squirm to get closer. In response, he settled firmly against her back and she moaned again. Forget the electric blanket— this man was a Grade-A blast furnace.

"God, could you do this every night?" she mumbled, dragging her arms up and resting her forehead on her stacked hands. The low rumble of his chuckle and the quick puff of his hot breath against her ear gave Monica another shiver. The sinuous stirring against her bottom, however, made her tense up, more aware than she'd been since his short stint as a xenoanatomy subject of how potently male—and how frighteningly alien—he truly was.

Uneasy now, she lifted her head and opened her eyes.

Oh yeah. This dream she'd gladly have every night for the rest of her life. She was squashed into a sandy, palm-dotted beach, the turquoise waters of the Caribbean rushing toward her and receding, the midday sun beating down on her back. Now, if only she had a fruity umbrella drink and the latest Michael Crichton thriller...

"You're asleep," came the soothing whisper in her ear, and she sighed as she laid her head down once more.

"I know, but it still feels weird. It's not often I have a dream where I know I'm dreaming. I think I like it." His scent was getting stronger and she lapped it up, breathing in greedy lungfuls as she lay basking in the fabulous heat.

"Who am I?"

"Kellen," she answered without hesitation. "You're *always* Kellen."

"You dream of me often." It wasn't a question.

"Sometimes." The stirring against her rear end became a nudging and she squirmed restlessly. "But not like this."

"You will from now on," he murmured, settling even more heavily against her backside.

"Promise?" Her question ended on a gasp as he slid one of his gigantic hands beneath her chest. She tried to twist away, ashamed of her inadequacy even in sleep, but he ignored her struggles and closed in on her right nipple. His thumb brushed over her, and the roughness of it through the weave of her thermals produced a rush of feeling so intense it knocked the breath from her lungs. He stroked over the tiny nipple again and again, and Monica thrashed under the weight of him. Her pulse was racing, her breathing erratic, so frightening were the sensations rippling through her.

Or was it the idea of waking up and feeling those sensations slip away as if they'd never been that made her so frantic?

"What are you doing to me?" she moaned. In answer, he pinched her nipple between his thumb and finger and pulled sharply. Lightning blasted down her body, striking hard between her thighs and ripping a strangled scream from her throat.

"Preparing you, little Terran." The reply was dark with humor and something else... Any attempt she might have made to figure it out was lost to the feel of his mouth opening against the side of her throat. His tongue licked out, scorching a trail of fire up to her ear, and she whimpered.

"Oh God, for what?"

His left hand edged beneath her thermals to pluck at her other nipple and she lurched, howling at the shower of sparks splashing into her belly.

He chuckled as he nipped at her earlobe. "For an alien invasion."

* * * * *

Monica woke with a start, jerking straight up in bed. Bright morning light pierced her eyes and she shaded them quickly with one hand, her head pounding in sync with the rhythm of her heart.

Bright morning light... Holy shit, what time was it?

"Ten-fourteen!"

She was out of bed and stripped to the skin before the echo of her shout died. Thankful there was no window in the bathroom, she left the vanity lights off while she gulped down more ibuprofen and brushed her teeth. Wrenching open the taps, she stepped under the cool spray and showered in record time despite the headache that knifed through her eyeballs. After toweling off her hair, she spritzed and sculpted it into its usual spiky disarray with her fingers, eyes slitted against the dim light. How long had it been since she'd had it cut, anyway? Seemed like it was just last week, but hell if the mop on her head wasn't getting shaggy again.

Squinting against the glare of the bedroom, she bypassed her makeup tray for the first time since arriving at Beaumont–Thayer. If her coworkers didn't all know she was a freak already, they would once they saw her today. The dramatic Goth makeup made her skin appear ashen, but without it, she looked positively cyanotic. Damn near purple, in fact.

Fuck 'em, she thought, tugging plain white panties up legs that were too long to be so chubby and stepping into a pair of wool socks. She'd just have to be careful not to close her eyes or someone might call a code on her.

It occurred to her that the pain had finally left her legs sometime during the night. Too bad it had ridden a bullet straight to her brain. God, if it wasn't one damn thing it was another. She sighed at the injustice of it all as she scrambled into ultra-thin long underwear and a set of scrubs. Once all her jewelry was in place—there was a limit to how much personal armor a girl could stand to leave off—she plopped large horn-rimmed glasses onto her nose. Contacts were out of the question, with her eyes already killing her.

"Hmm." Changing her mind, Monica slid the glasses off and tucked them into her breast pocket, then pulled open the top drawer of the highboy and rooted through her underwear until she found the rigid plastic case containing her prescription sunglasses. She hadn't worn them in months because there was nowhere to go and no way to get there, out here in middle of the great frozen north. Blowing a few specks off the lenses, she slid them on. Ah, much better. Now she could approach the window without breaking into a cold sweat from the pain.

She stepped to the bedside table and frowned to see the alarm on her clock turned off. Man, she must have been totally zonked to do that and not remember it. Then again, it had been a hard night, filled with bizarre dreams.

Erotic dreams.

Monica sank to her knees beside the bed with the intention of reaching underneath for her clogs, but...*wow.* She'd finally had her first erotic dream, and man, had it ever been a doozy. Heat trickled down her belly even as she sucked in a tremulous breath of dismay. *Oh shit—please tell me you didn't dream about* him! She had to work with the commander every day now, since her sudden transfer three weeks ago.

Maybe it had been Lieutenant Shauss. Yeah, that was it. That guy was everywhere she went these days, and he always seemed to be watching her, so whose fault was it if she was getting strange ideas?

Not hers, that was for damn sure.

Furious knocking made her jump.

"Hey, Gothchild! You in there?"

Shelley's voice was reassuring in its teasing concern. Sliding into her clogs, Monica shook off the feeling of impending disaster and grabbed her keys before throwing open the door.

"I decided to give bankers' hours a whirl," she joked with a sheepish smile as she stepped into the hall and headed for the evaluation clinic. After a couple of steps, she trod harder, trying to shove her feet further into the clogs. God, why did it seem like her heels were hanging off the open backs? Maybe these new socks were too thick—she'd have to change them at lunch. Assuming she got lunch. God, she'd better get lunch. After missing breakfast, it felt like her navel was kissing her spine.

"Even bankers go to work earlier than this," Shelley scoffed. "By the way, that's a charming shade of lavender you're wearing today."

"Bite me." They'd spent enough free time together that Shelley had seen her sans camouflage before, but apparently not often enough for her to resist commenting on it.

"And nice glasses. You tie one on last night or what?"

"Or what." At Shelley's look, she added, "I'll tell you about it at lunch, okay?"

"Fine, but you owe me. Your boss came into the clinic looking for you and stood about this," she held her thumb and forefinger a millimeter apart, "close to me, thank you very much." Shelley shuddered. "I don't know how you stand spending so much time around them, and I sure as hell don't get why you'd want to spend the next ten years living among them."

"Pansy," Monica dissed with a grin.

"You bet your ass, and like all good pansies, I belong firmly planted on Earth."

"That's just fine — more room in the cosmos for me, then. Did I miss anything important this morning?"

"Just your first orientation," Shelley said dryly. "But no worries — Dr. Emrich wanted to trade for the morning group anyway."

Monica stopped dead in front of the reception desk and stared at her. "I can't believe I slept through the start of orientation. My God, that's one of the main reasons I'm here, to help get these women — "

"Chill, Gothchild. Like I was saying, you're taking his afternoon session, where you'll get to orient just as many doomed women as you would have this morning, if not more. Now get a move on. The commander's looking for you, remember?"

"Right." Heat flooded her cheeks as the memory of her dream surfaced, and Monica looked away, her pulse spiking. She could lie to herself all she wanted, but it *had* been him. Damn it. Why couldn't it have been George Clooney all snuggled up to her backside, fondling her nonexistent breasts under the tropical sun? There wasn't a chance in hell she'd ever have to look *him* in the eye.

"So why aren't you moving?" Shelley asked when she hesitated.

"Just thinking."

"Well, think about doing your roots. Your hair is pretty funkedelic this morning."

"Already!" Monica's hands flew to her hair.

"And think about giving Laundry hell, too, for leaving you the wrong scrubs. You look like you're expecting a flood."

Monica glanced down at her woolly ankles and frowned.

"Gee, I'll get right on that. Anything else, Mother?"

"Yeah—get your rear in gear!"

* * * * *

Thankfully, other than the bevy of stone-faced guards lining the halls lately, the only soul she passed on the way to her airless little broom closet was Jasmine King, one of the shared secretaries.

"Don't tell me—your car wouldn't start," Jasmine teased, handing over a cup of fragrant coffee from the gourmet machine behind her desk. "Or was traffic murder?"

Monica bared her teeth in a snarl over the rim before taking a too-hot gulp. There were definite disadvantages to living where you worked, chief among them being that there was no excusable reason for being late. And there was no playing hooky, either, because the minute you called in sick, a gaggle of doctors was beating down the door, trying to take your vitals, palpate every inch of your skin and culture your every orifice. She knew this from personal experience and would never try it again.

Jasmine's grin broadened. "So, are you auditioning for the lead in a vampire flick today or what?"

"Everybody's a comedian," Monica muttered.

"Seriously, woman, you totally look like a corpse. And what's with the shades? Did you finally piss somebody off enough to take a swing at you?"

Tipping her sunglasses down, she glared at the lovely Jasmine, tall and elegant as ever in a beige business suit that emphasized her tasteful curves and made her peaches-and-cream complexion glow like she'd swallowed the sunrise. Was the little witch even wearing any makeup? If she was, it was good. Really good. Such understated perfection made Monica feel even more like the frump-slash-freak she was, but Jasmine was so nice — when she wasn't being a pain in the ass — that she just couldn't hold it against her.

"I have a headache, Stepford, and if you tell anyone, you'll need more than sunglasses to cover what I do to your face."

"Nice. Didn't you take some kind of oath to do no harm?"

"Knowing I was bound to run into people like you, I crossed my fingers."

Jasmine's short laugh made Monica hide a grin as she started down the line of cubicles toward her office.

"Hey, Monica — wait a minute."

She stopped and looked at Jasmine, who was waving her back with a furtive look on her face. Curious, Monica approached her desk once more, and Jasmine stood up and looked around before gesturing for her to come closer.

"The commander's been looking for you," she said in a low voice.

After the pulse spike waned, Monica crooked a brow at her. "Of course he's looking for me. I'm three hours late."

Jasmine bit her lip.

"Hello?" Monica prodded when she failed to say anything more. "What is it you're not telling me?"

"I'm not sure," came the frustrated reply. "I'm just getting a weird vibe lately."

"Vibe? What, is my aura shaking or something?"

Jasmine frowned. "Monica, I'm serious. Haven't you noticed all the guards in the halls?"

"Yeah. What about them?"

"Doesn't it seem like they're kind of...guarding *you*?"

Monica stared, her mind racing. Shit, she was probably right. No doubt the commander had sicced the guards on her out of concern that the pheromone incident might repeat itself. The jerk. She'd *told* him it wouldn't happen again, now that she knew to steer clear of the demonstrations.

"Don't worry," she said with authority. "I'll take care of it."

She strode down the hall, prickling with annoyance. It was bad enough he'd had her transferred without asking permission, and that he had Lieutenant Shauss skulking around keeping an eye on her. But to have posted a whole slew of guards to make sure she didn't molest some unsuspecting—

My God, does he think I'm going to attack him?

Cheeks burning, Monica slammed the door behind her and then immediately wished she hadn't. Fucking headache. She yanked her lab coat off a hook on the wall and pulled it on, then sank into the cheap imitation leather executive chair, holding her breath as it creaked under her weight. An impatient nudge of the mouse activated her computer, and she sucked down more coffee—hazelnut this morning, her favorite—and brooded while waiting for her e-mail folder to pop up.

Here she was, having erotic dreams about the commander, and he had her under guard! Why did *he* have to be the one who made her pulse spike, damn it?

Finding nothing in her inbox—surprise, surprise—she pulled a file from the mess on her credenza and tried to turn her attention to work. Spreading the folder open on her desk, she flipped past the first few pages until she came to the list of recruits for the afternoon orientation. There were seventy-two names in all, and though right now they were little more than ink on paper, a meaningless collection of statistics, soon many of these women would become her patients, her charges and perhaps even her friends. Tomorrow the first of their physical evaluations would commence, putting her one step closer to the launch pad.

A rebel yell nearly burst from her at the thought.

If someone had told her five years ago that one day she'd travel God knew how many light-years to help repopulate a planet decimated by genocidal enemies, she'd have sworn they were on crack. Or looked for the hidden camera. Everyone knew she was a total space nut and she wouldn't have put it past some of her coworkers to humiliate her on national television.

For as long as she could remember, Monica had dreamed of being an astronaut, but with a list of physical defects as long as her arm, she'd never stood a snowball's chance of making it into the space program. So she'd settled instead for studying astronomy, devouring science fiction novels and following every *Star Trek* and *Star Wars* incarnation with fanatical devotion. Her obsession with space hadn't made her many friends, but it had sustained her through her grandparents' defection and the resulting shitty eternity in Denver's foster care system, and then through the lonely and demanding years in medical school.

The stunning landing of the Garathani ship, broadcast worldwide on every channel, had alternately chilled her with distrust—they were shaking hands with politicians, for God's sake!—and warmed her with an unreasonable hope for the future. Then one miserably sunny morning, after a thirty-six-hour shift at the hospital, she'd answered a knock on her front door, wearing only a faded *X-Files* t-shirt and boxers and holding a half-eaten bowl of Cap'n Crunch, to find a couple of suits standing on her front porch—a less than stellar start to her interstellar career as Dr. Teague, Medicine Chick.

They'd flashed Secret Service IDs, eyeing her shirt with thinly veiled contempt as they sauntered in and turned off her TV without so much as an apology. Then they'd grilled her at length about the meaning of her life, and when she'd finally concluded it had no meaning and was ready to ask for one of their guns and eat it, they'd offered her the chance to do more, to be more. And she'd taken it, if only to find out what the Garathani might really be up to.

Of course, she'd had to sell her cute little English cottage in Kellen Gardens, which was like excising her own heart with a plastic spork from the Chicken Shack. You could have knocked her over with a cotton swab when, the day after she moved into the Beaumont–Thayer Compound, her orientation partner pointed out a tawny-haired seven-foot alien in an outrageously formfitting uniform and cooed, "That's Commander Kellen. God, isn't he just dreamy!"

What were the odds that she'd have another Kellen in her life so soon after giving up the last one? The name wasn't exactly ubiquitous, at least not on this planet. On Garathan, who knew? Maybe it was their equivalent of John.

"Kind of you to join us today, Dr. Teague."

Monica jerked, sending the empty coffee cup careening off the side of her desk and onto the utilitarian carpet.

"Thanks a lot, Commander," she muttered, leaning down without looking at him and trying hard not to blush. "Ever hear of knocking?"

Their fingers made unexpected contact over the smooth ceramic and she snatched hers back as if they'd been burned. *So much for not blushing.* When he set the cup on her desk without replying, Monica met his eyes briefly before looking away, her cheeks hot. Usually sunglasses lent her a certain feeling of anonymity, but not today. Today she felt absolutely naked in front of him.

"Thank you."

"Did you get up on the wrong side of the bed this morning, Doctor?"

His chiseled face was devoid of expression, but she could tell from his tone that he'd enjoyed asking her that. The man had an unusually good grasp of the subtleties of the English language—for an alien—and a well-known fondness for euphemisms, the more obscure the better.

Whether he was trying for amusing or annoying at the moment was impossible to tell, but at least he'd provided a convenient excuse for her behavior. He'd rattled her enough that she was no longer in the mood to confront him about the guards. She just wanted him *gone* so she could break down in peace.

"That about sums it up," she said, nodding.

"Why?"

Well, shit. *Go away, Commander,* her eyes telegraphed through the tinted lenses. Unfortunately, he wasn't getting the message. Planting his feet slightly apart and clasping his hands behind him, he stared at her like he'd heard something freaky was about to happen to her and he didn't want to miss it. His military posture threw the bulge at his crotch into prominent relief and only divine intervention could have kept her eyes from settling there. None was forthcoming.

Speaking of freaky things you wouldn't want to miss…

"Doctor?"

Suddenly drowning in drool, Monica swallowed hard and met his gaze again. The barest hint of a smile curved one corner of his mouth.

"I, um…I just didn't sleep well last night." Oh hell, she was blushing. Again. Damn that stupid dream! Until this morning, she'd felt pretty comfortable with Commander Kellen and the other Garathani reps. Now she felt off balance and embarrassed in his presence. And crabby. Hopefully, as with most dreams, the mood-altering effect would wear off soon and she would revert to her usual oddball self. Then she could tell him where to shove his guards.

"Perhaps you should return to your quarters and rest until the afternoon orientation."

"Thank you, but that won't be necessary," she assured him, sorting through papers like she had some earthly idea what she was doing. "Did you need something?"

"No. I was merely...concerned about you."

His hesitation made her look up.

"Oh. Well, as you can see, I'm fine." God, what she wouldn't give for a poker face like his! Those lapis eyes were disconcerting in their study of her. She'd thought herself accustomed to the unblinking Garathani stare, until this moment, when it was trained so intently on her.

Phantom sensations from her dream chose that instant to bedevil her, prickling her nipples and arrowing straight down between her thighs. *An alien invasion*, he'd said, and she'd known instinctively he wasn't talking on a planetary scale.

The heat that rushed up her neck this time was excruciating, consuming her entire face in a fireball of humiliation as her heart pounded beneath her breastbone. She closed the folder with hands that wanted to tremble and reached down to open a file drawer, desperate to escape his questing gaze.

His fingers curled under her chin and urged her face up for his inspection.

"You don't look fine, little Terran."

Little Terran. If his hot touch on her skin hadn't made her freeze, the echo from her dream sure as hell would have. Had he ever called her that before? It was hard to remember, with her brain shorting out like she'd plugged in one appliance too many. She'd certainly picked a hell of a day to leave off the war paint. Would this infernal blush never fade?

It was way past time to go on the offensive. Jerking her chin out of his hold, Monica stood up and met his eyes with steely determination. Okay, rubbery determination.

"I promise you, I'm fine." Drawing a shaky breath, she asked, "Why do you have guards watching me?"

"Ah." And here she'd thought his gaze couldn't get any more penetrating. His head tipped to one side, causing that gold and brown mane to ripple. "So that's what's bothering you."

"Damn right it's bothering me." She crossed her arms over her ribs. "It's true, isn't it? They're guarding *me*."

He regarded her impassively for a moment, then nodded slowly. "Yes, they are."

"Goddamn it, Commander, I told you I'd avoid—"

"They're for your protection, Doctor."

"*My* protection," she snorted. "What do I need protection for? You're the one who's—" Monica clamped her jaw shut to stem the flow of revealing words.

"I'm the one who's..." Kellen looked fascinated. "Do go on, Doctor."

"Well, you *are* a likely target for violence from xenophobic Earthlings," she improvised, absurdly pleased with herself for coming up with something plausible under stress.

"Your susceptibility to our pheromones makes *you* a far more likely target for the unscrupulous advances of desperate men."

"Oh, give me a break. They'd have to be pretty damn desperate."

"Which is precisely why we're on Earth, if you'll recall."

She noticed he didn't deny her contention. *Ouch.*

"Listen, Commander, I'm sure you think you're doing me a favor, but the fact is, I can't live under constant surveillance. You can just call off the guards now and I'll take my chances." *Such as they are.*

"I'm sorry, but I can't do that." Before she could object, he held up a hand and continued, "You may be willing to take the chance, but you're hardly the only one with anything at stake here. If you happened to be attacked, it's not inconceivable

42

that this entire program could be stalled indefinitely by the political fallout."

She ground her teeth. "But it's not—"

"Dr. Teague," he enunciated clearly, "feminine defiance can have unpredictable effects on my self-control." Planting his hands on her desk, he leaned into her face. "Perhaps you should concede this battle of wills before the guards have to drag *me* off you."

If there'd been anywhere to go, Monica would have taken a hasty step back. As it was, she just about swallowed her tongue.

"Are we done here?" the commander asked without backing away. She nodded vigorously. "I'm glad to hear it. The guards will remain, with the continuing stipulation that they're to leave your presence immediately if they become aroused."

"That's, um, good to know." Monica blinked repeatedly, desperate to regroup. Damn it, she'd let him put her on the defensive again with that ridiculous scare tactic. Eyeing him with renewed determination, she said firmly, "Now, unless you need something else, I have a lot of recruits to sort through."

It was his turn to blink, she noted with some satisfaction. But then his eyes darkened and he leaned in until his nose nearly touched hers.

"Are you *dismissing* me?"

Every self-preservation instinct screamed to life at the dangerous undercurrents rippling his tone, and deciding a tactical retreat was in order, Monica let her gelatinous knees drop her back into the chair.

"Gee, was I being too subtle?" The panicked breathiness of her tone kind of ruined the effect, but she stuck it out. "Some of us actually have to work around here."

"Mmmm." His response, like his expression, was unnervingly neutral. "As you wish, Doctor. But do plan to spend the better part of the morning in my office tomorrow. We have a number of details to iron out regarding recruit evaluations."

"I'll ink you in," she vowed, opening the file folder once more and fixing her gaze to the first typewritten page that presented itself.

The sound of her office door closing had never been more welcome. Monica yanked off her glasses and collapsed facedown on her desk with a long moan, the relief of having the commander gone so exquisite, it was practically orgasmic. Or so she imagined. If that persistent tingling down south got any more intense, she might find out for real, which was an eye-opening thought. God, he smelled *so* good, and she was *so* hungry…

Perhaps you should concede this battle of wills before the guards have to drag me off you.

Yeah, right. Obviously the man's reputation for strategic warfare was well-deserved. He'd certainly zeroed in on her Achilles' heel with ruthless precision. Jesus, the mental picture he'd drawn of guards fighting to drag his massive body off hers was enough to make her whimper. But not with fright.

Her stomach rumbled and Monica straightened with another groan, wondering how early she could possibly get away with taking her lunch hour. The groan turned to a laugh — page one of the recruit roster was stuck to her forehead. Yanking it off, she scooped it back in with the other documents and forced her mind back to the job at hand.

This unsettling distortion of her reality had better right itself overnight, she thought dismally, or she was in for a hell of a day tomorrow, too.

Chapter Three

ဆ

Barely an hour later, Monica slid her lunch tray down the line behind Shelley's. She'd gotten all kinds of funny looks on her way to the cafeteria, thanks to her cadaverous pallor, high-water scrubs and funked-out hair. A glance in the mirror on her way out the door had wrung a curse from her—for what she'd paid, that dye job should have lasted into her golden years.

"Jeez, Gothchild, are you loading up for some kind of dairy crisis we haven't heard about yet?"

Monica glanced down at her tray as she plopped a fourth carton of milk onto it and shrugged. "I like milk. So sue me."

She noticed that Shelley took two milks herself, but didn't comment on it. After all, she, at least, had the excuse of being six months pregnant. With twins, no less.

"You do realize a milk moustache really screws with your image."

Monica grinned as they scooted their trays down the line. "Beats a real moustache."

"And since when did you give up fruits and vegetables? Do you know what eating all that crap will do to your arteries?" Shelley shook her head, wide-eyed at Monica's lunch of two steaks, two ramekins of nutmeg-sprinkled custard and an extra-large slice of pumpkin pie with whipped cream. "You're not knocked up, too, are you?"

"You know better than that," Monica said severely. "Anyway, who died and made you the cholesterol cop?"

"Well, forgive me for wondering what the hell is going on with you," Shelley growled as they headed for an empty table at the back of the cafeteria. "For the better part of a year, you've eaten nothing but salads for lunch, and now you're suddenly sucking down calories like a war-starved refugee.

"And what makes it really freaky," she continued as they settled at the table, "is that you're losing weight anyway." She paused, looking hard at Monica. "You're not sick or something, are you?"

"Not that I know of," Monica said. She let her gaze slide away, wishing she hadn't switched out the sunglasses after her headache subsided. Sometimes Shelley's probing eyes saw too much. "And I'm not losing weight. I've gained five pounds in the last few weeks. Like I really needed that." She looked down at her tray and frowned. It was no wonder she was edging closer to that dreaded two-hundred-pound mark every day. But the strange food cravings she'd had lately were just too overwhelming to deny.

"Are you sure? You look thinner to me, especially in your face. Have you been working out? Maybe you're gaining muscle mass."

"Yeah, right," Monica snorted. "Me, working out." The mere sight of the gymnasium door was enough to make her hiss and writhe like a vampire confronted with a cross. She cracked open a carton of milk and guzzled it down in a few hard swallows, then did the same to a second before tucking into her steak.

"What in the..." She stopped chewing and shifted her food around in her mouth, disgusted to feel something hard in there. As discreetly as possible, she spat the whole mouthful into her paper napkin.

"What, are they serving teeth and toenails in the meat again?" Shelley asked. "I hate it when that happens."

Peeking at the mess in her napkin, Monica gasped. "Holy cow! You called it." She held up what looked like a tooth, narrowing her eyes as she examined it.

"That doesn't look like a cow tooth to me, holy or otherwise," Shelley said. "You didn't lose a tooth, did you?"

"I don't..." Feeling around, Monica was shocked to feel a gap on the lower left side of her mouth. "Oh my God, it *is* mine. I lost a tooth. Oh, that's just lovely," she groused. "Like I'm not already the walking freakazoid of the universe."

"Let me see it," Shelley prodded.

Monica handed the tooth to her with a sigh, tonguing the gap in her mouth, disturbed by the metallic taste of blood. That was all she needed right now, for her teeth to start falling out. She must have pulled some really bad shit in a previous life to be saddled with this crappy excuse for a body.

"This looks like a baby molar," Shelley finally pronounced.

Startled, Monica took the tooth Shelley held up and turned it over in her palm.

"Yeah, it is," she said, relieved. She'd almost forgotten that she still had a handful of baby teeth. The dentist swore she had adult teeth hiding in there somewhere, but they'd never shown any eagerness to emerge. "Maybe I'll get a quarter from the Tooth Fairy."

"A quarter," Shelley scoffed. "No way! Those babies are worth at least a dollar nowadays."

"Works for me." She dropped the tooth into the pocket of her lab coat and got back to her steak. It was kind of weird trying to grind up the tough meat with her new gap, and of course, it had to be on the side that she favored for chewing.

"Don't look now, but your boyfriend's back," Shelley muttered behind her hand.

For one shocking second, Monica thought she was talking about the commander and felt scorching color surge all the way up to her scalp. It was almost a relief to realize Shelley was referring to her new shadow, Lieutenant Shauss.

"Just ignore him," she advised. "That's what I do. I'm sure Commander Kellen asked him to keep an eye on me to make sure I don't, you know…" She couldn't bring herself to say it out loud. *Get drunk on their sex hormones.*

"I don't like the way he's looking at you," Shelly insisted. "You need to nip his little *thing* in the bud before it becomes a problem."

"I saw his *thing* in xenoanatomy," Monica snickered, "and believe me, it's far from little."

"Damn it, I'm serious! He's looking at you like…" she trailed off, biting her lips.

"Like?" Oh, the suspense was killing her. Truly, how often did a prime cut of male look at her like…anything?

Looking both directions first, Shelley leaned forward and hissed, "Like he wants to bonk your brains out."

Smothering a laugh, Monica told her, "God, Shel, you are too much. Maybe you need to see a therapist or something. Sounds to me like you have your own little *thing* to deal with."

"Fine," Shelley said, obviously insulted. "Just don't come crying to me when you wind up naked in chains on the cover of some alien BDSM mag."

There was no holding back this time. Monica slapped her hand over her mouth and doubled over, shrieking with laughter, and barely missed dipping her bangs in her whipped cream. She laughed even harder when Shelley just sat there, munching on her taco salad with a bored look that said, *You're sooo immature.*

Then she caught a glimpse of Lieutenant Shauss as she turned to wipe her eyes and the last of her giggles lodged in her throat. He was just smiling at her, nothing too unusual about that. But it was the *way* he was smiling…

Shit! Heat flashed in her belly and she quickly looked away, shaken. Shelley was dead-on about how he was looking at her and Monica had no clue how to react. Damn it, she wasn't *going* to react. There was a reason men didn't look at her like that and she'd damn well better remember it.

"Mmm-hmm," Shelley hummed knowingly, still chewing.

"Just ignore him," Monica repeated less firmly than she would have liked. *And maybe he'll go away.* He didn't, of course, but she concentrated hard on chewing her steak and tried to shove him toward the back of her mind.

Which became even more difficult when Shelley whispered, "I think Jasmine has a crush on him."

"On Lieutenant Shauss?"

When Shelley nodded, Monica slumped back in her seat and stared at her. The Stepford secretary, crushing on the cover-model alien? Oh, now that was too funny. "No way."

"Way. Watch her the next time he's around."

"He's always around, and I've never noticed anything."

"That's because you're not keyed in on boy-girl stuff. Alien-girl stuff," she corrected with a grimace.

Monica turned her attention back to her steak, not wanting to travel any further down that road. *Alien-girl stuff.* God, maybe she and Jasmine had more in common than she knew.

"So what do you think it means?" Shelley finally asked. "Losing the tooth, I mean."

"Is it supposed to mean something?"

"Well, you only lose your baby teeth when your adult teeth are ready to come in, right?"

"Yeah, when you're anything close to normal, which we both know I'm not. With my luck, they'll all just drop out and I'll have to gum my way across the galaxy."

"Oh come on, Monica." Shelley pushed away the crumbs of her salad and tore open the mouth of her milk carton. "Think positive, for a change. Maybe this is the start of something big for you."

Monica shuddered. "God, don't say that. Anytime something big happens to me, it's usually something that really, really sucks."

Shelley arched a brow at her. "Oh yeah? So tell me, Dr. Gothchild, what tall, brainy astronomy freak is going to be one of the first people on Earth to leave our solar system in just a few months?"

"Okay, so that doesn't suck," Monica admitted. "But it hasn't happened yet, has it? Something big right now could definitely screw that up for me."

Like the pheromone thing. She shuddered again at the fresh reminder of how close she'd come to being scrubbed from the mission roster. She didn't remember much about that day, but according to Shelley, Dr. Snow had stopped by her quarters to check on her less than ten minutes after the commander dropped her off. If Shelley hadn't stuck around to run interference, totally trashing Monica's eating habits and promising to help her make better nutritional choices from the cafeteria's offerings, things could have gotten really ugly, really fast.

"You'd better be careful what you say," Shelley warned as she smoothed a hand over the basketball that was now her belly. "I swore I was going to forget one of my birth control pills someday, and look at me now, the classic victim of self-fulfilling prophecy — with double indemnity."

"Yeah, well, the difference is that unconsciously, you really wanted to get knocked up by your foot-dragging fiancé. My conscious and unconscious, on the other hand, are in total agreement about leaving the solar system. The two are as one," Monica concluded in a sucky Kung Fu accent. "At peace with the universe and all who reside therein."

Shelley rolled her eyes. "You're so full of shit, Grasshopper."

"Confucius say, it take one to know one."

"Very profound. But seriously, I still think this tooth thing is significant somehow."

"Well, I, for one, hope you're wrong." Monica shoved her dinner plate aside and laid into the pumpkin pie. "I'm finally happy with the way my life is going and I'm not about to let it change course now."

* * * * *

"Commander, how is our little daughter of Sparna faring today?" The ambassador's voice floated over the com screen behind him.

Our little daughter? Turning his chair to face it, Kellen told him, "She shed one of her milk teeth just a moment ago."

Pret's eyes widened. "Are you certain, Commander?"

"Definitely. It's in the pocket of her lab coat at the moment. I'll retrieve it and examine it for verification, of course."

"And how do you propose to do that?"

Kellen smiled, baring his own large white teeth and wondering if Pret knew about the Tooth Fairy. "You're better off not knowing. Plausible deniability."

Pret sighed. "You're probably right."

"She's also grown more than an inch taller in the last week and gained five pounds in the last two."

"Mother of Peserin! That degree of acceleration can't be safe. Or comfortable."

Kellen frowned as he nodded. "She's experiencing pain in her legs at night, and it will no doubt grow worse."

"Perhaps it's time to remove the good doctor to the *Heptoral*. Terran physicians will be of little use to her, especially when they have no idea what her condition truly is."

"Not yet." Kellen looked as forbidding as he could.

"We can't wait too long, Commander. If they figure it out first, we might never get her off the planet."

"Have no worries on that front, Pret," Kellen growled. "I'll level North America before I leave here without her."

"As you will."

When the connection was broken, Kellen lounged back in his chair and stretched his long legs under the massive custom-made mahogany desk, staring blindly at the darkened screen. He wasn't as unconcerned about his little doctor's accelerating transition as he pretended. In fact, he was more worried than Pret might imagine.

In the weeks since she'd become his aide, he'd grown somewhat attached to the little xenophile. Despite her annoyance at being commandeered as his aide, she'd displayed an almost childlike excitement at the prospect of having more concentrated contact with the Garathani contingent. She'd warned him, though, from the very first day, that her number-one priority was still her service to the females she would be tending and if he didn't like it, he could just transfer her right back to the general pool.

It hadn't taken long for him to appreciate Dr. Teague's blunt assistance in handling all matters Terran. Even better, her interactions with the other Terrans, which he observed on a daily basis, afforded him considerable enjoyment. She was a prickly little bundle of contradictions who held herself aloof from the tight-knit community and took great pride in lobbing frequent and well-aimed verbal grenades at several of her more condescending colleagues.

If she'd made any effort to fit in, she might have been a favorite of the group. As it was, she would be lucky to have any Terran companionship at all once aboard the Garathani vessel. It was unfortunate her jumpy little nurse friend had enlisted for domestic service only. While Kellen would be pleased to fill the gaping hole in Dr. Teague's social life once they departed, he regretted that she would be so completely alone when her Sparnite transition began in earnest. He dreaded the physical ordeal she faced as much as he was impatient for it, and he liked her enough to almost wish it would pass her by.

Almost being the operative word.

Already, the pain she was experiencing grated on his conscience, which admittedly was a somewhat egocentric reaction on his part. His weren't the only pheromones that had initiated her transition, after all. But he was the one who stood to benefit the most from it, and it was up to him to make certain that she suffered as little as possible, which was why he'd finally lain with her last night, poised on that cusp between heaven and hell.

He'd made many stealthy excursions into her quarters over the last three weeks and implemented a number of measures designed to enhance his awareness of her, not the least of which was the insertion of a hypodermic biomet unit under her left arm. The tiny multipurpose sensor sent him a continuous stream of data via cerecom link, ensuring that at any given moment, Kellen knew more about the doctor's physical condition than she did herself. It was through the biomet, as much as his own quiet study of her as she slept, that he'd learned of her rapidly developing leg pains.

What she needed now was the relief that only intimate contact with a Garathani male could provide, and he intended to see that she got it as often as she needed it. However, that relief was not without its price for either of them. Such contact tested the limits of his self-control even as it stimulated her already erratic transition. But he couldn't just sit idly in the haven of his flare field each night and watch while she writhed in agony upon her narrow bed. His discussions with one of the Garathani physicians had convinced him that going to her was his only course of action.

So he'd lain with her, covered her with his warmth and bestowed the analgesic properties of his pheromones, all the while stoking the fires of both her maturation and his own lust with inquisitive hands. He'd enclosed them both in the versatile bubble of his flare field, deceiving her eyes and easing her mind with its vivid images as he gave her the barest taste of the pleasures of the flesh.

Kellen groaned as the memory curled through his groin.

My, oh my, Commander, Shauss drawled in his head. *Guess who's emitting now...*

Chapter Four

෨

"No way, Commander."

Monica's head jerked vigorously in denial, her temper threatening to slip its fragile leash. She stood toe-to-toe with the expressionless knothead, wound tight with anxiety about getting in the face of a man who'd nuked a whole civilization, but unable to back down now that she'd made her stand.

Talk about a self-fulfilling prophecy, she thought with disgust. It was only nine a.m. and already her day was showing signs of taking the express handcart to hell.

Yesterday had gone from bad to dog shit. After lunch, she'd stumbled her way through the orientation packet as if she'd received it at the last minute instead of designing most of the damn thing herself, earning a lot of confused and doubtful looks from her flock of recruits. The commander's watchful presence at the back of the theater had done little to curb her nervous rambling, and by the time she'd blathered her way through the final page, she was ready to spit in his eye.

She'd marched straight to her room with her head once again pounding like a bass drum and kicked her dresser so hard, her last full bottle of foundation had rolled off and cracked open on the thin carpet, spilling into an ugly stain. Too tired and upset to eat dinner, she'd tossed her lab coat and scrubs on the floor and crawled right into bed, desperate for the asylum of sleep. Of course, then she'd suffered incredible leg pains and tossed for hours before drifting off.

Today hadn't started out much better. She'd managed to wake up in time to put her face on, but hadn't been able to find any scrubs long enough to cover her ankles. Then she'd shrugged into the rumpled lab coat she'd discarded so carelessly the night before and been both surprised and amused to reach into the pocket and find a dollar instead of a tooth.

Wondering how in the hell Shelley had accomplished that, she'd actually headed for breakfast with a smile on her face. Then Shelley had totally denied her role as Tooth Fairy and made a big show of speculating about who might be responsible. Not that it was such a humongous deal, but Shelley had decided to make it one. All the blasted woman had to do was fess up and they'd have had a good laugh about it. Instead, she'd maintained her wide-eyed innocence and Monica had left the cafeteria bristling with annoyance.

All the stresses of the last twenty-four hours had led to her present condition—puffy-eyed, woolly-brained and spoiling for a fight with the irksome Commander Kellen.

Her hyperawareness of him hadn't faded away overnight, as she'd hoped. Oh, no. Thanks to the explicitly sexual dreams riding her in those meager hours of pre-dawn sleep and the vivid flashbacks still riding her this morning, she was more exquisitely sensitive than an exposed nerve and ready to scream with the frustration of it.

Once again, she'd fallen asleep on her stomach and he'd lain over her like a living blanket. But this time, after teasing her meager breasts without mercy, he'd slid one of his hands down into her panties as he rocked against her ass. She'd tried to crawl forward, away from his rough fingertips as they stroked her pubis, and he'd pressed all his weight down on her, forcing one of his long fingers into the shallow cradle of her cleft. Even now, she could hear herself keening as that finger pulsed gently against her flesh, and even now, she was profoundly grateful to know it was only a dream. The idea of Commander Kellen exploring her malformed genitals made her intestines twist with fear and shame.

And damn it, yes—need. God, it sucked to wake up throbbing with sexual arousal. Why had she ever wished for such a thing, when there was no hope in hell it would ever be fulfilled?

Her nipples were sore now, stinging with every brush of scrubs against long underwear, and the glands that surrounded them were swollen and warm to the touch. Damn it, she was going to have to forget the undershirts and find a training bra or something. Did they even make them in her size? Oh, that was going to be fun, asking the burly, cigar-chewing quartermaster to hunt down a thirty-eight double-pancake for an ultra-late bloomer.

Her life was shit. Complete, egg-sucking shit.

Kellen interrupted her bitter thoughts. "I'm afraid I must insist."

"Ditto!" she snapped back, humiliation and resentment pricking the back of her neck. "I'm sorry, but there's no way in hell I'm going to let you guys clutter up the women's eval rooms. Those evaluations will be uncomfortable enough for them as it is."

"If they were so concerned with personal comfort, they would not have volunteered for copulative services," he countered easily.

Monica cringed. Copulative services! God, could they possibly have thought of a term less personal or caring?

What really pissed her off was that he was right. Most of the applicants who'd been accepted for evaluation had rated themselves "indifferent to" being observed in intimate situations. The remainder had actually checked the "excited about" option, which made her squirm with discomfort. These women couldn't care less who saw them being probed and measured. It was her own sense of propriety, of personal dignity, that railed at the idea of these mega-sized alpha males playing voyeur while the recruits were subjected to such intimate examinations.

For all intents and purposes, the women were going to be little more than well-paid Garathani whores and broodmares, but she would do her damnedest to make sure they were all treated with respect. After all, they were the ones stepping up to the plate to save the commander's whole godforsaken race. At the moment, Monica wondered if they were even worth saving.

"Forget it. You can just take my word for their suitability."

"No, Doctor, I can't," Kellen explained with exaggerated patience. "Council decree requires two Garathani witnesses."

"To do *what?*" Her voice had risen a full octave, but she was beyond reining in her anger. "Do you intend to take a peek into the speculum when I do the pelvic exams, or maybe palpate their uteruses yourself?"

"If I deem it necessary, yes."

"Oh, that does it." Monica reached out with both hands and shoved at his massive chest with enough force to make Kellen fall back a step. His shaggy head tilted to one side as he watched her and the sight of his wary stance sent fierce satisfaction sizzling along her veins. He *should* be worried!

"Why don't you just beam back to the mother ship, Captain Jerk-off," she shouted. "And find another planet to harvest your sex toys from!" She shoved him again, as hard as she could, and he took another step back. A red haze of fury tore through her, sending waves of heat rippling over her skin, making her shoulders hunch defensively as she continued to rage at him.

"These women, these human beings," *shove*, "you're so damned callous about, are willing to give up everything they've ever known just so you and your cohorts can get your fucking rocks off!" *Shove.* "And in return, you'll show your appreciation by ogling them while they're lying there helpless," *shove*, "with their feet in stirrups and their legs spread wide, you dirty, thankless son of a bitch!"

The brisk knock at Kellen's office door froze her mid-shove.

"Everybody okay in there?"

Jasmine's tentative inquiry snapped Monica out of the *Twilight Zone* with the force of a roundhouse kick. She felt the tears streaming down her blistering hot cheeks, heard the respirations that were as harsh and rapid as her bounding pulse and was immediately racked by shudders. She wrapped her arms around her waist as if to ward off a sudden chill.

Kellen still watched her, his back nearly to the wall now, his face as unreadable as ever.

"We're fine, Miss King," he said calmly. "Just a little misunderstanding. You may return to your duties."

After a pregnant pause, Jasmine's uncertain "Okay, then" floated through the door.

"Oh my God," Monica hiccupped. "I'm so sorry, Commander. I don't know what just happened here, I swear I don't." A sob wrenched from her throat.

For just a moment, she thought everything was all right. Kellen's face softened into what might have been compassion and he took a step toward her. Then her stomach growled and she suddenly became aware of the thick, savory sweetness of pheromones bathing her respiratory tract.

Commander Kellen was aroused.

By her.

"Stop!" she cried, putting up her shaking hands to hold him at bay. "Don't you touch me!"

* * * * *

Empran, dispatch Ketrok to my office immediately, Kellen ordered. At first he'd been bemused by her show of temper. Then arousal had set in. If the shouting hadn't done it, the pushing definitely would have—nothing fired his blood more quickly than a physical confrontation. The temptation to lay her over his desk and show her the error of her ways had wound deliciously through his belly, but he'd ignored it, allowing the fire to mount slowly even as he allowed her to propel him backward across his office.

He'd never been more thankful for his steely control over the demands of his flesh than at this moment.

*Dispatch confirmed** came the reply.

Hopefully the Garathani doctor would know what to do with Monica. Obviously some major upheaval was taking place in her body and Kellen was at a loss about how to handle her rising hysteria. Color blazed under her pale skin and beads of sweat trembled on her brow and upper lip. Peserin's eye, what must she be going through?

Taking that last step back, pressing his buttocks and shoulders against the wall, he raised his hands in a gesture of surrender. "It's all right, Doctor. I'll stay right here."

"See that you do," she said tremulously as she hugged herself. Then she blinked repeatedly before she doubled over at the waist and gasped.

"Monica, what's wrong?"

"Stay back!" she screamed. "I mean it, stay back!"

"I will," Kellen promised urgently. "Just tell me what's hurting you."

"My stomach," she gasped. "My head, my eyes..." Then she crumbled to her knees and laid her forehead on the floor with a ragged cry. "What's happening to me?"

Empran, I need Ketrok NOW!

Ketrok ETA nine seconds.

The last time Kellen had felt so powerless, he'd watched his mate and young daughter succumb to the final destructive wave of the Narthani bio-war virus. They'd died in such unbearable pain that it had splintered his mind and ripped out his soul.

This helplessness was just as maddening. He wanted to slam his fist into something, drive it hard enough to crush his very bones. Instead, he locked down the impotent rage and maintained his position behind the door, unwilling to frighten Monica further by sweeping her up into his embrace as every instinct screamed that he should. She was rocking now, scraping her face roughly against the carpet while she cried out in agony.

Then he saw the blood streaming down the legs of her scrubs, pooling around her knees, and felt his entrails turn cold.

Chapter Five

ജ

Waking had never been such a chore.

Monica knew it was time. The lights were bright on the other side of her closed eyelids and she felt relaxed and rested as she hadn't in weeks. Still, it was so nice to just lie here and drift. She'd had amazing dreams, tons of them, and no pain at all that she could remember. Someone must have slipped her some damn fine meds.

"Monica, can you hear me?"

Soft fingers brushed her hair back from her forehead and she sighed with contentment.

"Hi, Shelley," she murmured without opening her eyes.

"Hey, Gothchild, how you feelin'?"

"Marvelous." Her chest felt kind of heavy and she didn't have enough energy to lick a postage stamp, but otherwise, she'd never felt better.

"That's good. Can you open your eyes for me now?"

"I don't know. They're pretty heavy."

"Just try, okay?"

Her sigh this time was long-suffering. "If you insist."

Her first thought was that someone had been doing some funky renovations in the hospital wing. Everything was blue, a startling iridescent blue.

"*Hello!*" she exclaimed weakly. "Was there a sale on spray paint at Home Depot?"

"Not exactly." Shelley's smiling face came into view. "You're aboard the *Heptoral*." At Monica's blank look, she clarified, "The Garathani ship."

"Wow, really?" Monica tried to sit up, but the wave of nausea that washed over her when she moved convinced her that was a really bad idea.

"Just lie still, okay? The commander will explain everything when he gets here."

Shocks of excitement skittered down her spine. She was on a spaceship! She turned her head and looked around, unsurprised by the sleek, Spartan appearance of what must be one of the ship's four infirmaries. Hers appeared to be the only bed out of six currently occupied.

"What's wrong with me?" she finally thought to ask, anxiety welling in her chest.

"You're fine now, sweetie," Shelley assured her.

"So what happened, then? Why am I here?"

"I'd rather let Commander Kellen explain that, if it's all the same to you."

"But why?" she demanded.

"Quit haranguing your faithful sidekick, Monica. She's under orders to leave the explanations to me." Kellen's voice swept over her like a balmy summer breeze and her eyes closed reflexively.

Forcing her lids up again, she countered the dreamy feeling by mustering a glare as he stepped up beside the bed.

"Commander," she acknowledged. "Care to clue me in about what's going on?"

"I'll do that, just as soon as Nurse Bonham has assured herself that you're well."

"If she can stare daggers like that, she's definitely on the mend," Shelley declared with a broad grin. Then she leaned down and planted a kiss on Monica's forehead. "I'm so glad you're okay. Don't ever scare me like that again, you hear me?"

"Do my best," Monica agreed thickly. How had she ever lived without friends?

"I'll come back as soon as I can." When Shelley reached the door, she turned and said severely, "Be nice to the commander, Gothchild. He saved your life. If he wasn't so big and scary, I'd have kissed *him* instead of you."

"It's not too late," Kellen interjected quickly, but Shelley just smiled and left the room. He turned to Monica. "I'm not that scary, am I?"

His plaintive tone earned him a grin.

"To a five-foot-two pansy, yeah, you're that scary."

"But not to you."

"Nah. You're just a big marshmallow." Planet Narthan notwithstanding.

"You didn't seem to think so at our last meeting."

The frown pulling down his brow curled something in Monica's stomach. Vague memories of that confrontation teased the edges of her mind, but she couldn't recall the details with any accuracy. She did remember being terrified, but she couldn't imagine he'd been the cause of it. More likely, she'd been scared out of her wits by whatever the hell had seized her body.

"I think I was really out of my head with pain that day. I hope I didn't say anything to hurt your feelings." It crossed her mind that he might not have feelings, at least not as she knew them, but she wasn't taking any chances. "How long has it been, anyway?"

Kellen's eyes were dark as they watched her.

"Ten days."

"Holy crap, really? What was wrong with me? Did it require surgery? Why did you bring me here? And how did we—"

"Let's take one question at a time, little Terran." He smiled. "Yes, you required some relatively minor surgery. We arrived here by molecular flare, which is an advanced technology we haven't yet revealed to the Terran representatives. The nature of your emergency made speed of the essence, which is why we risked using it."

"Why am I totally not surprised? You'd be fools to lay all your cards on the table if you didn't have to," she murmured.

"Exactly, and we're far from foolish. Hopefully," he added grimly.

"I notice you skipped right past the 'what was wrong with me' question."

"I'd hoped you were still too groggy to catch that."

"Sorry." His hesitation made *her* hesitate. What if something awful was wrong with her?

"It's nothing life-threatening," he hurried to say, divining her fear. "At least not now that the crisis has passed."

"So why the sidestepping?"

"Because I'm not looking forward to your reaction."

"*Now* you're scaring me," she growled. "Just spit it out, Commander."

"Perhaps it would be better to show you." He sat down, very carefully, on the edge of her bed. "Empran, station one, elevate head twenty degrees."

Monica was startled to feel the mattress rising silently under her head.

"Nifty. Is that what you wanted to show me?"

"Hardly." His expression didn't match the dry tone. "What I'd like you to do, Monica, is to place your hands on your breasts."

"Excuse me?" She blinked at him. "When did we go from hinky to kinky?"

"Indulge me, please."

"Oookay," she drawled, sliding her hands, stiff from disuse, gingerly up her ribs. The extravagant mounds of flesh that met her questing fingertips were...

Definitely not hers.

"What the *fuck*?"

* * * * *

"You brought me up here to give me breast implants?" she asked, disbelief sending her dark brows into her hairline.

Kellen slanted a look at her, doubting that she seriously believed that scenario.

"No, they're all you."

Her eyes blinked rapidly as she digested that, her hands unmoving on her newly bulbous breasts. "All right, we've done show, now *tell*," she demanded in a dangerous tone.

"We transported you up here because your body was undergoing a violently accelerated maturation and your immediate needs were beyond the scope of Terran medicine."

He was surprised when she let her head fall back on the bed and rolled her eyes.

"Good God, this stupid body of mine never has done anything the normal way. Only I could go from thirty-eight flat to thirty-eight C—"

"D."

"Thirty-eight *D* in just over a week. Holy shit, I'm a D-cup? How weird is that going to be when I go back to the compound? Nobody will believe they're real."

Kellen was just debating whether or not to tell her she wasn't going back to the compound when her eyes widened again. "Maturation, huh? I suppose I've got... Turn your back," she ordered. Kellen obeyed without question, turning to face the door. "Damn it! *That* development I could have done without. Now I'm going to have to wax."

Ah. She disliked the thick, silky patch of curls between her legs. He'd have forbidden her to remove it, but decided to save himself the grief. Where they were going, wax wasn't even an option.

"I can't believe all this happened in less than two weeks," she murmured. "You can turn around now."

She'd pulled the blanket up to her chin.

"It didn't happen without considerable trauma to your body," he said gravely. "Dr. Ketrok likened the process to a series of catastrophic earthquakes on your planet. He induced a light coma to help you through the worst of it and you've slept naturally for nearly seventy hours since then." The urge to draw her into the protection of his embrace was almost overwhelming, but he restrained himself. "The violence of your transition made you a shocking sight, especially those first few days, which is why I refused to allow Nurse Bonham to see you until today."

Kellen looked away from her momentarily, still shaken at the vision of her kneeling in more than a pint of her own blood. "The maturation of your reproductive organs was particularly vicious. Do you remember hemorrhaging in my office?"

She nodded slowly. "Vaguely. It seems more like a dream."

"I'm not surprised," he agreed. "You were in shock. The hemorrhage was precipitated by the explosive buildup of your endometrial lining, which couldn't be expelled because your hymen was abnormally thick and solid. The pressure finally became great enough to rupture your membrane and a number of the larger vessels perfusing your vaginal tissues."

Her cheeks were stained with color as she turned her face toward the bulkhead, which was somewhat surprising, considering her profession.

"That was the *minor* surgery?" she asked incredulously.

"I was trying not to frighten you."

"You weren't there for it, were you?"

She looked at him then, her gray eyes wide and vulnerable and begging him to lie. But he wasn't about to begin their relationship with untruths between them. He'd already misled her once about the nature of her reaction to their pheromones, though his explanation was true in the strictest sense of the word — it was just incomplete.

"I was," he said softly. The river of blood pulsing from between her thighs had disturbed him more than any battle injury he'd ever witnessed, and as Ketrok raced to seal the ruptured vessels before she bled out, Kellen had whispered his first prayer to the Powers since the death of his House. It was only the first of many such prayers to pass his lips over the ensuing days.

Monica looked away again. "So, it seems you've seen every inch of me, then," she said bitterly. "Why is that, Commander? What gave you the right to be privy to all my secrets?"

Kellen considered her profile, so radically altered since the onset of her Sparnite transition, and felt unexpected sorrow for her. She'd appeared so very young when they first met, so tender and innocent despite her attempts to harden her look with the outlandish makeup and piercings, that it made the change all the more jarring.

Though the Garathani doctors had done their best to anticipate her nutritional needs and supply the calories necessary to sustain her through the hyper-metabolic episodes, Monica had lost a substantial portion of her fat reserves and it showed most clearly in her face. But even if she hadn't lost the baby fat that was a hallmark of Sparnism, she would still look vastly different. Her facial structure had grown longer and stronger, as had the bones of her body. He wondered if she would even recognize her own reflection.

Over time, Monica would adjust to her new appearance, and though it might take longer, she would eventually learn to accept the reality of her true origins, as well. Her sudden sexual maturity and its ramifications, however, would no doubt lead to countless trials for all of them. He was tempted to delay informing her of that aspect of her life until she'd had at least a few days to work through the other changes, but

Kellen didn't think he'd be doing any of them a favor by putting it off.

As much as he wished it were otherwise, he and Shauss would have to mate with her long before she was ready in order to protect their claim. As the only Garathani female within four parsecs of this ship, Monica was a prize that many would sacrifice their honor, their fortunes, perhaps even their very lives to possess, and only a child of his House in her belly would guarantee her protection.

And Peserin's damnation if the thought of putting one there wasn't raising his staff.

"The Garathani Council gave me that right," he answered, running a gentle fingertip down the newly hollow cheek she'd presented to him, "when they awarded you to me."

A muscle in her jaw stood out in stark relief as she clenched her teeth and Kellen could hear her breathing become quick and shallow, but she didn't look at him.

"Awarded me to you," she repeated with deceptive calm. "I'm not sure what that's supposed to mean, Commander, but no one, especially your goddamned Council, has the authority to *award* me to anyone."

"That's where you're wrong, little Terran," he confided in a silky voice. "Or should I say, little *Garathani*?"

Chapter Six

🕰

She'd never thought herself slow on the uptake, but Monica finally had to look at him, uncomprehending.

"Little *what*?"

His look was chiding. "I'm certain you heard me, but I'll repeat myself, *little Garathani*. And that *is* what you are, Monica."

She licked her lips nervously. "In what sense?"

"In every sense."

"Damn it, could you be any more vague?" she raged suddenly, fear twisting angry knots in her stomach. "What the hell are you talking about?"

"Please be calm, little one," he tried to soothe her. "I have much to tell you, and it may not be easy for you to accept in the beginning. But for your own sake, you must make the effort."

"Just tell me!" she shouted.

"Very well, then. Your father was a Garathani scout," he said baldly. "He—"

Monica felt her jaw come unhinged as her brain temporarily froze with shock.

"—was part of a reconnaissance team dispatched to Earth more than thirty—"

"I knew it!" she shouted. "Goddamn it, I *knew* this wasn't the first time you people had been here! Everybody was acting like that landing was some great historic first," she snorted, "when you'd already been here for *decades*. Were you trolling for playmates even then? Oh my God, you were the ones abducting humans and conducting experiments on them, then

70

sending them back to Earth to look like nutcases, weren't you? Do you have any idea how many lives you ruined—"

"On television, they slap people in the face to bring them out of hysterics," he remarked in a casual but curious tone.

"Do it and you die, asshole," she shot back. "Now let me out of this bed."

"Monica, you will be very sick if you attempt to—"

"Let me up!" she screamed, struggling with the light blanket that covered her. Kellen sighed and stood up, moving back out of her way as she swung her legs over the edge of the bed and lurched upright.

At once, a watery stream of vomit spewed from her mouth and landed with dull splash on the floor. The humiliation that seized her then would have just about finished her, if the weakness hadn't gotten to her first. She listed hard to the right as dizziness struck, darkening her vision for a mind-bending instant. Fortunately, Kellen managed to grab her before she fell into the cesspool she'd created.

"You know better than to rise so abruptly after an extended illness, Dr. Teague." After easing her back onto the cushy mattress, he disappeared into an adjoining room. Moments later, he was pressing a cool, damp cloth to the back of her neck and wiping her cheeks and chin with another.

"Your boots," she murmured. He was standing right where she'd hurled.

"Are fine. The interior of this vessel is lined with a biologic pad that feeds on discarded organic material," he explained. "It consumes everything from the skin cells we shed to the waste we excrete to the microbes that would harm us, and in return produces many of the gases and nutrients we need to survive."

Monica roused herself enough to peer down at the floor, and sure enough, all evidence of her disgrace had disappeared. Thank God. But did that mean everyone just whizzed against the nearest wall? Surely not. They had to have designated facilities for that.

Didn't they?

Kellen sat down beside her again and her heart thumped hard against her breastbone. God, he was big. How could she have forgotten how big he was?

"It's not all bad news, you know."

"Do tell."

"The Tooth Fairy left you seven more dollars and you now have twenty new molars."

She sucked in a breath. "Oh, no way! That was you?"

"Guilty, I'm afraid."

"Wait—twenty new molars? How the hell many teeth do I have?"

"Forty-four, the full Garathani complement. And your vision is now quite a bit better than the average Terran's. You can see at twenty feet what most of them can see at eight."

She thought for a minute. "So that line you fed me about halethoid mutations was total crap?"

"No, it wasn't. The halethoid mutations cropping up on your planet are a natural part of humanity's evolution. You carry nearly all of them because of your Garathani genes; thousands of years from now, all Terrans will likely be what the Garathani are now. The only reason their evolution has lagged behind ours is the inordinately high levels of bondridon emanating from Sol."

She arched a brow. "Are you telling me we're all Garathanis on the inside?"

"No, I'm telling you there's a reason why Terrans and Garathani are compatible for mating. We're descended from the same race of beings. In your biological terms, we are a slightly different species of the same genus."

"Uh-huh."

"I know this is a lot of information to digest all at once," he said with a sigh, "but please, just let me finish my explanation of how you came to be."

"Can I stop you?" she asked sourly.

"No, but I can stop you," he threatened without heat. "It's not uncommon for Garathani females who can't hold their tongues to be gagged by their mates."

"Oh, that's really nice. Do you tie them up, too?"

"Only to fuck them," he drawled.

Monica stiffened, her breath congealing in her lungs as her ears buzzed from the intense bass vibration of his reply. Issuing from his mouth, the f-word was a spider that skittered down her spine. She'd never heard Kellen or any of the other Garathani use foul language and this wasn't exactly the time she would have chosen for him to start.

"That's better. As I was saying before, your father was part of a reconnaissance group that spent two years on Earth gathering information about the various cultures. I'll leave it to him to share the details, but obviously he had intercourse with your mother, which resulted in conception."

"Leave it to..." Monica's eyes bulged. "You mean he's still alive?"

"Yes, he is. I believe your name is a bastardized version of his."

Her smart mouth automatically kicked out, "Bastardized—how appropriate," while her brain shrieked, *Oh my God, your mother did the nasty with an alien!* For some reason it hadn't occurred to her that her conception might be the result of intercourse. Instead, her imagination had fallen victim to its years of sci-fi conditioning and conjured visions of impregnation through some anonymous, technologically superior means of embryo delivery with a name like the Pregomatic-9000. Or, at other end of the spectrum, an ugly, torturous needle in the navel.

Obviously her own mother been served from behind by one of these massive soldiers. Oh jeez, she'd had his spur up her—

"You have no cause to disrespect yourself or your parents in such a manner." Kellen frowned. "Your father is one of the greatest warriors of our time, and to have been sired by him is an incredible honor. It's my understanding that he was intimate with your mother only once, the night before he was to be recalled, and he had no idea that a child had resulted from the union. Not until…"

A sardonic smile dimpled his cheek. "It pains me to seemingly confirm your basest suspicions, but yes, we did collect a number of human subjects beginning nearly ten years ago, after the bio-war attack, and yes, we did conduct experiments with them."

When she opened her mouth to lambaste him, he clamped his hand over it.

"However," he said loudly, "they were not tortured or mistreated in any way, nor were they returned to Earth to face the ridicule of others. They were all women who had no immediate family and many of them have since become highly valued members of our society. It was through those experiments that we learned that interspecies breeding was possible."

She swatted his hand away in annoyance but kept her lips pressed into a mutinous line, allowing him to continue.

"Our scientists were astounded to find that a chemical in Garathani semen triggered immediate ovulation in Terran females, resulting in conception in nearly every encounter. So far, nearly six hundred and fifty hybrids have been conceived by the females we appropriated from your planet, three hundred and twelve of whom still live."

"Three hundred and twelve?" Monica gasped. "That's a mortality rate of over fifty percent!"

Robin L. Rotham

already had mixed ideas about gender dominance, the Council had deemed it prudent to limit the education of the recruits to Garathan's current social order. Technically, the new democracy afforded females equal rights, but it was still in its infancy and, for the moment, run exclusively by males, and the sooner the recruits adjusted to their minority status, the better off they'd be.

Monica, however, was an entirely different kettle of fish. As a Garathani female, and the minister's daughter at that, she would have every right, and indeed be expected to eventually [lear]n the bigger picture of Garathan's history. No doubt she [wou]ld assign unjustly vengeful motives to his treatment of [her] making the mastery of her even more difficult. And she [didn'] even know about Shauss yet.

[Sh]e winced again. Once she was awake and had time to [think ab]out what he'd said, she would probably arrive at the [conclusion] on her own and hit the proverbial ceiling. She was [well v]ersed in current Garathani mating rituals, after all— [and did]n't expected to participate.

[Rem]embering her enthusiasm for all things Garathani, [he could onl]y hope that she would one day accept him and [Shauss with t]he same enthusiasm. That she would have to [come to term]st for mating with her prior to her acceptance [was a foregone c]onclusion. She was as intractable as a drunken [Yheng, an]d despite her diminutive size, no doubt twice [as strong. It m]ight take years of sleeping with his dagger [strapped on b]efore she finally gave herself to him and [Shauss for preser]vation.

[It wou]ld be in everyone's best interests for him [to accept]t their attentions in advance, though [he held little] hope of that happening. He could try [when Shauss] returned to the infirmary in the [morning.]

[He c]onceded that wasn't a promising [thought. To h]arm anyone in recent memory, [Shauss] hadn't taken much exposure to

---

Alien Overnight

"Experiments are not without their risks, Doctor. Unfortunately, a significant percentage of the females we took were too small to mate with our males. Still more were unable to carry the fetuses to term, and of those who were able to carry successfully, many were unable to deliver vaginally because of the size of their fetuses. Most of the fetal deaths resulted from babies too large in wombs too small, and sadly, a number of the females expired from the same cause and its complications." He leaned closer, his gaze pinning hers. "Why do you suppose we're so particular about the physical requirements for the recruits? The last thing we want is for the females who would serve us to suffer unduly or perish for our cause."

Monica was dazed and not a little horrified by the tale he'd just told her. Women, many women, and their babies, too, had already sacrificed their lives in the race to save the Garathani people, and this information was not being provided to the reproductive candidates. They could very well be signing up for…

God in heaven, her own mother had died within days of giving birth to her!

"This situation is unacceptable, Commander," she said unsteadily.

"I refuse to debate the morality of our actions, Monica. We are making every effort to ensure that the females selected are able to bear the children we plant in their wombs and that's all I have to say about it."

"Well, good, because I have plenty to say about it!"

"After I'm finished, you can flay the skin from my bones with your razor-sharp tongue all you'd like, but please contain yourself until then."

"Fuck you, Commander," Monica snarled, turning to face the wall again. Her wits scattered to the four winds when Kellen curled his long fingers under her chin and forced her to look at him.

75

"Believe me, you will," he said arrogantly, fire blazing in his eyes. "Just as soon as you're declared fit."

* * * * *

Perhaps that hadn't been the best way to inform her of her new lot in life, Kellen thought ruefully, scrubbing the nutty-smelling cleanser through his hair as the shower pounded his body.

After her eyeballs had threatened to pop from their sockets, they'd rolled back in her head and she'd fainted dead away. Ketrok hadn't been pleased to find his patient unconscious again and had ordered him out of the infirmary.

Kellen ducked his head under the spray and tried to let the steaming water rinse away some of his tension along with the suds. Peserin, but the brat could be aggravating! He'd invented the bit about Garathani females being bound and gagged in an attempt to silence her, but even as the words fell from his lips, he'd known their fiction would become reality as soon as he pried her away from Ketrok. If her impassioned protection of the recruits was any indication, she would present quite an erotic challenge in the mating bed, and his cock was near bursting at the prospect.

The past two weeks had been the worst kind of torture ever devised, holding her as she lay helpless, caressing her body and soothing her with his warmth and his scent, all the while going stark raving bananas from the backed-up blood strangling his gonads. *Stark raving bananas.* He grinned. He could see the phallic fruit in his mind's eye, peeled from its skin and ranting madly at not being fed into the orifice it was meant for.

No doubt Monica would bite off his banana, should he try to feed it to her.

The thought was enough to make him wince, but the imagery was so tantalizing, he cupped himself and groaned with a comic blend of trepidation and lustful curiosity. What

would it be like to push the bulk of his throbbing flesh into her mouth and feel that velvet heat laving him, knowing that she could emasculate him at any moment with a single snap of her jaw? How tempted would she be to try it, knowing that he could snap her neck with a single flick of his wrist?

Squirting a puddle of scrub into one palm, Kellen beg lathering his groin with rough sensuality. He'd considered questions like these, or their inherent control and trust, outside the dark realm of his fant feminine fists that had ruled Garathan prior would have slammed down hard, and wi finality, on any male who expressed inter insisted on, receiving oral sex. *It serves no u* rationale for their females' rejection of was true enough, given that males fellatio the way females could from as true that their females were q performing such a service, an do anything they didn't care

Kellen had roared "Girls rule, boys droc Only Terrans could down to a flippa had appealed t his compute reminder been decor thi

ship
citizen

78

their arts and entertainments to convince him that their idea of charm differed vastly from his, and now that he thought about it, his little ex-Terran seemed less susceptible to charming than most.

Then there was the fact that he was not her favorite Garathani at the moment.

Perhaps he should let Shauss try his luck with her.

* * * * *

"The little Sparnite witch tried to gut me!"

Shauss swore viciously as Ketrok painted the ragged edges of his belly wound with regeneration gel and pressed the accelerator to it. "And with my own dagger, no less!"

"What precipitated her attack?" Kellen demanded.

"Only the Powers know," Shauss replied. "I'd barely sat down and expressed my pleasure in her recovery when she struck."

"Has she been confined?"

"Yes, Commander," the doctor replied without looking up from his ministrations. "She was too weak to put up much of a fight after her initial assault."

Although Shauss' discomfort eased almost immediately, Kellen's did not. He paced the surgical bay, brimming with fury, and not just at the homicidal little doctor. Hadn't it crossed his mind that she might resort to violence? He should have cautioned Shauss more strongly.

"Calm yourself, Commander," Shauss said with a rueful grin. "That was a lesson I needed to learn for myself. I'll never be caught off guard again."

"Nor will I," Kellen assured him, still frowning ferociously. "But her actions cannot go undisciplined."

"On that we agree, my friend. Did you have something in mind?"

"Several things," he said with a nasty smile. "But most of them wouldn't be appropriate for a convalescent, not matter how feisty she's feeling." Ketrok's ferocious frown widened Kellen's smile. "No, Doctor, as tempting as it is, I won't spank her. Or fuck her," he added. "Though she deserves both, and more."

"I'd fuck her," Shauss said darkly, "*while* I spanked her. If she's fit enough to skewer me, she's fit enough to be skewered herself. Ow! Not so hard!"

Ketrok eased the accelerator back slightly, but kept his scowl firmly in place. "Until I declare her fit, keep your penises in your pants and your hands to yourselves or I'll see you both before the Council."

"Killjoy," Shauss muttered. Then his grin reappeared. "Actually, if our little GaraTer had so shamed any warrior but me, I'd be more inclined to reward her show of courage."

"Don't tell her that." Kellen rolled his eyes. "She's going to be difficult enough to master as it is."

Shauss opened his mouth, obviously prepared to assert otherwise, then closed it again with a look of chagrin. And rightly so, as he was the one whose body would bear the scar of her intransigence.

"No," Kellen said. "She's made up her mind to fight us, and it's up to us to make her reconsider her position."

* * * * *

God, what had she done?

One minute she was losing the fight to keep Shauss from prying his blade, still dripping with his own blood, from her nerveless fingers, and the next she was surrounded by this breathtaking blankness. It was like someone had pressed the mute button on the TV, only it wasn't just sound that was blocked.

White noise. That was the only way to describe what she was seeing and hearing.

In that first instant, she'd wondered if she was about to pass out. Before Kellen's little shocker, she'd only come close to fainting once in her life. It had happened at the end of a taxing double shift at the hospital and she'd heard that same hissing sound and thought it was one of the unused oxygen valves leaking, until the edges of her vision started to darken. But her vision was fine now—she could see her legs, crossed tailor-fashion under the blood-spattered covers, and her hands in her lap, wringing the edge of the blanket. Yet the noise and the whiteness persisted and it was as if the world had been reduced to her body and this bed. She reached out to the side with her fingers, stained with Shauss' blood and shaking like nobody's business, then jerked them back when she encountered a barrier that sent fierce tingles up her arm.

Her fingers... Monica stared at that hand, front and back, like she'd never seen it before. And maybe she hadn't. It didn't look like her hand. The nails were long and sturdy, and the fingers seemed even longer and certainly bonier than before. For God's sake, they looked like talons!

What had she done? Monica wondered again, fear curdling in her belly. She drew up her knees, wrapped her arms around them, heedless of the blood, and rocked. She'd just tried to kill Lieutenant Shauss, had grabbed the wicked-looking dagger from his belt and buried it to the hilt in his gut. And why?

Because she'd smelled the spice of his Garathani pheromones.

After the commander had left her the previous evening, she'd lain on her bed, the very bed that was now the only object left in her world, and tried to digest all that he'd revealed. Their parting shots had chased round and round in her thoughts.

Fuck you, Commander.

Believe me, you will. Just as soon as you're declared fit.

Commander Kellen intended to mate with her. There was no other way to take his reply, and the very idea of it boggled her mind—and scared the living shit out of her. He was an alien. He was over seven feet tall. He was larger than life in places she didn't care to think about and would only get larger.

And she herself was…what? Did she even know what she was anymore? All her life she'd been different, set apart from the world by a deformed and undeveloped body. Now, instead of flowering gently into womanhood, as she'd always dreamed, she'd burst violently, almost overnight, into…

Pain. Terror. Confusion.

Alienhood?

Whatever it was, it certainly didn't feel like womanhood. Her body might have undergone some sort of freaky maturation process, but the rest of her had yet to catch up and it was hard to imagine that her deformities could have magically disappeared. Although these days, nothing seemed quite as impossible as it used to. She'd checked the impulse to feel around down there—the temptation was strong, but her awareness of possible unseen observers was stronger.

If the commander didn't realize that she'd been born with congenital defects, he might be in for a nasty surprise when he reached between her legs. And if her body had somehow miraculously transformed itself into a more acceptable form, she could be in for a nastier surprise. Because although she was well-versed in the mechanics of sex, she had no firsthand experience of it. None. She'd never even been kissed, for God's sake!

She'd tossed under her blanket for hours, agonizing over the possible scenarios she faced. Then Shauss had stepped into the infirmary first thing this morning, and she'd seen his possessive look, the not-so-subtle anticipation in his gaze, and that's when it had hit her like a boot to the head that necessity, along with Garathani law, required all males to share their mates. Possibly with more than one partner, depending on their rank and circumstances.

Shauss intended to mate with her, too.

A whimper sounded deep in her throat, muffled by the strange field that separated her from reality. It was the lightning realization of what these two mountains of alien flesh planned to do to her, coupled with the insidious aroma of Shauss' pheromones, that had triggered her ill-advised attack. Monica shuddered at the memory of Ensign Hastion plowing into Carrie Ray from behind, reaming her vagina and anus simultaneously, and a tear streaked down her cheek. That couldn't happen to her. She would die before she'd become the impersonal receptacle for their lust, their desire for children.

On some level, she was aware of the irrational and absurdly hypocritical nature of her reaction. She'd been more than happy to plan this very fate for hundreds, hopefully even thousands of other women, to accompany them across the galaxy while they eased the needs of these mighty beings, and to monitor and nurture them while they carried their alien babies. It had seemed like a calling then, like the true reason for her existence had finally been revealed.

Now it seemed like some monstrous plot to…

Hysteria edged her laugh at the idea someone might plot to get her into bed. Her! Monica Teague, the original oddball. Like the commander could have planned her love of the stars or her strange fixation on his name. Like he could have arranged, somehow, for her neighbors to be transferred overseas, giving her their cute little border collie named Kellen. And her first major crush on Aidan Kellen, her undergrad humanities professor, who'd inspired her to doodle *Mrs. Monica Kellen* in every notebook margin for two full semesters. And her house in Kellen Gardens.

Her house.

The thought of it crushed her chest, made a sob of longing erupt from her throat as her tears rained down, creating big wet circles on her knees.

* * * * *

"Do we have to do this now?"

The doubtful inquiry made Kellen sigh as he observed Monica's abject misery from outside the field. She was still such a child…

"You know we do," he said resolutely. "To put it off would only frighten her further."

"She's little more than a child."

The echo of his own thoughts made Kellen's gaze slide to Shauss.

"So you don't want to mate with her."

"I didn't say that."

"She has no choice in this, Shauss, and we can't let her imagine that she does."

"I know!" Shauss bit out. "Sorry, Commander. I just didn't expect to grow so fond of her so quickly."

"Tell me, Shauss," Kellen asked blandly, "is it her foul mouth or her handiness with a blade that's endeared her to you so completely?"

The barely restrained rumble of Shauss' laughter made the commander grin. "Okay, let's do it."

Chapter Seven

ဢ

"I take it you figured out who my second is."

Kellen's wry comment made Monica look up sharply. The world was back. Or at least the infirmary was back, along with the two objects of her fevered, if not downright hysterical, imaginings. Wariness kept her silent as she stared at them, leaning further into the wall, drawing her knees even closer.

They were out of uniform.

Their expressions said they were out of patience.

And they were out of their fucking minds if they thought they were going to have her now. Monica steeled her jaw, looking away. But not too far away.

"Do you know the meaning of the word discipline, Monica?"

She didn't even blink, wouldn't give them the satisfaction, but her pulse skittered anxiously. She'd known she would be punished for harming the lieutenant, had been trying to brace herself for whatever was coming.

"Look at me when I address you, little one," Kellen demanded softly.

Name, rank and serial number. Wasn't that all prisoners of war were allowed to give up? But this supposedly wasn't war and these men already knew all that about her, and more. Much more. So she simply ignored them, ignored *him*, even as that act of blatant defiance made her breath turn choppy. The man did have a history of charbroiling people who pissed him off.

Out of the corner of her eye, she saw Kellen and Shauss draw up two contoured chairs beside her bed and settle themselves in them.

"I feel like I should have popcorn and a box of Milk Duds," Shauss said in a conversational tone.

Annoyance raised her hackles, which admittedly was a step up from cowering in fear. The asshole was mocking her!

"Do you even know what popcorn and Milk Duds are, ET?" she sneered.

"Refreshments available for purchase at a show," he answered promptly. "And frankly, you look like you're about to put on quite a show."

Kellen's low chuckle was just as infuriating. "I doubt she intends to put on quite the show she's going to."

Unable to stand it, she let her angry gaze fly to his. "Why are you doing this? I thought you were nice!"

Slouched low in his chair with his fingers laced across his belly, Kellen replied, "I can be very nice. But right now you require disciplining, as much for your own safety as for ours. Can you define discipline for me, Monica?"

She glared at him, heart thumping. "Look it up yourself."

"Unnecessary. In your case, discipline will involve training you to submit to my authority without question."

His subtle emphasis on the word *submit* robbed her of breath for a long minute, and she looked away again, dismayed to feel a fierce, dark tingle in her belly. If she didn't know better, she'd almost swear it was...anticipation.

"Ha! Like that'll ever happen."

"Oh, but it will."

Monica's chest constricted at that quiet promise and it felt like every cell in her body was being sucked toward him. She tensed against his magnetic pull, furious that this new and improved body was just as weak and defective as the old one. She *would not* desire such a controlling bastard.

"Fuck that."

"Such profanity withers the flower of your mouth," Shauss berated lyrically.

Monica rolled her eyes. "Fuck that, too."

The Garathani officers looked at each other as if to say, "Well, we did our best," and stood up. A frisson of panic slid down her spine, and damn it, continued right on down into her crotch. Jeez, she was getting more twisted every day!

"Empran, activate neural restraint, subject Monica Teague," she heard Kellen order.

"Neural restraint activated," a marginally feminine voice responded.

Monica gasped as she collapsed into a puddle of her former self. Her head sagged against the wall and her arms fell away from her legs to rest heavily beside her. She couldn't move!

"Don't be frightened, Monica. Your nervous system is working perfectly," Kellen said gently. "Neural restraints only affect voluntary movement from the neck down."

A wave of anxiety washed over her when the two huge males moved in to rearrange her body. Her eyes darted wildly between them as Shauss took her shoulders and lay her down on her back while Kellen grasped her ankles and pulled her limp legs out flat. Shauss backed off then, but Kellen wasn't so quick to release her. He smoothed his warm, dry palms up her shins and over her knees, her thighs…

Because her head had come to rest facing away from them, her whispered plea bounced off the wall. "Don't look at me."

His hands continued in their upward path as if he hadn't heard her, taking her gown along for the ride. They slid along the sides of her hips, her waist, and carried her arms up alongside her head as he tugged the garment completely off her. Monica squeezed her eyes shut tight when he returned her arms to her sides and gently tilted her head to face them.

"You will learn to submit," he murmured in her ear.

"You will be sorry for this, asshole," she breathed back, disgusted at the tremor that stole much of the fervor from her promise. She was naked. Dear God, she was naked in front of the man who'd haunted her dreams and made her feel things she'd never expected to.

In that instant, the scent of pheromones whispered into her nasal passages and her eyes flew open.

"Brave words, for one so completely at our mercy."

Monica gasped with fury at the amusement lacing Shauss' taunt, then gasped with something else as both men pulled their tunics over their heads and dropped them to the floor. Their pheromones were thickening the air now, making every breath she dragged into her lungs a chore.

God, it *so* wasn't fair how gorgeous they were! Shauss had left his hair hanging free, and the long straight fall of black and pale blue silk raining across his shoulders was enough to make her mouth water. His chest was impossibly wide, leanly muscled and liberally furred with silky black hair, and she wanted nothing more at the moment than to rub her face in it, to knead it like a cat and purr with the joy of it.

Who'd have thought neural restraints would be a good thing?

Kellen's naked torso was deeper and browner, bulging with a leashed power that made her bones feel watery. *Oh, crap...*

"You don't want me," she choked out, forcing her eyes to his face.

"I have an erection that says otherwise." Kellen's eyes glinted as he stood there, arms akimbo, and damn it, she just had to look. And then gape, heart pounding, at the ridge trying to fight its way out of his loose-fitting black pants.

"I'll see your erection and raise you two blue balls," Shauss quipped, causing her eyes to skitter to the left. God, she shouldn't have looked.

"I'm deformed!" she gasped.

"In what way? You look perfect to me. Good enough to eat, in fact."

Shauss' deliberate words sparked a fire of confusion in her chest and cheeks; pleasure that such a beautiful male thought she looked perfect, embarrassed remembrance that she'd once said those very words to the commander, and oh God, yes, desire, thick and heavy, at the mental image his words evoked. When she'd said them to the commander, her intention had been purely innocent, but Shauss' tone was far from that. Blood pounded in her head from the odor of their arousal, coursing downward through her veins to pool in her nipples and belly, and between her thighs. Her palms and the soles of her feet were beginning to burn.

"My genitals," she managed to squeak. "They've never been right." And at the moment, the way they both smelled made her wish that wasn't the case.

Kellen's reply immediately made her wish she'd kept her mouth shut.

"Maybe we'd better take a look."

* * * * *

Empran, reflect full-body image, station one.

At his nod, Shauss stepped to the head of the bed and took Monica's tousled head between his palms, turning it so she looked directly up.

Her eyes widened in shock as the flare field solidified overhead, reflecting her naked figure.

"What is that?" she gasped.

"That's you."

"That is *not* me! I don't look like that."

"You do now," Kellen told her.

"I don't know what you're trying to pull, but there's no mirror up there. It's a trick."

"You're right, as it happens. That's not a mirror, but a molecular flare field, like the one we used to transport you up here. And the white field we used to confine you." At his silent prompt, Empran momentarily switched the field to white mode before restoring her image.

Kellen tried to see her as she would be seeing herself for the first time. Her hair, having grown more than a foot since she'd last seen her reflection, was now a motley tangle of brown and ash-blonde, with chalky black ends. Her face had become long and hollow and her eyes, away from the yellow cast of her home planet, looked nearly purple, their sockets deep and dark.

Tendons stretched in a neck as long and fragile-looking as a sumiswan's, and her collarbones, ribs and hipbones stood out in stark relief against her sunken torso. Her limbs, already long, were now the stuff of Terran stick-figure legend, and it would take many weeks of supplemented feedings to return her to her previous healthy plumpness.

Her breasts, however, were remarkably lush and Kellen could see she was having difficulty drawing her gaze away from them. Even in her supine position, they were round and firm-looking. Their overnight appearance hadn't yet allowed her skin to stretch out enough for them to spill to her sides.

"Ketrok says your breasts will eventually soften and settle more naturally onto your frame," he told her. "Although with the difference in Garathan's relative gravity, they will never hang quite as they would have on Earth."

They were beautiful, no doubt exquisitely tender from their rapid emergence, and the mere thought of that was enough to spark an inferno in his veins. Already he could hear the impassioned cries that would burst from her as he suckled their virginal nipples, the same cries he'd drawn when he'd fondled them in their immaturity. She had been confused at first, then perturbed by her raging response to the light pain of his pinches and tugs. If he hadn't been wary then of waking her too fully, he would have latched on and sucked until she screamed for release.

Towel or bucket?

Kellen glanced at Shauss, puzzled.

For the drool.

He narrowed his eyes. *Keep it up, Shauss, and she'll be a grandmother before you see her breasts again.*

Shauss barely managed to disguise his snicker as a cough, keeping his face out of Monica's line of vision.

Kellen had to turn away himself, fighting a smile. Peserin, but it was a job being the disciplinarian when lust and humor joined forces to chisel away at his resolve. Then his gaze landed on her newly furred mons and humor fled in the face of aching desire. Determined to stay on track, he ran a hand down her thigh, and disregarding her involuntary jerk, pulled her knee outward until it rested against his abdomen.

"Don't!"

A quick glance told him her eyes had closed once more, her face flushed. With shame, he realized. She truly thought herself malformed.

He looked at Shauss and felt a different sort of smile creep over his face. Surely between the two of them, they could think of a variety of pleasant ways to clear up that little misconception for her.

* * * * *

"One of the cruelest ironies of this disaster which has befallen our race," Shauss murmured, his measured breaths loud in her ear, "is that Garathan's males, who are unable to attain satisfaction by our own hands, emerged unscathed."

"While our females," continued Kellen, as if on cue, "who could and quite often did pleasure themselves and each other while we waited on them for our relief, nearly died out."

Warm fingers trailed up her inner thigh and paused to trace the valley where it joined her pelvis. She should be freaking out. Really, she should. Any minute now, she would.

Maybe.

Oh God, she was feeling good. Tickles were flaring out from her abdomen, making her nipples stand up and beg for attention, making her toes curl reflexively. Every deep breath she took chilled her out further, and paradoxically wound her up tighter. This was kind of what she'd thought to experience in high school, back at the girls' home, where she'd gotten lonely enough to try smoking pot with a couple of wacked-out roommates and wound up paranoid and puking for six hours instead. She'd never tried another consciousness-altering chemical again, but if their effect was anything like this, it was no wonder people became addicted.

She felt those wandering fingers brush over to her other thigh and push it gently outward and knew she really, *really* should be objecting, trying to draw away from their prying eyes. But it was just too much trouble.

"Monica." God, she loved the way Kellen said her name in his slightly stilted accent. It was thicker now, like he had marbles under his tongue. "Look at yourself."

Obeying without thought, she opened her eyes and had only an instant to stare at the strange woman who hovered above her, thighs fallen open like a stringy, over-baked chicken's, before the image mysteriously morphed into…

Hardcore porn?

Holy shit, that was a close-up of her whole new fur-lined package, ten times larger than life and way too personal. She squirmed inwardly as fingers the size of baseball bats loomed in the view and gently spread her labia open for an excruciating inspection.

"You, my dear doctor, have a *lovely* little Garathani vulva," Kellen purred appreciatively from somewhere out of her sight.

"As flawless and sweet as any I've seen," Shauss agreed. Without warning, his face was over hers, still trapped between his palms, and his full lips were brushing hers upside down. Electricity arced between them as the delectable roughness of his tongue stroked her lower lip, leaving it wet. "And I'm going to taste it before I fuck it," he promised before he pulled away.

Something curled hard in her abdomen at his words and washed down into her wide-open pubis, making her gasp and whimper and arch uncontrollably on the bed.

"This..." Kellen's finger stroked lightly up her cleft, drawing her splintered attention back to the image once more. It looked like there might be, oh Lord, not another... "This, Monica, is your spur nook."

"My what?" She tried to blink away the pheromone fog that enveloped her. "What are you talking about?" The term rang a bell, but she just couldn't think.

"That part of you that houses the center of all your pleasure," Shauss murmured. "That part that will receive the fullness of our spurs."

Their spurs. Spur nook... Her eyes widened. She had a spur nook?

"Does that mean I won't have to..."

How to ask this delicately?

And at this point, was delicacy even a possibility?

"Take it in the ass?" Shauss supplied helpfully.

Okay, no delicacy. She resisted the urge to ask where he'd learned such a phrase.

"Right."

"No, you definitely won't." Kellen sounded pretty firm about that and she sighed in relief.

After a strangely expectant pause, Shauss appeared right in her face again and added in a silky tone, "Unless you want to."

"Oh man, you're the wild child, aren't you?" she snorted, vaguely disgusted, highly amused and, damn it, disturbingly intrigued. "Gotta try everything, no matter how gross, at least once, right?"

He kissed her again, this time sliding his tongue between her lips, grazing her teeth. Monica couldn't help it, she really couldn't. She opened up and sucked him inside her mouth before he could get away. God, if she could only move her hands, she'd have them twisted so tight in that beautiful hair, he'd never get away. Yummy, yummy, yummy...

Shauss pulled away, breathing harder than she was.

"I'll do anything you let me get away with," he answered in a tone so deep, it was almost inaudible.

Chills broke out on her skin. He wanted her bad, any way he could get her, and she really should make things harder for him than she was.

"Don't hold your— Aaah! What are you *doing*?"

Shauss draw back once more, allowing her to see the magnified view of Kellen's shiny-wet pinkie finger advancing slowly into that strange new opening.

"You didn't think you had a clitoris, did you?"

Chapter Eight

ఠ

Kellen halted his invasion at the first knuckle and began to rub against her in light circles. Satisfaction roared over him as her back immediately arched off the mattress and a shout burst from her throat. Shauss looked equally pleased at her responsiveness, leaning down once more to join his mouth with hers. She latched onto him fiercely, and he grunted with approval as he plumbed her recesses with his tongue. Intriguing. Kissing wasn't an activity his people normally indulged in.

Watching the delineated muscles in Monica's throat rippling as she worked to devour Shauss, Kellen pressed his finger a fraction deeper and frowned. Her nook was somehow not quite what he'd expected, almost too narrow for...

Then his brow cleared. Perhaps her Terran genes hadn't manifested themselves as disastrously as he'd begun to think. Kellen withdrew his finger, provoking another muffled cry, and bent down for a closer look. Instead of clinging to the deeper recesses of her nook, as was typical of Garathani females, Monica's little clitoris hovered just inside the orifice and arousal was puffing it into the open air.

"My, my," he murmured. "Somebody wants to come out and play." Under Shauss' curious gaze, he wet a larger finger in his mouth and stroked it into her several times, each penetration deeper than the last, maintaining a light, careful friction as he tested the limits of her nook. It was a mercy that small kernel of sensitized tissue was drawing outside, which meant his spur would fit—barely. He hated to think what they'd both have gone through otherwise. Unlike her vagina, which would stretch far enough to accommodate the head of a newborn, her nook tunneled through her pubic bone and thus was fixed in size. If Shauss happened to have a thicker spur…

Perhaps the man's arcane fascination with anal penetration would stand him in very good stead indeed.

Kellen glanced at him and knew by the narrowed eyes that his amusement was showing. He didn't bother enlightening him. Shauss would figure it out for himself when the time came.

His testicles drew tight when a heavier touch made Monica scream into Shauss' open mouth. She was very close to orgasm, he thought with considerable envy.

Then he saw Shauss' hands sliding down her neck toward her breasts.

Me first.

Without pausing in his oral ministrations, Shauss slanted a nasty look his way.

Why don't you do the honors down here? At Shauss' raised brow, he explained, *Since I'll claim the right of first mating, I suppose I must allow you the first…meal. You did say you wanted to…*

I want to.

Monica's whine of dismay when Shauss pulled away so abruptly would have made Kellen smile if it hadn't been so damnably arousing.

"Where are you going?" she cried, eyes still closed, head rolling restlessly back and forth. Ah, there was nothing like two males emitting in close proximity to reduce a female to a shameless mass of quivering want. And there was no doubt Monica herself was actively emitting now. Her fragrance was unusual but arousing, light and sharp and…alien. He'd never scented any female quite like her.

Kellen moved up and took her chin between his fingers. She tensed at once, eyes flying open. From this close, they looked even more enormous, more vulnerable.

Still linked with her biomet, he felt her pulse begin to sprint. Interesting. And she was trembling. She obviously felt more threatened by him, *much* more than by Shauss, which was at once intriguing and disturbing.

"I will never hurt you," he murmured. "I will never take you against your will, and I will *never*," he swiped his tongue briefly over her closed mouth without breaking eye contact, "leave you unfulfilled. But I *will* have your obedience, Monica Teague."

She appeared to have run out of defiant comebacks, so he turned at once to her breasts. A glance told him Shauss was positioning Monica for his convenience, so to prepare her for the storm about to strike her body, he dipped his head and indulged himself.

Empran, deactivate neural restraints.

* * * * *

"Oh God, please!"

Kellen's luxurious mane crackled in her grasping fingers as he laved her breast from base to summit in long, unhurried licks and deposited swaths of moisture on her sensitive skin. Her nipple prickled, drawing upward, wet, rigid and needy, and his tongue probed delicately at the puckered flesh, drawing teasing circles that made her squirm with anxiety. She arched instinctively into the heat of his mouth, but the light suction he offered wasn't nearly enough.

"Harder, damn it!" she heard herself shriek, beyond caring about anything, *anything* but the hunger consuming her. He obliged immediately, caught her nipple between the rough slide of his tongue and the roof of his mouth, the almost painful edge of his teeth, and sent urgent signals blazing downward into her crotch. At the same time, his fingers plucked boldly at her other nipple, twisting, tugging, and the shock of it all, the pure, amazing sizzle of it, made her yowl out loud, made every muscle in her body pull tight, searching, needing so damn bad…

"By all the Powers…" Shauss sounded amazed. "Look at her. I haven't even touched her and she's about to come."

Kellen pulled harder in response, and time seemed to bend and hover on an indrawn breath while something so searing, so totally overwhelming, gathered in her body… The sight of Shauss' thick thumbs pulling the lips of her vulva wide, exposing the moisture that glazed her pink folds and streamed into the crevice between her buttocks, stretched her taut. The visible quivering of her vaginal tissues pushed her over the edge. She broke with an ear-splitting scream, buffeted by wave after wave of released energy as the powerful contractions wrung her, straining her neck and arching her shoulders off the mattress in agonizing pleasure.

Awareness returned in an improbably slow rush as the tide receded, leaving her trembling and breathless. She must have cried, because the hair at her temples was coolly damp and she could feel little puddles in the inner shells of her ears. Pulling her hands free of Kellen's hair, she reamed out the annoying moisture with her fingertips while she tried to catch her breath. His ravenous pulls had gentled, but he still fed at her breast, kneading the other with obvious enjoyment. And Shauss still held her open, as if he were down there just watching, waiting.

"Very nice, little virgin," he purred.

And as if by some unspoken command, the view above changed, revealing her once more from head to toe.

"Oh shit." Shauss' big hands were suddenly smoothing her scrawny drumsticks even wider, and he was wedging his shoulders between them. "Shauss, no!"

He turned his head far enough to grin upward at her, making his hair cascade against her most sensitive flesh, and she writhed in anguished delight. His shiny, beautiful hair was going to get all sticky…

"Like that, do you?"

Kellen's voice startled her. His head was up now, leaving her breasts to the mercies of his hands, and she could see him watching with rapt attention as the other man deliberately trailed his hair over her again.

"I haven't bathed!"

Not looking away from the action, Kellen murmured, "You've been bathed daily."

Oh God, she didn't even want to think about who might have done *that*.

A fine tremor settled into her joints when Shauss reached to pull all that hair to one side over his shoulder and laid his jaw against her thigh, rubbing the surprising smoothness of his skin against hers as he inhaled deeply.

"Please don't—"

She'd almost said it. Oh God, she'd almost said, *please don't stop*, and that was apparently what he'd heard because he drew his tongue through her folds at once, slowly, expertly, careful not to block her view.

Monica jumped at the insane rush of sensation.

"Jesus Christ, Shauss!" she swore roughly. "Were you a porn star or something before you joined the troops? Because you could probably make a really great living—"

He did it again and she reached instinctively to push him away, terrified by her own response. But Kellen was there to block her, snagging her twiggy wrists and pinning them to the mattress beside her head. And damn the bastard, he stayed right there, staring at her face with blazing dark eyes that refused to blink, to allow her even one split-second of retreat. She tried to yank her hands free and then gasped.

The neural restraints were gone. When in the bloody hell had that happened?

And when she would have struggled in earnest, Kellen grinned down at her. She couldn't fight her way out of a snotty tissue right now and he knew it.

"Rat bastard!"

He adjusted his grip on her wrists, hunkering down with his elbows propped on the mattress above her shoulders, bracketing her head. His breath was sweet and earthy and strangely familiar as it gusted from his open lips, his eyes unyielding as they bore into hers. Pride refused to let her look away.

"Nook only, Shauss," he murmured. "Eat away."

* * * * *

He had to give the little hellion an A for effort. She thrashed against him for exactly six point two seconds, keeping her gaze locked on his.

Then Shauss must have figured out which end was up, because her eyes widened and she gasped and stiffened like she'd grabbed an open circuit. Kellen had had no idea how fortuitous his choice of a second would be. Oh, he'd known Shauss was an excellent soldier, a good friend to have at his back when evil threatened and all that, but he'd had no real concept of the man's skills in matters such as this. Considering how few years he must have had to accumulate sexual experience before the attack, he was remarkably bold. And, it seemed, kinky.

It was an intriguing idea. There had never been a Garathani word for that particular quality because, despite the relatively recent and necessary implementation of mate-sharing, kinkiness hadn't existed on Garathan, or at least had never been acknowledged as such. Their females had always enjoyed each other's bodies, but it had been considered only natural—they could pleasure themselves and each other, so why shouldn't they?

Of course, that was also back before men's word became law in such matters.

Ah, times were definitely changing, he smirked to himself.

Monica jerked hard beneath him, and though she tried to hold it back, whatever Shauss was up to down there squeezed a sharp whimper out of her. Her bewildered eyes clung stubbornly to his, though they narrowed against the pleasure of Shauss' attentions.

"Is he pushing his tongue into your nook, little Garathani goddess?" Kellen wondered aloud, gathering her wrists into one of his hands over her head and stroking the velvet hollow of her cheek with his forefinger. "I would be, though perhaps I'd take the time to nibble at your charmingly outgoing little clitoris for a while first."

Don't you have something better to do with your tongue right now than wag it at her?

Kellen smothered a grin at Shauss' taunt, momentarily tightening his hold on Monica as she bucked against him. Strangled moans broke from her almost continuously now, and tears were trickling from the corners of her lovely wild eyes.

Bending to capture one of the salty drops with his tongue, he shot back, *Absolutely. But first I want to see what yours is doing to bring her to tears.*

Watch and learn, then, Commander.

Kellen rolled his eyes, but craned his neck to see exactly how Shauss was punishing his would-be assassin. The scene that met his eyes almost made *him* weep.

With one slender thigh over his shoulder and the other pinned to the mattress by his forearm, Monica was utterly defenseless against him. He'd spread her labia from above and below, and in between, his busy mouth was making quite the meal out of her.

As Kellen watched, Shauss lapped languidly at her tender flesh, stroking from bottom to top several times before stopping to circle her vaginal opening. Then he dipped just inside, drawing a stuttering moan from Monica, and when the rigid scoop of his tongue reappeared, it bore a considerable pool of her secretions. He looked at Kellen and swallowed, his eyes black with lust.

Fire streaked over Kellen's skin. Doing nothing but cradling Monica's face and watching the gamut of expressions that flitted across it had taken the edge off his desire, but that relative easiness passed abruptly. He felt his own eyes grow heavy and his cock turn to stone once more as Shauss resumed his intimate explorations.

The tendons in Monica's inner thigh stood out starkly as she dug her heel into his back, no doubt barely conscious that her reflexive action would force Shauss' face deeper into her drenched flesh. But Shauss had more than enough strength to counter the upward thrust of her hips, and after several more passes, he opened his mouth wide over her and shoved his tongue deep enough into her nook to earn a full-fledged screech.

When Shauss' eyes drifted shut and his jaw hollowed repeatedly, Kellen knew he was working her clitoris in earnest. Swallowing hard, breathing harder, he dropped his head beside hers, nuzzling her ear with his lips and drinking in her stream of whimpers like the powerful aphrodisiac they were. They turned to grating sobs when he sucked the delicate skin below her ear into his mouth, eating at her with barely controlled savagery. By Peserin's hand, when he was free to slide between her thighs...

"I'm going to fuck you, Monica Teague," he growled against her flesh. "Fuck your beautiful little cunt until you scream yourself hoarse, fuck you 'til you can't even *crawl* away from me, and then I'm going to fuck you again."

Monica went wild in his arms, screaming his name—*his* name!—over and over, and Kellen felt the back of his neck prickle with the possibility that he might never be the same once he'd had her. He turned to savor the sight of her convulsing body, drawn so tight, curved upward so viciously that only the back of her head touched the mattress. Her thighs had clamped around Shauss' ears, both feet pushing hard against his back, and his hands gripped her hips as he devoured her, grinding her flesh into his ravenous mouth.

It was the most incredibly erotic sight he'd ever hoped to see, and he prayed to the Powers that he could get out of this bay with his honor intact. The primitive urge to claim his mate, to sip at the fount of her passion himself and then drive his tortured flesh into her weeping, untried wells, was quickly becoming more than he could resist.

The very last gossamer-fine thread of his control was about to snap.

* * * * *

Kellen hadn't kissed her.

The realization still rankled twenty-eight hours later.

Monica stood before the mirror—excuse me, *flare field*— and glared at the new girl in town. Talk about bed head! She'd brushed the tangled mass for ten minutes straight, 'til the bristles went through without a snag and her chalky split ends swirled around her shoulders, and she still looked like she'd out-snoozed Rip van Winkle by at least a decade. Hell, forget bed head—she just looked flat-out bizarre. Kind of like a giraffe. A giant fucking Chia Pet giraffe, with two overripe grapefruits strapped to its chest. Directly under its chin. And damn it, all the holes in her ears had closed, too. And her teeth were furry! Her fucking teeth were furry, and she'd played *you swab my tonsils and I'll swab yours* with Shauss.

The thought made her flinch as she squeezed a thick line of blue gel onto her toothbrush. *He'd* kissed her, all right, and weak-willed wimp that she was, she'd tried to suck the taste buds right off his tongue, which would no doubt have been a relief for him, considering her total break with oral hygiene. He probably deserved it for being such a conceited ass, but it still bothered her to have inflicted her mothball breath and sloughed-off epithelial cells on him.

Kellen hadn't even given her a chance to inflict them on him, and it was just plain stupid how much that hurt.

She passed her toothbrush once, twice, under the faucet Ketrok had pointed out earlier. She'd never have found the thing for herself, it was so odd-looking. And that toilet... Now there was a piece of engineering Earth's manufacturers could take a lot of cues from. She'd used it standing up, like a urinal, only facing away from the wall. The elongated basin was narrow enough in the middle to slide between a woman's thighs and automatically raised and lowered according to each user's needs.

But that was about the only thing she'd found to like around here. She jammed the brush into her mouth and scrubbed harshly. It was going to bug the living shit out of her that Shauss had kissed her first. If anyone should have gotten get her first kiss, it was Kellen. Not that he was anything special. Just his name, Kellen, and that weird niggling feeling that all this was somehow meant to be. But apparently he hadn't deemed her worthy of kissing. Worthy of a big, nasty hickey, yes. But not a single kiss.

Monica shook her head, brushing off the pain as she hid the stark purple blotch behind the fall of her hair.

And as for what else Shauss had done first...

She spat in the sink and rinsed, her mind shying away from the memory of her utter and complete meltdown. Grudgingly, Monica admitted to herself that she'd probably owed him that first kiss, and maybe a few more, for operating on his abdomen without anesthesia, much less informed written consent. Hell, it would be a miracle if she kept her medical license, assuming she ever set foot on terra firma again. But the penalty he'd exacted, *they'd* exacted...

She slammed the door on those thoughts and concentrated on trying to tug her scrubs top down low enough to cover her sunken bellybutton. It wasn't working. All the clothes Ketrok had brought her from the surface were about four inches too short, tops and bottoms. And forget about her shoes—she'd count herself lucky if she still fit into a women's size. She was six-foot-three now. Six-foot-freakin'-three! And who knew if she was done growing? God, was Shelley ever in for a major shock. Monica had always topped her by a few inches, but now the difference was over a foot. Meet the new Mutt and Jeff…

And she'd thought finding a date was impossible before.

A date. She touched her lips with her fingertips. If Kellen had his way, she'd never go on a date, at least not with anyone but him or Shauss.

"Who do you belong to, Monica?" he'd demanded after he and Shauss turned her inside out with their hands. And their talented, hungry mouths… *Don't even go there*. Exhausted and nerveless, she'd tried to shake him off, but he'd held her face to his and insisted, "Say it, Monica. You belong to us."

"All right," she'd snapped weakly. "I belong to you, you arrogant prick!"

"Say, 'I belong to Kellen and Shauss,'" he'd come back forcefully. "And leave off the insults or suffer the consequences."

Already overwhelmed and excruciatingly aware of Shauss' mocking presence, she'd gulped down her pride and muttered, "I belong to Kellen and Shauss." And said the *you prick* part silently. And he'd seen it in her eyes and grinned. The prick.

So here she was, subjugated by her two alien lovers.

Not!

Monica shook her head 'til it rattled. No fucking way had she worked so hard, come so far, to spend the rest of her life playing sex slave for two swaggering comet jockeys. They'd just see who belonged to whom.

Satisfied that she was lean, mean and ready to rip doors from their hinges with her sparkling bare teeth, she struck out for the ship's command center.

Chapter Nine

➻

And ran face first into the infirmary door.

Shit! Hadn't Kellen and Ketrok, and even Shelley, simply walked up and let the silvery pocket door open spontaneously, like on the *Enterprise*, only without the *shhhp* sound effect?

"Now what?" She eyed its smooth, knob-free surface with loathing. Then something Kellen had said clicked in her head. "Empran, whoever you are, would you mind opening this door?"

"Egress not authorized," the same voice she'd heard earlier informed her.

"The hell you say!" Monica bristled. "What does a girl have to do to get authorization?"

"Egress requires the authorization of Commander Kellen."

Rolling her eyes, she barked, "Fine, then put me through to the commander."

"Unable to comply."

Monica was just winding up to let Computer Bitch have it when the door slid open and suddenly Shauss stood less than a foot away, his dark eyes heavy-lidded, lips curled in a provocative smile. Her pulse shifted into overdrive and she backed up two quick steps without thinking.

"Going somewhere?" he inquired, advancing on her. She'd barely had time to make a quick assessment of the open door and her chances of making it around him when it closed behind him. Damn it!

His hand shot out and grabbed the nape of her neck, yanking her to him before her struggles could even begin.

"Did you miss me?" he murmured into the hair at her ear as his other hand slid down and got a firm hold on her ass, pulling her upward and anchoring her against him.

"Like hell!" All her pushing and fighting did was make her breathless and dizzy, but she just couldn't give in. Oh God, he had a hard-on and was grinding it into her with surgical precision. If she didn't get away soon, she might prove herself a disgrace to womankind by coming from his manhandling alone.

"I missed you like hell too, angel." His breathing grew louder as he rubbed his chin in her hair. "I've barely slept at all for remembering the sweet tang of you on my tongue." Weakness seized her and she dropped her forehead against his throat with a low groan. "If I'm never allowed to do more than sup from the delectable spread of your thighs, I'll die a happy man."

"What are you, a fucking poet?" she moaned. "Just shut up!"

He laughed and hugged her tighter. "A poet, maybe. The fucking awaits Ketrok's sanction."

"Arrogant prick," she said without heat. He was getting to her again, she realized, sucking in his edible fragrance with frustrated resignation.

"Be nice and I'll take you to your surprise," he promised with a delicate nibble at her earlobe. Ah, God…that felt too good!

"What surprise?"

"My kiss first."

She managed to pull her head back far enough to glare at him. "You can kiss my ass!"

"Even better," he agreed at once, arching one brow in exaggerated surprise.

"Oh, for Pete's sake…" she muttered. Grabbing his head, she strained upward and slammed her closed lips against his. He opened at once, cupping the base of her skull in his fingers and tilting her until he could push into her mouth with his questing tongue. Her own fingers twitched in the silken fall of his hair, and she was a goner. She raked through the endless mass, shivering at the cool slickness trickling over the backs of her hands. His tongue was a restless marauder, velvety and supple as it swirled in her mouth, drawing on hers with the skill of a snake charmer.

"No," she cried helplessly when he pulled away. Then she flushed with mortification at the self-satisfied smile on his face. "You got your kiss, you arrogant prick," she growled. "Now let me out of here before I kick your ass."

* * * * *

As if the mossy biologic pad under her bare feet weren't disconcerting enough, it didn't take Monica long to notice that every Garathani they passed in the corridors stopped dead in his tracks and all but panted after her. And here she'd started thinking that maybe, just maybe, she wouldn't feel like such a sideshow freak anymore. After about the fortieth glazed stare, she couldn't take it anymore.

"What in the hell is everyone's problem?" she demanded, keeping her arms crossed over her ribs and her shoulders hunched low. Every single one of the fucking losers was looking at her chest. "Jesus, do you have a trench coat or something? I feel like I'm having that 'Oh my God, I'm at school in my underwear!' dream."

"You're imagining things," Shauss dismissed without so much as slowing down. Doing a slow burn, Monica fell a step behind and flipped him off.

"Here? Now?" he invited over his shoulder.

"What, do you have eyes in the back of your head, too?" she grumbled, determined to stay behind him. Then it dawned on her that they'd all stopped looking at her. Seriously. Not only were they not staring, they were deliberately averting their gazes as she passed.

These people were really beginning to creep her out.

* * * * *

Kellen studied Monica as she stalked into his private dining area behind Shauss, reassured that she was none the worse for wear. The transformation in her this morning was nothing short of astounding. Her eyes were sharp, her lips pouty and moist and her skin was finally losing some of its ghostly translucence. In point of fact, she looked primed for a fight.

His cock twitched boldly at the thought. *Later*, he promised himself.

She stopped beside the table, arms akimbo, and frowned at him. "If you're my surprise, I'm kicking the lieutenant's ass all the way back to the infirmary."

Kellen shook his head with a secretive smile.

"You're looking rested," he said, delighted when she pinkened. Despite Ketrok's attempts to rouse her for meals, she'd slept the clock around twice after her sensual disciplining and certainly looked better for it. "I trust you enjoyed your breakfast."

Flopping into the seat next to his, she grimaced. "Actually, it was kind of weird. Like a burger and fries from the Chinese buffet, if you know what I mean."

"I'm afraid I don't."

Eyes rolling, she ordered, "Just give me what you guys eat next time, okay? Either that or let me cook my own eggs."

"As you wish," he agreed neutrally, though he was quite pleased. Monica had been one of the few Terrans at Beaumont–Thayer adventurous enough sample Garathani cuisine, and the only one to actually enjoy a few of the dishes. *Coptier, cancel the cheeseburger and French fries. The doctor will be sharing our meal.*

Very well, Commander, came the long-suffering reply from the galley.

"So, what are we doing here? Is it lunchtime already? What's my so-called surprise?" she asked with a pointed look at Shauss, who'd settled in the seat across from hers.

"Isn't luncheon with the commander of the *Heptoral* surprise enough?"

Monica glanced at Kellen. "Was he dropped on his head as a little lieutenant, or was he born this way?"

"He's a freak of nature, I'm afraid."

"Freak is right," she snorted.

"Wait 'til you see me naked." Shauss grinned rakishly. "And you can sneer all you want, my bloodthirsty little Sparnite, but the burst of pheromones you just emitted tells me—"

"Save it for the mating chamber," Kellen interrupted when it looked like Monica was about to resort to violence. "Both of you."

* * * * *

"So, are we ever going to get to my surprise?" she wondered aloud after she'd sucked the last succulent bit of meat off an Adorana sea quill and dropped the delicate fanned bone into the pile on her plate. *Ah, full at last.*

Though she'd managed to do it justice, the sight of their meal had initially made her blanch. The table had practically groaned under the weight of the exotic repast, a dozen or more offerings presented on two large round metal trays, without the benefit of serving dishes. Everything was plopped in unappetizing piles, their individual juices running together to create an alarming moat of—*sludge* was what came to mind—around the edge of each tray. The diners were given smaller metal plates, heavy red mugs of Malascan ale and glasses of water, which, in the absence of cutlery, Monica planned to use as a finger bath. For all she knew, that was what it was for anyway.

She'd raised her brows when the steward slapped three mounds of dark bread—they were too misshapen to be called loaves—directly onto the tabletop. Plainly, refined manners weren't a requirement for dining with the commander. It wouldn't surprise her a bit to see the men toss gnawed bones and other debris over their shoulders, instead of discarding them on their plates—wouldn't the biologic pad eat that stuff, too? The medieval staging had tempted her to pound the table with the closest thing she saw to a turkey leg and shout, "Bring on the next remove!"

Restraining herself, she'd listened carefully and repeated after Kellen as he told her the Garathani names of the various dishes—the turkey leg was actually arm of firi—and fed her small samples with his fingers. The heavy breathing factor had put a stop to that after the third dish and she'd started picking out her own little pieces to nibble. Some of the foods were so grotesque-looking, she'd had a hard time touching, much less tasting them. Had they looked that bad before they were cooked? Hard to imagine they could look any worse, but she made up her mind never to raid the ship's refrigerator for a midnight snack, just in case.

Fortunately, nothing had tasted as bad as it looked, and a few items had really tripped her trigger, particularly the sea quill. Kellen and Shauss had very kindly left most of that for her. In return, she'd divided her ale between their two rapidly emptying mugs, still gagging from that first—and last—bitter sip. Someone needed to introduce their brewers to the Germans.

"So impatient," Kellen teased, holding a long, slimy pekki shoot over his mouth and sucking it down like a spaghetti noodle. After licking the juice off his fingers—hadn't these people ever thought of napkins?—he continued, "You must have been a trial to your grandparents before holiday exchanges."

"I was a trial to my grandparents every day," Monica replied, trying for a smile and not quite succeeding. Noticing the uncharacteristic seriousness of the face across the table, she prodded, "Don't think so hard, Shauss. You might hurt yourself."

"Don't change the subject, Monica." He reached over and picked up the piece of too-chewy bread she'd left on her plate and sopped up some sludge from the tray. When he offered it to her, she shook her head with a shudder that made him smile. "Why do you think you were a trial to them?"

Entirely too fascinated by the muscles bulging in his jaw as he chewed, she looked at her plate, cursing her traitorous hormones.

"Because I was."

"How do you know?"

"When someone who's supposed to love you gives you up for adoption, it's a pretty good sign you've been a trial to them," she said evenly, picking up one of the quill bones and swirling it in the sludge pooled on her plate.

Kellen frowned. "You were adopted by strangers?"

"No, I was given up, but never adopted. Nobody wants to adopt a thirteen-year-old with physical and emotional issues." Her palms were starting to sweat. She'd thought nothing could make her more uncomfortable than Kellen and Shauss seeing her naked, but apparently that wasn't the case. "Can we drop this please?"

"When you've clarified the matter to my satisfaction." God, the man's arrogance knew no bounds! "Where did you go if you weren't adopted?"

It was obvious he wasn't going to let go until she'd spilled, so, taking a deep breath to steady herself, Monica launched into the tale with exaggerated patience.

"Into foster care. I stayed in a couple of private foster homes at first, but mostly I lived in a state-run home for girls." She sighed at their blank stares. "Look. I was a problem child.

It was hard being raised by grandparents who were almost seventy when I was born. It seemed like I was always too noisy or too clumsy, always breaking things and getting in trouble, and I acted out a lot because it didn't seem like they loved me."

"I'm certain that wasn't the case."

She looked at Kellen, exasperated. How could a man feel enough bitterness to blow up a planet and still have such a Pollyanna view of life?

"Actually, I think it was. They came from an era where an illegitimate child was considered an embarrassment, and the fact that no one had any idea who my father might be was even worse. Honestly, now that I think about it, I'm surprised they ever took me home from the hospital. If my mother had died a little faster, they probably wouldn't have."

Kellen and Shauss were both frowning now. "Punishing children for the sins of their forebears is barbaric. A child is a gift to be treasured and I can imagine no circumstance under which any Garathani would relinquish one," Kellen commented.

It occurred to her that he'd had no qualms about punishing the children of Narthan, but she thought it would be imprudent to say so.

"Well, they sure as hell relinquished me. And really, I can't blame them," she admitted. "As naughty as I was as a young child, it was nothing compared to how I acted once my other shortcomings became obvious."

"Shortcomings?"

She raised her eyebrows at Shauss. "Remember me, your bloodthirsty little Sparnite?"

"Sparnism is a matter of physical immaturity, not deficiency," Kellen dismissed.

"Yeah, well, Sparnite differentiation isn't included in most junior high school curricula," Monica said wryly. "And even if it was, the kids still would have treated me like shit. At that age, different equals bad. Period. That's when I started fighting. I fought with the other kids, with my grandparents, with my teachers…" God, now that she'd started, she couldn't seem to shut up. "Eventually I worked my way up to fighting with the authorities, and when the state stepped in, my grandparents took their chance to bow out of my life forever. End of story." She forced a smile. "On the bright side, they left me enough money to pay for medical school and a nice house, so I think I came out ahead of the game."

Kellen's expression said he still wasn't about to let the matter drop, so she squared her shoulders and stuck out her chin. *To hell with prudence.* "It seems like you guys know everything there is to know about me now, so how about we shrink your head for a while, Commander? Tell me, how does it feel to know you wiped out millions of women and children who probably had nothing to do with the bio-war attack on your planet?"

Although she maintained her belligerent pose, her heart kicked a little faster with every second that passed. Kellen took a leisurely swallow of his ale as he watched her with something that began to bear an uncomfortable resemblance to compassion and she finally had to look away.

"Is that how you think of me, Monica? As nothing more than the mass murderer of innocents?"

The mild, almost reflective tone of his inquiry was baffling. If someone had asked her a question like that, she'd have gone off the deep end, ripped them a new one in defense of her duty and honor and righteous outrage. But instead of being offended, he sounded almost like he felt sorry for *her*, like she was the one who had something to learn here.

Unable to help herself, she glanced at him again and was immediately sucked in by the velvety blue magnetism of his eyes. Jesus, he looked like he actually cared what she thought of him, like the idea of her viewing him as a murderer pained him. And the hell of it was, she *didn't* think of him that way and never had. In fact, the more time she'd spent around him, the harder it was to believe that he could be so…heartless. Kellen was many things—funny, arrogant, astoundingly intelligent and sometimes downright infuriating—but he'd never struck her as heartless.

"When I became a fleet officer," he said without releasing her gaze, "I swore an oath of allegiance to Garathan. I vowed to protect the lives of her people and to obey my leaders in the furtherance of that objective. Even had I not been required to assist in the final disposition of over two million corpses, even had I not watched while my mate writhed in anguish upon her deathbed…" His eyes narrowed. "Even had I not held my beloved daughter against my breast while she cried her final, bloody tears, I would still have done my duty. I am a man of honor, Monica, because without honor, a man is nothing."

Monica's vision clouded with tears of her own as she nodded, unable to speak. Jesus. It was one thing to read an impartial account of a global disaster years after the fact, but to hear it fresh from the lips of one who lived through it was…unbearable.

Her voice was husky when she finally asked, "How old was she?"

"Three years and one quarter."

Monica swallowed, drawing a shaky breath. *Three years old.* God, she probably would have launched the attack herself, if it had been her daughter. "What was her name?"

"Keleschi."

"And your wife?"

"Mate," he corrected. "She was Dendriin."

Something about the way he said it made her ask, "Did you love her?"

Way to sound jealous, Monica.

"And how would you define love, little Terran?" He leaned farther back in his chair, still watching her with calm, inquisitive eyes. "If by love you mean fulfilling my vows to her, then yes, I did. Our union was arranged by our mothers, with satisfactory results for all parties involved."

Monica blinked and then choked off a laugh. "Wow. Okay."

"Does my answer displease you?"

"No, no. That's just...how things are on Garathan, I guess. I'll get used to it." So why did it make her chest ache, and not just for him?

She looked at Shauss, almost afraid to know about his background. "What about you?"

"I lost no one."

She frowned as he stared back impassively. *I lost no one.* What did that mean? No one he loved had died or he'd had no one to lose?

Dessert arrived at that moment and she lost the nerve to ask. The rest of the meal passed in a pregnant kind of silence, like something sweet but fragile had sprung up between them and no one wanted to ruin it.

"Well, that was interesting," she finally said, pushing her plate of...something very *brown* away almost untouched. She hoped to hell it wasn't their idea of chocolate cake because she was in for some really shitty birthdays from now on if that was the case.

When they finally stood, she did too, and the steward hurried in, offering warm, damp cloths. Kellen watched her as he wiped his fingers, and the obvious compassion in his probing inspection set her teeth on edge. Why in the hell did he feel sorry for her? He'd probably suffered a thousand times worse than she ever had.

Turning away, she used her towel with excessive enthusiasm, scrubbing at her hands 'til they glowed pink and swabbing any remaining traces of sea quill from her lips and chin. Then she dropped it on the table and faced them with her best *let's get down to brass tacks* look.

"I'm ready for my surprise now."

* * * * *

It wasn't the surprise Kellen had planned for this moment, but it seemed appropriate somehow. Taking an impromptu detour from their destination, he led her through several of the outer corridors, her revelations still roiling in his mind.

She'd had no family, no protection. None. The fact made him angry, while the knowledge of her lonely early existence made him ache in ways he hadn't thought to experience again after the deaths of Dendriin and his beloved daughter. It was no wonder she'd grown such a prickly exterior.

"Oh my God!" Monica gasped beside him, her eyes wide and luminous as the floor-to-ceiling view field opened in front of them, revealing the swirling blue and white surface of the planet below. "Is this a window?" she asked, reaching out but not quite touching the membrane.

"It's a molecular flare. There are no true windows on the *Heptoral*, but the view field reflects exactly what you would see through a window in the same position."

"Can I touch it?"

"Your touch will distort the image, but it will cause no harm." Shauss was standing behind her, looking down on her head with a subtle concern that matched his. He made no move to touch her, no doubt recognizing as Kellen did that any display of affection, coming so close on the heels of her personal disclosures, would probably be construed as pity and rejected accordingly. And no doubt loudly. Possibly violently.

"Wow," she breathed, her eyes following her own index finger as it traced over the field. "I'm in space. I'm really in space."

"Technically, you're in orbit," Shauss corrected.

"Could I breathe on the other side of this wall?"

"Of course not."

"Then I'm in space." Her sigh this time was one of utter contentment and Kellen felt oddly compelled to echo it. To impress her further, he sent a cerecom command to Empran and Monica gasped as the field's view suddenly magnified, in one-second increments, drawing them closer and closer to the Earth's surface. When the desired magnification was attained, they were looking at an image of the Beaumont–Thayer Compound, an image so clear that he could see the tops of several heads as people walked about the grounds. "Oh my God, I can't believe it! That's the compound, isn't it? Jeez, talk about spy technology! That's frickin' amazing!"

"I'm glad you're pleased."

She turned to look at him then, and his chest stilled at the sight of the first truly warm smile she'd bestowed on him. "Thank you, Commander. This was the perfect surprise."

Commander. Kellen knew better than to think she'd used the formality as a sign of respect. Even in her delight, she distanced herself from him. "Ah, but this wasn't the surprise. That awaits you down the corridor." Turning, he offered his arm and waited. After a long hesitation, she slid her fingers carefully into the crook of his elbow.

* * * * *

He should have known her mellow mood would be fleeting.

Despite the detour, they'd arrived at the Council chambers nearly a half-hour early, and if the wait hadn't soured her disposition, Shauss' irrepressible manner would have.

"Does the term *hurry up and wait* mean anything to you?" she'd asked after the first five minutes.

Just returning from the head, Shauss had bypassed his own seat and gone to her, perching heavily on the arm of her chair.

"I know something we could do to pass the time." His intimate tone and the way he leaned into her had made her strain away from him, baring her teeth in annoyance.

"In your dreams!"

"I believe that would be in *your* dreams, sweetheart," Shauss taunted. Kellen saw the bright blush staining her cheeks and cringed in anticipation of her eruption.

"Make that, over my dead body," she fired back, shoving at his hip. "Get off, you arrogant prick!"

Maybe you'd better back off and let her settle down before we see the minister.

Shauss rose at once and resumed his seat, but he wasn't quite done with her. "By the way, Monica, I'm keeping track of your foul language, and just as soon as Ketrok clears you, I intend to spank your sweet little ass, one swat for every infraction." At her gasp, he added, "Five for every time you call me an arrogant prick, which means you're up to twenty already for that one alone."

When her outraged eyes swung to his, Kellen shrugged. He'd enjoyed her smile, but nothing appealed to him like her fury. "I agree wholeheartedly, though I have…somewhat more enjoyable punishments in mind."

"That's bullshit!" she shouted.

"Twenty-one," Shauss ticked off.

"Aaaah!" Monica screamed. "That's not fair." When Shauss opened his mouth, she added, "And if you say nobody ever said life is fair, I'm going to ram your balls up into your windpipe, you got it?"

Kellen managed to suppress his smile and narrowed his eyes at Shauss. *That wasn't exactly what I had in mind when I said to let her settle down.*

"The minister will see you now," came a tranquil voice from the open door of the Council chambers. Kellen stood at once and nodded to the page.

"Thank you, Milnon." He held out his elbow once more. "Dr. Teague..."

No. He wouldn't. He *couldn't*.

Monica didn't move, but pinned him instead with a penetrating stare. "There's no way you're— *Please* tell me you're not taking me to meet the Minister of the High Council."

Kellen looked honestly confused. "I thought you'd be pleased."

"Pleased! Are you insane?"

The fresh-faced page started, eyes wide, as she jumped to her feet.

"What—" Kellen began.

"For God's sake, look at me!" She swept an agitated arm down her front. "I'm dressed for clam digging, not rubbing elbows with heads of state! My bellybutton's showing," she enunciated with a snarl, volume gradually increasing. "My hair's a rat's nest, I have no makeup and I can't fit into my fucking *shoes*!

"So no, Kellen," she roared in his face, breathing hard, hands on her hips. "I—am—not—*pleased*!"

Three things hit her at once—the scent of pheromones drowning her nasal passages, the dangerous glint of lust in Kellen's slitted eyes and Shauss' wicked murmur, "Twenty-two," from directly behind her.

Heart pounding, she froze like a rabbit stalked by big hungry cats, twitching with awareness as heat slithered through her abdomen and twisted its throbbing tendrils between her legs. One false move and she was seriously fucked, and for some incomprehensible reason, she was feeling compelled to make that move.

"It sounds to me, Commander, like your female is more than fit for mating."

The smooth rumble was like an ice cube dropped down the back of her shirt and she pivoted to face the legendary Minister Cecine in all his flame-haired glory. Deep-set eyes dancing with amusement in a long, narrow face drew attention away from the scar that zagged down one cheek and under his chin. His fists were propped on his hips, holding open his ceremonial robes and showcasing all seven and a half lean feet of him. "Perhaps we should postpone our interview until you've helped her work off some of her frustration."

"But I—you—" Monica went cross-eyed with fury. The Garathani leader was smiling at them all indulgently, as if they were sweet little newlyweds anxious to be off for their Hawaiian honeymoon. "You've got to protect me from these assholes!"

"Twenty-three."

As if it were attached to someone else, Monica watched her hand fly out, saw it land hard across Shauss' cheek. Aggravatingly, though her fingers stung from the force of the blow, not only did his head not snap back, but the man didn't so much as flinch. In fact, nobody reacted to her slap, but the tension level in the room skyrocketed.

"Thank you for your understanding, Minister," Kellen acknowledged with a dip of his head. "Shall we try this again tomorrow?"

"I look forward to it."

Cecine turned on his heel and stalked back into the Council chambers, followed closely by his page. Monica's breath caught in her throat as the door slid closed behind them with silent finality.

Oh shit, she was in for it now.

Chapter Ten

ဆာ

Lust was a dense, invisible fog in the air, and she was suffocating in its seductive caress.

Run! Run! RUN!

Monica tried, but the instant she heeded the impulse, hands like iron snagged her wrists and halted her flight with a suddenness that jerked her off balance. Exploding with adrenaline, she fought silently, jumping and kicking and twisting against the two men who held her, determined to escape the inescapable. They each managed to snatch one of her ankles from midair and then she was suspended there between them, still writhing, every muscle straining, unwilling to accept their domination. At least not without a fight.

Sweat beaded on her skin while she struggled, easing the friction of their hold and creating an intimately moist bond with their hot hands—and God help her, she finally groaned with the sheer primitive thrill of it. Reason gradually pushed back the mindless tide of panic and she was both dismayed and excited to feel the slickness drenching her panties, to realize that resisting these powerful men, who were obviously determined to fuck her into submission, was satisfying some perverse inner appetite even as it inflamed another.

She could fight their relentless desire until the end of time, but she was helpless in the face of her own.

"No!" she cried out as her body sagged between them, drained of energy.

In that moment, in the silence broken only by her ragged breathing, she waited, eyes closed, until they dropped her ankles one at a time and hauled her upright. Neither of them eased his grip on her wrist.

"Do you go peaceably to my quarters, or do we carry you?" Kellen inquired, his tone implacable. The fucker wasn't even breathing hard.

Swallowing her retort, she said with dignity, "I'll walk."

* * * * *

Monica kept her head down, hiding both her nerves and her excitement as they led her through the vast, winding blue corridors and into a long atrium. Kellen slowed his strides as they entered, and the cavernous room, which had been humming with conversation, grew abruptly still for their endless passage to the other side. Even without looking, Monica could feel the weight of a hundred or more eyes following her, assessing her, and the knowledge that her state of disgrace must be obvious made her cheeks grow hot.

Annoyed at Kellen for prolonging her humiliation, she twisted against his grip, and in an instant she was crowded between two impossibly hard bodies.

"Perhaps I should let Shauss take care of your spanking right here," Kellen growled into her ear, shoving his free hand into the hair at her nape and forcing her face up to his. God, he looked angry. And horny.

"Take a look around you, Monica," he whispered without releasing her gaze. "You are the only woman here, a fresh young beauty on a ship full of men who have not touched female flesh for a decade or more. Do you really want to risk the kind of riot that could ensue if Shauss were to bare your virgin ass before them all? I doubt he'd make it to three swats before you were at the bottom of a very large pile."

Although the silly teenage girl in her had stopped listening at "fresh young beauty", the rest of her was appalled. She didn't dare look, but the rustling and murmurs that now filled the silence were unnerving. When one lone voice from across the room begged with plaintive humor for her to take the risk, she stiffened, her face on fire. They'd all heard every word Kellen said to her.

Without warning, he lowered his face to hers, sweeping past her lips and teeth to plumb her depths with his tongue. *Finally...* Consciousness faded once more as he surged strongly in and out, not finessing, not caressing, just fucking her mouth with his own, plainly establishing his ownership of her for the benefit of his men. And as much as she wanted to hate him for ruining this first engagement of their mouths with his caveman tactics, only his hand at her neck kept her from sinking to the floor in a puddle of molten need.

"Who do you belong to?" he finally demanded tightly, breathing hard enough now to stir the hair at her neck.

"You," she whispered, dazed and lost in his darkening eyes, in his savory scent.

He squeezed the back of her neck until she cried out and demanded again, "Who do you belong to?"

"Kellen and Shauss," she choked.

"Tell them all."

"I belong to Kellen and Shauss!" she shouted now, blinking back tears of rage. The arrogant prick was going to pay for this.

* * * * *

An eternity later, she was no closer to making him pay.

"Empran, this is *subject* Monica Teague," she snarled. "I demand that you release me immediately!"

Once in Kellen's quarters, they'd stripped her naked and pushed her into a large rounded shower, where she was pounded six ways from Sunday by jets of steaming water. Shauss had pointed to the dermal scrub dispenser on the wall and she'd soaped herself from head to foot, supremely conscious of their eyes following her every move.

After she'd rinsed off and dried herself with the enormous and fabulously absorbent towel Shauss handed her, Kellen had pushed her to the center of his sleeping chamber, her back to the door, and ordered Empran to place her in tension restraints. Then he'd posed her like some fucking life-sized action figure and dragged his tongue through her mouth one more time before they both left the room.

And here she'd stood for what seemed like hours, her feet shoulder-width apart, her hands behind her head, elbows back, and her impossibly high breasts thrusts out so far she could see them without looking down. It was a classic arrest stance, and for some reason her wayward thoughts kept drifting to the more intimate aspects of detainment. Like frisking. And cavity searches. And nightsticks. And hell if it wasn't inspiring a hot, slick trickle down the inside of her left thigh.

She must be one sick puppy.

"Release not authorized."

"Fuck!"

"That's twenty-four, I believe." Shauss strolled into her line of vision, smirking. "Not counting whatever I decide you've earned for disrespecting me in front of the Minister."

Monica felt her cheeks pinken. Again. Damn it, when had he come in? Unable to think of anything to say that wouldn't get her in deeper, she kept her mouth shut and glared at him.

"Ah, she's learning," he goaded, stepping close and stroking a forefinger back and forth over the fluffy curls covering her mons. Oh, he smelled good. It was obvious from his damp hair and silky, loose-fitting garments that he'd cleaned up, too, but it wasn't soap or cologne teasing her senses. Unable to control the bump of her pulse or the heat that washed over her, Monica focused on the blank wall beyond his head and tried to empty her mind. He was *not* going to get to her.

Then his nosy finger edged downward.

"What have we here?" he murmured. Seeing his smile out of the corner of her eye, she inwardly cursed her own lack of control, profoundly thankful he couldn't read the racy thoughts she'd been entertaining while he was gone. "I think someone enjoys being at our mercy, Kel."

Her pulse doubled instantly and she had trouble getting air into her lungs.

"Oh, she really likes you," Shauss drawled then, wiping his damp fingertip over the pulse point in her throat. "Just hearing your name makes her heart race."

Monica ground her teeth, wishing she could smack him again, no matter what the cost.

"That's nothing," came the amused reply. "Hearing hers makes me harder than a crunite pillar."

Shauss stepped aside, and suddenly there he was in front of her, the fearsome Commander Kellen, big, bare-chested and beautiful enough to make angels sing. He snagged her eyes before she could look away, and her heart threatened to pound its way out of her chest. Without saying a word, he reached out and touched the damp hair between her legs. But the touch was startlingly cold, making her gasp loudly.

And then the cold was sliding in, the warmth of his hard finger pushing it up high inside her vagina, and she gasped again when he withdrew a bit and shoved in once more to make sure whatever he'd inserted was firmly seated.

"What..." She trailed off as he withdrew, breathing deeply as tingles started to radiate from the cold, and chills erupted on every inch of her skin. "What did you do to me?"

His smile was not reassuring. He drew his finger, wet with her secretions, across her lower lip before answering.

"I gave you a muscle relaxant to ease my alien invasion."

"But I thought you said my hymen was gone," she said, confused.

"There's more to a virgin's pain than the piercing of her veil," he assured her, pushing his finger between her lips, her

127

teeth, touching it to her tongue. "Especially for one as small as you." Rubbing her tongue, he invited, "Taste your desire for me."

Obeying without thought, she sucked the tip of his finger and knew the perversely arousing taste of her own body. Then his words finally sank in. *Alien invasion.*

This might be the wickedest thing he'd ever done. Of course, some people would consider reducing several of Narthan's cities to rubble wickedness of the highest order, but that had been a matter of honor. And duty. And cold, personal revenge. Tormenting Monica—that was hot, unadulterated pleasure.

The dawning comprehension in her eyes was priceless, and fortunately, he'd charged Empran with storing the images of this claiming for his future enjoyment. Monica probably wouldn't be pleased to know about them, much less view them with him, which only tickled him more. He'd truly never realized his own potential for sexual iniquity until this hardheaded little Sparnite was sprung on him. Now he couldn't wait to see how else he could shock her.

Of course, Shauss had a few nasty shocks of his own to deliver.

The thought made Kellen tighten with pained arousal and he smiled, anticipating her reaction to his next revelation. "Empran, enclose three, flare field image Caribbean beach."

Monica's eyes widened to comic proportions as the beach scene of her dreams appeared around them. "You pervert," she hissed. "You touched me when I was asleep!"

"You were in pain," he said simply. "It would be unconscionable of me to allow you to suffer when it's within my power to ease you. Which is why," he added, "I inserted the penetab. I'd never heard of such a thing, 'til Ketrok enlightened me this morning. Feel free to thank him for his foresight the next time you see him."

Shauss moved up behind her and caressed her buttocks with his hands, compelling a squeak and a reflexive jerk from Monica.

"What are you doing?" she asked, sounding breathless.

Shauss leaned forward to tug at her earlobe with his teeth and answered, "Easing the way for *my* alien invasion."

He wouldn't...

"Hey!" He'd separated her buttocks and was drawing moisture back from her dripping vagina with a gentle finger, pushing it little by little into her anus. "That hurts!"

"Hence the need for this." His voice was dark with meaning, and suddenly the coldness of another penetab was breaching her tender flesh, with his thick finger right behind it. When she tightened against the intrusion, he informed her, "It's going in whether you want it or not, so try pushing against it instead. That's supposed to make the passage easier."

"Goddamn it, Shauss, you said only if I wanted it!" she cried.

"That was before you slapped me," he replied. "But I'll make sure you want it."

"Fat chance! Nobody really wants—"

Monica sucked in a huge breath as Kellen's hot mouth latched onto one of her nipples. "Oh God. Oh shit! Please, please..."

Strange waves of cold, scarlet heat billowed up from her bottom as Shauss explored her there, the curious noises he made plucking at her over-amped senses like gunshots. He started to stroke carefully, in a little, out a little, over and over, and Kellen's strong suckling magnified those strange waves into a churning ocean of blood-red need.

"So, little Sparnite," Shauss breathed against the side of her neck, taking a sucking bite of the delicate skin. "Let's see how you like having the tables turned."

Monica's chest heaved with the effort to maintain control when one of Kellen's hands caressed its way past her belly and over her pubis, down into the moisture that overflowed her labia. She didn't have enough coherent thought left to ask Shauss what he was talking about.

"You're about to lose your virginity to not just one, but two men who haven't spilled their seed for twenty years between them," he murmured as Kellen stroked her wet curls lightly.

"Kellen gets to fuck you first." Electricity arced through her veins at the words. "He'll lay you back and spread your beautiful pussy wide and try to eat his way up to your throat from the inside. Then, when he's swallowed all the delicious, musky cream he can, he's going to stuff that quivering little slit with too many inches of rock-hard cock for you to take. And yet you'll have to take them all so that when his spur is up, it will stuff your nook every bit as full."

Monica trembled hard when Kellen treated her other nipple to the same forceful suction, leaving the first to the tweaking twists of his other hand.

"And when he's got your aching holes stuffed nice and tight, he's going to ream them both, fuck them hard enough to make you scream, and the best part is, you'll be so far out of your mind, you won't even know if it's pleasure or pain." She screwed her eyes shut tight, moaning loudly when his finger sank deeper, twisting as it went. "And it could very well be pain, because there's only so much a penetab can do to prepare a novice for a ride like that. But I doubt you'll care by then."

Monica was amazed to still be standing under the erotic onslaught. Shudders slid down her back and goose bumps rose on her arms and legs as the heat built inside the orifices they'd prepared. The soles of her feet were burning hot and her breath was huffing in and out of her like a steam engine.

"How do you like my dirty talk, Monica?" Shauss asked. "I studied hard, just for you." When she could only whimper, he chuckled deeply. "She's speechless, and I haven't even gotten to my favorite parts yet."

"You were slightly off on this detail," Kellen commented as he released her nipple with a smacking suck and gripped her hips with both hands.

Monica's eyes snapped open at the sound of him dropping to his knees and the image that greeted her was like a punch in the gut.

Her Caribbean beach had disappeared and in its place was a reflection of the three of them, decadent in its clarity. She was struck by the layers of flesh before her, Kellen's wide, powerful back tapering into a narrow waist, her own unfamiliar face, arching neck and voluptuous breasts, and above her, Shauss' face, angular and darkened by the flush of heavy arousal. As his eyes stared back at her, he slowly, deliberately pulled his finger out of her ass and shoved it back in hard, all the way up to his palm, propelling her right onto Kellen's waiting tongue.

The hoarseness of her scream as he drove his tongue into her nook made Kellen glad he was already on his knees. He'd waited too long to hear it again, and lived an eternity for the taste of this moment, more exhilarating than a thousand hard-won battles, of this woman, so sensual and strong, and this fluid, as inebriating as the finest of wines.

Patience was a concept beyond his comprehension. Even as he opened his mouth wide over her trembling nook, laving her clitoris with each rough pass of his tongue, he plunged his two middle fingers into her vagina, fucked her with them until her wetness slid down his palm, and reveled anew in the screams that resulted. When his extended index finger brushed the back of Shauss' hand, the surge of awareness almost took his head off. She was full of them...

He felt the tremors rocking her legs and knew her pleasure was at hand. Drawing back with regret, knowing he must indeed be insane, he uttered the one word he knew would enrage her.

"Stop."

Chapter Eleven

ஐ

"You bastard!" Monica cried as Kellen stood up, the aborted orgasm tickling her innards like a backed-up sneeze. "You're inhuman."

She almost came when Shauss tugged his finger free of her. Almost.

Damn it!

Kellen grinned in her face. "I suppose I can't argue with that."

"I suppose you know I'm going to lay you out when you turn me loose," she blustered, furious to have let them take her so far out of herself again.

"I look forward to it" was his smug rejoinder. "But first things first. I believe punishment should always come before reward, and you're due quite a spanking."

"What!" Her eyes bulged. "Like leaving me hanging like this, *literally*, isn't punishment enough?"

"Oh, not nearly enough," Shauss purred.

"You guys are just twisted."

"Objection noted. Now, Monica, listen to me very carefully," Kellen advised. "When I release your restraints, you will go directly to that chair and lean over the back. If you refuse to cooperate, you'll be restrained for the punishment, as well. Do you understand?"

She glared at him.

"Yes, Master," she sneered. He looked inordinately pleased at her response and Monica had to roll her eyes. "I was being sarcastic, Einstein."

"Twenty-five."

"Hey, that's not swearing!"

"It was an insult, just the same."

"I called him the most brilliant man in history!"

"Implying exactly the opposite."

"Shauss, you'd better watch your back," she threatened in her most dangerous tone, "because I'm never going to forget this."

Her restraints were released abruptly and she crumpled into an undignified heap on the floor. "Thanks for the warning, asshole," she muttered, swatting away Kellen's helpful hands and climbing awkwardly to her feet. The long confinement had left her joints stiff, her fingers numb.

"I'll let that one slide, since we didn't catch you," Shauss conceded.

"Thanks for nothing."

Anxious to get it over with, Monica didn't even bother trying to get away, but marched right to the upholstered chair and leaned over the back. It was just high enough that when her head and elbows hit the seat, her toes left the floor.

"Well, get on with it," she sighed into the odd, slithery fabric.

The first blow wasn't what she expected. It landed immediately, sharp and painful, and she jumped, screeching, "Hey, watch it!"

The second was worse, this one on the other cheek, and she instinctively reached back to shield her rump, only to have Kellen grab her wrists and hold them with one hand in the small of her back. Refusing to act like a wimp, Monica bit her lip and took it, flinching but not making a sound as Shauss' hard slaps rained down on her ass. Trying to tamp down her anger, she chanted silently with every strike, *I stabbed Shauss, I deserve this, I stabbed Shauss...*

When the count reached thirteen, her entire ass was on fire. At fifteen, she noticed the blaze was working its way down toward her thighs. At twenty, she inhaled sharply. The pads of his fingers landed in her wet, tender folds, evoking a starburst of sensation that she couldn't quite decide was good or bad. Two more like that finally had her whimpering, though the jury was still out on the good-bad thing.

Shauss moved around to the side of the chair, and the resulting change to the angle of his next slap was enough to make her scream. His palm had landed right on the crease between her buttocks, his fingers on the lips below, and when he smacked her again, the reverberation through her swelling tissues was intolerable.

"You can't do that!" she cried hoarsely, straightening her dangling legs and squeezing them together in an effort to head him off. Kellen's fingers pinched her hamstring, and when her body jerked into a defensive curl, they slid around her thigh and pulled it out to the side, holding her wide open to the other man's ruthless attentions.

"Who's going to stop me?" Shauss growled.

He came at her again, two, three, four more direct strikes on her stinging clitoris, and she stiffened at the tightening knot of lust in her belly.

"Oh Jesus," she choked. "Not like—"

His rhythm went into double-time, and then a wave of sensation more intense than anything they'd made her feel before sizzled through her body. It burst like thousands of rolling pinpricks under her skin, deep in her muscles, cascading outward from her belly in a rush so incredibly dense she couldn't even breathe, much less scream.

The jury was in and the verdict was disastrously, humiliatingly *good*.

* * * * *

"So it's true then," Kellen commented gruffly as he pulled her upright. He'd let her lie there for several minutes to catch her breath, but now it was his turn. And he wanted her fighting. He *craved* her fighting.

Shauss backed away and sank into the opposite chair, his hands shaking visibly as they lay over his tented pants. He let his head fall back against the upholstery, watching the two of them, his eyes glittering slits in his face. Kellen hadn't mated in front of a witness since his ceremonial claiming of Dendriin nearly eighteen years in the past, the supposed breaching of an innocence she'd long since bestowed on another. That had been a mere formality, performed in the detached presence of their mothers, but this... The intently involved carnality of Shauss' observation was truly electrifying.

"What's true?" Monica asked languidly, using both hands to brush her hair back from her face.

"Earth girls *are* easy."

His taunt landed with deadly accuracy as her eyes whipped to his, her jaw clenched and her cheeks reddened.

"I told you," Shauss rumbled, amusement rife in his voice.

"Yes, you did," Kellen grinned. "And here I thought your devotion to Terran cinema was such a waste of time."

Monica's gaze slid away, no doubt in an effort to shield her from his probing.

"A century's worth of quality American films to choose from and you watched that one?" she sneered. Out of the corner of his eye, he saw Shauss' hand slide along the ridge of his erection with lazy frankness, no doubt for Monica's benefit. The hiss of her indrawn breath almost made him laugh. The man was an absolute genius at riling her.

"The title suggested it was pertinent to our situation," Shauss was saying. "Though I must confess I was disappointed by the lack of sexual content. If I'd known enough to look for an X-rating in those days, I might not have watched it."

"Why am I not surprised you're into skin flicks?"

"How else are we to learn what pleases Terran females?"

"Oh please," she snorted. "Those films are all geared to men's tastes, not women's. If you really want to know what women enjoy, read romance novels."

Grasping her chin in his fingers, Kellen forced her attention back him.

"But we already know, don't we? All it takes to make you come like there's no tomorrow is a good spanking." Encouraged by the tightening of her jaw, the increasing roughness of her breathing, he pushed harder, telling her in a silky voice, "Go on, Earth girl. Lie on the bed and spread your legs for me, and I'll slap your tasty little cunt into another orgasm."

She came out swinging.

"I am *not* easy," she raged as her palm connected soundly with his jaw.

"How would you describe yourself, then?" he asked, savoring the heat of her palm print on his skin. "Wanton?"

Teeth bared, Monica smacked him again, her fingertips stinging his left ear.

"Shameless?"

This time she aimed higher, narrowly missing his eye with her fingernail.

Leaning over her, he growled, "*Deviant*?"

"You fucking bastard!" she screamed, launching herself at him. Kellen was ready for her.

Fury and lust formed a searing cocktail that surged through her veins like one-hundred proof whiskey, inciting her to a level of violence she'd never suspected herself capable of. She snarled like an animal as she pounded at the unyielding flesh of Kellen's chest and shoulders. When he lifted her off the floor, she kicked at his shins and tried to get a knee into his groin.

The next thing she knew, he'd thrown her on the bed and followed her down, holding her against the mattress with one hand on her diaphragm while he pushed down his pants and kicked out of them. Even as she drew blood with her vicious scratches to his arm, reaction to his nudity flooded her, immediate and extreme.

"Holy shit," she squeaked, squirming hard against his hold, pushing ineffectually at his wrist. He knelt there beside her, his thick quads bulging, and used his free hand to lift his balls in blatant anticipation, letting her look, letting her get good and freaked out by the sheer, inhuman size of him.

I'll never hurt you.

The sudden memory of his promise made her blink. Good God, how could he help but hurt her? His erect penis, a dark-veined, angry red, was bigger than she'd imagined one could get. Almost as startling was the flesh-covered bone of his fully emerged spur, about the size and shape of a man's finger, curving down to brush the tight skin of his erection. Kellen had every intention of shoving both of those organs into portions of her anatomy she hadn't had the chance to explore yet, and it scared the living hell out of her. He had never seemed more alien to her than he did at this moment.

"That's not going to fit!"

"I'll make it fit." His emphatic pledge was anything but reassuring, and she struggled madly as Kellen kneed her legs open and lowered his body between her resisting thighs. He gripped her wrists and held them to the mattress above her head, resting his weight on his elbows.

Watching her face with blazing eyes, he made a definitive adjustment of his hips and lodged the head of his penis against her streaming vaginal opening.

"Are you ready for me to fuck you?"

She groaned and tossed her head, shutting him out, wishing he'd stop with the domination crap and just do it.

"Answer me, Monica," he insisted.

Something in his tone, a tentative harshness, made her look at him again. His face was hard, searching hers for...

Surely not *permission*?

I'll never take you against your will.

"What if I say no?"

She caught her breath as he shifted, sliding his fullness slowly up and over her clitoris and then down again. "Are you saying no?"

"No!" she gasped as he repeated the motion.

"What are you saying, Monica?" he insisted, sustaining the gentle teasing motions of his hips. "Tell me what you want."

And I'll never leave you unfulfilled. God, he'd damn well better not.

"Just quit talking and do it," she panted.

"Do what? I'm not sure I understand."

"Fuck me, you asshole!"

He snugged against her vagina once more and she squirmed impatiently, trying to lure him inside.

"Ask me nicely." Monica froze, blinking in disbelief. Ask him? *Nicely*? Bitter words hovered on the tip of her tongue, desperate to take flight, but oh God, the need for him, for that thickness pressing just inside her aching opening, made it impossible for her to speak them.

Throat dry, she whispered, "Please."

He nudged a fraction deeper, causing her muscles to contract in delicious, pained ecstasy.

"Please what?" he asked, his tone all silk and steel.

Tears of humiliation and unbearable arousal slid down her temples as she tried to push her hips up, to force the union of their bodies. He was far too strong for that.

"Please, Kellen—please fuck me." Once she'd said it, she couldn't stop. "Please, oh, please, *please*! Oh God, I need you."

His grunt as he dropped his head to her shoulder sounded like it could have been a prayer of thanksgiving. It was immediately forgotten as he battered into her without further ado. The shock of his invasion made her back arch violently, but her defensive action only pulled him deeper, and their simultaneous groans broke harshly in the quiet room.

"Never mind," she squeezed out between gasps. "Forget I said that!" Holy crap, he was going to break something if he tried to go any further.

He ignored her and pushed ahead, gaining another couple of inches, and they both groaned again.

"Stop, Kellen, just stop. Oh God, I told you it wouldn't fit! Get off me!"

"Monica, try to breathe through it," he gasped. "This won't last long, I promise you."

Desperate for any kind of relief from the biting fullness invading her, she obeyed, breathing deeply as he held there. Kellen's magnificent hair was strewn across her face, flavoring her indrawn breaths with its delicious, clean fragrance, and she rubbed her cheek against it distractedly, letting one of the thick locks trail between her lips, over her tongue. God, it even *tasted* good…

He drew back and thrust again, and then again, forging deeper inside her straining walls with every push. Splinters of fire, at once painful and enticing, danced along the edges of her internal tissues, and one more tear slid down her temple.

"I'm sorry, *sziscala*," he sighed as his tongue made a delicate foray at the corner of her eye, licking up the salt tear and leaving its own wet trail.

140

"Then take that damn telephone pole somewhere else," she muttered tremulously.

He smiled at her then, his eyes at half-mast.

"Oh, but we're almost to the fun part now."

A fireball surfaced at the base of his spine when his spur finally edged into Monica's silken nook, sending fingers of flame down to his testicles. Kellen gasped as he let the weight of his lower body settle onto her pelvis, nearly out of his mind with the rapture of being clasped so tightly within her folds.

He felt the flutter of her indrawn breath and knew fierce delight. The steely bone of his spur was flattening her clitoris against the edge of that snug little nook, and she was no doubt beginning to feel the pangs that were only a prelude to the tumult that awaited them both.

Resisting the temptation of her parted lips, he began to work himself forward and back with aching intent, his thrusts cautious and shallow at first, then gaining in momentum as she writhed beneath him. He let go of her wrists when she tugged against his hold and was exultant when she ran her delicate hands urgently over his face. The curtain of his hair rendered this moment private, and Kellen devoured her with his eyes, certain nothing would ever be this perfect again.

As the rhythm of his thrusts began to deteriorate, his scrotum tightened in warning and every muscle in his body began to shake. Deepening the tilt of his hips, he slammed both rigid spikes into her, over and over, determined to hold out against this brutal need until she'd peaked. Monica returned his urgency, wrapping her arms tightly around his neck and raising her hips to his as she began to sob out her own need.

Long, shaky groans rattled from his chest, tightening his neck, pulling his head back as the years of deprivation rose up to conquer him, brooking no further delay in the payment of their penalty. He couldn't wait for her.

"Forgive—" The fireball at his spine contracted in a chill, and then his groans became shouts as it finally exploded, engulfing his body in a shattering inferno. And even through the tortured convulsions wringing him, he watched her eyes, saw them widen at the scalding streams of his seed flooding her and then close tight as she too lost control, screaming out his name while the world dissolved around them.

* * * * *

Holligan to Commander Kellen.

Would that annoying buzz in his head never cease?

Ensign Holligan to Commander Kellen.

Kellen raised his head from the damp, fragrant curve of a feminine neck, blinking and disoriented. Mother of Peserin, he'd fallen asleep on top of Monica! Feeling the slight rise and fall of her rib cage beneath him, he heaved a sigh of giddy relief that she wasn't dead, but merely dead to the world.

As he lifted his weight off her gingerly, his head swiveled to find Shauss, still slouched in his chair, his eyes trained on their wilted bodies, his carnal appetites apparently banked. For the moment.

"How long have we been…"

"Forty minutes."

Kellen grimaced. "My apologies."

"None necessary." Shauss nodded with unprecedented good nature. "Your show made the wait worth every minute, though I wouldn't have minded some popcorn and Milk Duds to round out the experience."

Holligan to Commander Kellen.

What is it, Ensign?

The surface pod bearing the Terran females has arrived.

Terran females? Still muddled, he frowned.

They're slated to dine with Dr. Teague, Sir?

ham

ted," she mumbled, unable

her. "So, Shelley said you

*

ng from the interior of this
n told him.

vn to the pod bay for a
wasn't what he'd expected

gn stepped back from the
o the anomalous energy

asked with a frown.
had to guess, I'd say it was
ck."

g they were able to access
Heptoral's, someone might
sed undetected within our

ood last?"

y, Kellen broadcast, *All*
n board. Empran, dampen all

d the tranlift, he added
Monica and don't let go.

"Damn it, I'd forgotten about that," he sighed. "Nurse Bonham and Miss King are on board." Yet another surprise he'd scheduled for his lusty mate. He could only hope she was more appreciative of this one than the last.

Thank you, Ensign. Escort them both to my table.

"Luckily, I did remember," Shauss remarked. "Which is why I'm sitting here serenely instead of frothing at the mouth."

"Why didn't you wake us? You could have…" Kellen's lips twisted in a wry grin.

"Hurried to get mine?" Shauss looked amused as well. "No, thank you. I prefer to take my time. Besides, it was fun watching the little Sparnite try to breathe under your weight."

"Has any female ever accused you of being a gentleman?"

"Not one."

"I wonder why," Kellen snorted. He still hovered above the slumbering Monica, and looking down at her once more, his eyes softened with affection. "Perhaps this one can change that."

Shauss' reply was barely audible. "It wouldn't surprise me at all."

Something in the stubborn thrust of Jasmine's chin told her the little bulldog wasn't about to give up the chase. Fortunately, that last bite of pizza got stuck halfway down her gullet, saving her from answering for a precious few minutes while she choked and gagged and had the ever-loving crap beaten out of her back.

"What do you mean?" she finally asked as casually as she could, eyes still watering as she sipped at the cola they'd brought aboard.

"Aw, give it up, Monica," Shelley chided. "When the commander told Snow he'd brought you up here, he said it was because he'd claimed you as his mate."

"He did?"

"Mmm-hmm. Him *and* Lieutenant Shauss," she added meaningfully.

Okay, now she really was blushing. She didn't know why, but the idea that everyone down below knew she'd…*hooked up* with two aliens made her squirm with discomfort. It shouldn't. Hell, for all the attention any of them had paid her, present company excepted, she might as well have been swinging from the compound's art deco chandeliers while doing it with half the Garathani delegation.

They couldn't possibly have ignored her more than they already did. Ever since she'd said the state song of Montana was "Embraceable Ewe" at the compound trivia night, most of them had looked at her like a particularly diseased sputum sample. Humorless bastards.

Well, to hell with 'em.

"All right, then," she admitted defiantly. "Yeah, I guess I'm mated to both Kellen and Shauss."

"Oh my God, you mean you've…"

And she'd thought Jasmine's eyes couldn't get any rounder.

"No, Jasmine, I haven't. Not yet, anyway."

"And…it wasn't what I expe to meet their gazes.

Jasmine finally took pity on wanted a haircut?"

* * * *

"I'm getting an unusual read surface pod, Commander," Hollig

"What kind of reading?"

Kellen had been called do potential security breach, but this to hear.

"Take a look, Sir." The ensi diagnostic panel and pointed signature.

"Do you recognize it?" Kellen

"No, Commander, though if I some kind of nonstandard flare tra

"Elaborate," Kellen snapped.

"Hypothetically, Sir, assumin sufficient energy apart from the create a flare field that could be u vessel's. Perhaps stow away—"

"Who was transported in this

"The two Terran women, Sir."

Eyes narrowing dangerous security details, full alert. Intruder o flare activity.

As his feet pounded towa urgently, *Shauss, put your hands on N*

* * * *

"What the hell?" Shelley's squeak as she stared past Jasmine made them both turn and look. "Where did you come from?"

Monica rolled her eyes when she saw the robed figure standing in front of the door.

"Chill, Shel. It's just Ambassador Pret." She nodded a polite greeting to the diplomat. "Good afternoon, Ambassador."

"Dr. Teague." He inclined his own head graciously. "You're looking well."

"But how did he get here?" Shelley insisted. "He didn't come through the door. He just popped out of this sort of air-bubble thing."

"Oh. Well, I'm not really at liberty to say," Monica said apologetically. "But it's no big deal."

She was surprised when the man walked up to her chair, right through the pile of black hair clippings, and stood close enough that his robe touched her elbow. The Garathani were generally more circumspect—

"Hey!"

In less than a heartbeat, Shelley and Jasmine and the entire lounge had disappeared.

* * * * *

Clutching two handfuls of his uniform, Kellen slammed Ensign Verr against the bulkhead. "What do you mean, *she's gone?*"

Fury and fear mingled in an ugly, highly unstable mass of energy that was eating away at his gut. If he let it loose, he might kill someone. If anything happened to Monica, it would no doubt kill *him*.

"A thousand deaths curse me, Commander!" the guard wheezed. "The flare faded before I breached the door."

"Pret took her."

Shauss' words echoed with barely suppressed violence, freezing Kellen to the floor as he stared into Verr's purpling face.

"And you know this how?"

"The women."

Dropping the ensign to the floor, he turned on his heel and stormed across the room. The force of his palms slamming onto the tabletop made both women flinch.

"Tell me what you saw," he demanded, trying unsuccessfully to tone down the brutality in his voice. Each clasped the other's hand before one of them answered.

"It was the ambassador," the secretary confirmed with a brief dip of her head. The other, Monica's nurse friend, just nodded mutely, her chin trembling.

Out of the corner of his eye, he saw the minister sweep into the room, but he was too focused on his objective to acknowledge him.

"Did he say anything?"

"Not really," Miss King answered again. "Just, 'Hey, Monica, you're looking good,' that kind of thing, and then *bam*! They were gone in this…this bubble of light."

Holligan, scan the surface for flare tracks matching the signature you found in the pod.

Kellen stared grimly at the pair, his mind churning. The little blonde, near to bursting with her pregnancy, stared back, tears welling in her eyes. She looked as if she wished to make an inquiry, but was too afraid of him. The secretary, though… Something about her posture, her expression, wasn't sitting well with him. Instinct made him lean into her face.

"You are being dishonest," he charged flatly.

She paled at once and her breath began to stutter in her chest. "No! I swear I've told you everything I know."

Boring into her with his gaze, Kellen saw complicity in Monica's disappearance.

Surface scan negative, Commander.

Aware that the rage bubbling in his blood might cause him to kill her before he got the information he needed, Kellen looked at Cecine and ground out, "Minister, this female has cost Lieutenant Shauss his chance at a mate. He must be compensated."

Cecine didn't blink.

"Lieutenant, the female is yours," he decreed emotionlessly.

Kellen trained his eyes on the secretary's panicked face once more.

"Take her, Shauss," he ordered. "And make it as painful as you possibly can."

Chapter Thirteen

ဢ

This couldn't be good.

One minute she was sitting at the table having a nice, uncomfortable chat with her two closest friends—okay, her two *only* friends—and the next she was falling on her ass in some kind of cave. She squinted in the sudden dimness, making out the squared-off walls and ceiling. Maybe she was in a mine shaft.

Whatever else it might be called, it was for sure a dark, dank hole in the ground, and she hated the dark. And the dank. And she especially hated holes in the ground.

Pret stood over her, and his expression didn't improve her outlook any.

"I suppose I have you to thank for this?" she asked cautiously, taking one crab-walking step backward before scrambling to her feet.

"Indeed." Artificial light, eerily blue, emanated from some sort of lantern hooked to the wall, and the more her eyes adjusted to it, the scarier the ambassador looked. He'd always been tall and gaunt, but the lighting made him look like some of the cadavers she'd studied. "But you may save your thanks for after our mating."

Hell, no. He did not just say that.

"I'm sorry," she laughed incredulously, "but I think you have me confused with someone who'd actually touch you without containment gear."

"I would advise you, Dr. Teague," he said as he shrugged out of his robe, "to sheath that blade you call a tongue before you find yourself without it. Commander Kellen may be tolerant of your insolence, but you will find me considerably less forgiving."

"Well, forgive *me* if I find you considerably less appealing than a baboon's shiny hiney," she fired back, absurdly relieved to see that he wasn't naked under there. Pret's body was positively spidery in the dark one-piece suit, and not in that lip-smacking Tobey Maguire way.

"I will make you eat those words."

"Kellen and Shauss will make you eat your own dick if you lay a hand on me," she said, looking around for the exit.

"On the contrary, my dear. Apparently Lieutenant Shauss has yet to finalize his claim on you, and though my preempting of his rite might be politically incorrect, it is in no way a violation of our laws."

"In other words, you snooze, you lose, huh?"

"Exactly. And I'm far from unreasonable. Shauss is certainly welcome to stand third once you've borne my babe." His lips twisted. "Just don't expect me to watch—the idea of those two rutting on your delicate body turns my stomach."

"Gee, that's big of you." Her scornful words sounded pretty brave, but Monica was getting scared now. Could this be true? Was it really open season on her ass? "If this is all aboveboard, why are we hiding down here?"

Instead of answering, Pret grabbed her.

"You really must pay better attention to hygiene after copulating," he said tightly as he wrestled her, kicking and scratching, to the ground. "You stink of Kellen's stain."

"You're going to *be* Kellen's stain, you prick, because that's all that will be left of you when he's done," Monica ground out as she fought to get out from under him. The stone floor was scraping the hell out of her back. God, he was strong for a beanpole! Of course, he had a good six inches on her and he hadn't just emerged from the Sparnite wringer.

Tearing one arm free of his hold, she raked her nails across his face and heard him howl, felt his blood and skin cells accumulate under her nails with primitive satisfaction.

His backhanded blow made her see stars.

* * * * *

"No!"

The female tried to lurch from her seat, but Shauss seized the back of her collar and yanked her upward. She erupted into a flailing tangle of flying arms and legs, clearly terrified. Kellen felt nothing but impatience as he waited for her to break.

"Stop it!" the nurse cried, clearly frightened out of her wits. "She didn't do anything!"

He regretted that she must witness this tactic, but he hadn't the time to reassure her now. "Calm yourself, Ms. Bonham. This shouldn't take long."

Jasmine King scrapped quite well for a female her size, but Shauss had both arms twisted behind her back and locked in his left hand in short order. His right moved immediately to the waistband of her skirt, ripping the garment from her in one smooth sweep. Shock rendered her briefly inert, but when he tore the white scrap of fabric from her privates as well, she exploded into frantic motion once more, air bursting from her throat in shuddering sobs. Her insubstantial footwear had long since flown off and Kellen imagined being nude from the waist down must have struck the worst kind of fear into her heart.

"Shauss, please don't!" she gasped as he tripped her with a sweep of his foot.

"What's the matter, Jasmine?" he returned harshly, shoving her facedown on the floor. "Don't you want me?"

"No!"

He knelt beside the writhing secretary and pinned her hands in the small of her back. "That's funny — I heard you did."

The blonde was sobbing now and care for Monica's feelings, if not for hers, led Kellen to lean down and whisper, "Be calm, little one. He will not complete his assault." She didn't look up, but her shudders seemed to ease.

Shauss held the woman down with one hand while he deliberately drew out the unzipping of his uniform and tortured her with the ominous rasp of it. In a surge of frenzied strength, she yanked one hand free and tried to reach underneath the hem of her blouse.

"What are you up to now?" Shauss growled, recapturing her hand and rolling her to her side.

"Don't do this, Shauss, please don't!" she begged, eyes glancing off the fiercely erect penis he'd exposed. His spur was rearing, as well, and Kellen began to wonder if the man would be able to call a halt before he did her real damage.

"What were you trying to do?" Shauss ground out, shoving her blouse up to expose the small electronic device affixed to her rib cage. He and Kellen both leaned closer, then looked at each other with no small amount of horror. Shauss ripped the device from her, peeling away a layer of her skin in the process, and held it in front of her face. At the sight of it, her expression said she'd lost all hope.

"Why would you do this thing for Pret?" the minister demanded, crouching beside her head. "Do you have any idea of the kind of pain this death would cause you?"

"D-death?" He'd thought her pale before, but she was suddenly whiter than her blouse. "He said it would tr-transport me out of h-here," she fumbled, her teeth clattering in the sudden quiet.

"Miss King, this device is a feyo shell," Kellen said menacingly. "It will incinerate you and anyone you're touching from the inside out."

"Jasmine?" The blonde looked more horrified now than when Kellen had ordered the attack. "You *helped* him?"

"How did he convince you?" Shauss asked angrily. "Promises of money? Power? Technology?"

"Nothing!" Jasmine cried, cringing away from the sight of his still-vivid arousal, her thighs drawn up and pressed tightly together. "He came to me and said that Monica didn't want to be with you, that she was miserable and had begged him to get her out of here, and I thought it was true because I heard her yelling at you in your office that day before she disappeared! Please, Commander, I swear to God, I was only trying to help her!"

"Where has he taken her?"

"I don't know," she sobbed.

Shauss immediately shoved her back to her stomach and threw himself atop her, forcing her thighs apart with his knees as her screams escalated once more.

"Tell me where he took my mate or I and every soldier on this ship will fuck your ass into useless, bloody shreds!" he roared.

"I don't know!" she screamed back at him. "All I know is they're underground somewhere!"

Kellen slammed his fist into the table, making the blonde jump. A flare track was undetectable under the planet's surface.

Then he looked at Cecine.

"Ketrok hasn't removed her biomet."

* * * * *

"You will submit," Pret ordered, breathing roughly with the effort to subdue her.

"*You* will wish you were dead before Kellen is through with you," she hissed, adrenaline whipping her into a frenzy of motion beneath him. She managed to turn her hands back against his restraining grip and gouge deep into his wrists with her nails, and his yowl of rage was all the reward she needed. "And after he and Shauss have carved every inch of your flesh into a screaming mass of exposed nerve endings, I'm going to get my digital camera out and take your picture—"

"Silence!"

"—and post it on alienassholes.com—"

Pret tore the neckline of her suit open and pulled it down, baring her breasts as he confined her arms in the bunched fabric. She felt the pinch of his nails as he reached between her legs and gave a forceful tug, ripping the smooth fabric away and baring her to the chill and his insidious fingers.

"—under the caption, 'Touch Monica Teague, just once, and this could be you!'"

He reached for his zipper and jerked it downward.

"What do you think, Ambassador?" she continued to taunt, determined not to give in to the fear storming her. "Do you think that will discourage anyone else from attempting to take me from them?"

"It would me," came Shauss' half-amused growl from the darkness.

Chapter Fourteen

ఴ

Pret stiffened over Monica, then scuttled off her when Kellen snarled, "Those words will serve even more effectively as his epitaph."

"Kellen!"

Monica's glad cry seized his soul even as Kellen seized the back of Pret's suit, trying to drag him to his feet. The slippery diplomat tore his arms free of the fabric and dived across the rough-hewn floor, leaving the suit and his boots behind and rolling to his feet in a surprising display of agility.

Though keeping his attention focused on the crouching Pret required sparing her only a glance, Monica's exposed breasts and the torn crotch of her wrapsuit made the animal caged within him howl with rage. He was dimly aware of Shauss helping her pull the garment back over her shoulders and climb to her feet, but he had eyes only for the man who was about to die.

"Injure me at your own peril," Pret told him self-importantly, the tremor in his voice belying his confident manner. "I have done nothing illegal, and to harm me is to incur the wrath of the Council."

"Assaulting a Garathani female is not illegal?" Kellen demanded, stunned by the man's gall.

"As she is yet unclaimed by a second, Dr. Teague is subject to mating by any male who has the courage to take her."

"Courage, my ass! Try cowardice, you miserable cocksucker!" Monica's exclamation made Kellen grin, but it was her muttered "Could somebody please hand him a pair of boxers before I puke? Jesus, haven't you guys ever heard of underwear?" that dissolved the destructive ball of energy in his belly, fizzed it outward into his organs, his limbs, his skin, his brain, until he felt consumed by the sheer joy of her.

"Taking an unclaimed female may not be illegal, but attempting to murder a Terran is." Kellen found Pret's nervous twitch quite gratifying.

"I have attempted no such thing."

"Murder?" Monica squeaked. "Who?"

"Jasmine King," Shauss replied. "He used her to elicit information about you and then tried to eliminate her, and us alongside her, with a feyo shell."

"Ouch! Jasmine was trying to get information for *him*?" Monica shuddered. "No wonder the little bitch was so snoopy at lunch."

"Don't be too angry with her," Kellen cautioned. "She'd heard us arguing and Pret had her convinced that you hated being with us and had asked him for assistance in escaping."

"And she's paid the price for her gullibility."

The finality in Shauss' voice made her look at him, her heart suddenly thumping.

"What price?"

"One very similar to the price you almost paid for our negligence."

"The price I almost paid," she repeated blankly. Oh jeez, he couldn't mean...

Kellen clarified, "In order to secure her cooperation, I ordered him to rape Miss King. If I hadn't, we might not have found you in time."

Horror prickled under her skin. "Shauss, you didn't!"

"No, I didn't," he agreed with a grim look. "But I would have. Believe me, there's nothing I wouldn't have done to get you back. *Nothing*," he spat in Pret's direction. "If her actions had lost you to me, she would have taken your place in my bed and suffered the rest of her days for it."

Pret chose that moment to try darting past Kellen, but the larger, stronger commander had him facedown on the ground and pressed under his heel in an instant, yipping in pain. Barely noticing the disruption, Monica stared back and forth between her two mates, her heart thudding thickly in her ears. Did she even know them?

"Kellen?" Nerves made her lick her lips.

"He would have had my blessing." The steel in his voice told her he meant business.

"A Garathani female is worth that much, then?" she asked, depressed by the idea. They only wanted her because she was a rare commodity, like diamonds. No, wait—those weren't really rare, just tightly controlled. Hen's teeth—now *those* were rare.

And of course they would do anything to retain possession of the prize they'd staked their claim on, up to and including the rape of an innocent woman. *Rape*! How could she possibly love—

"The only daughter of the minister is worth any price!" Pret declared.

Oh shit. *Oh no.* She *so* did not love either of these barbaric—

Her eyes widened as the shock of Pret's words finally registered over the shock of her own realization. "The only daughter of..."

"Minister Cecine is your father." Kellen watched her face.

Her father. Cecine was her father. Hell, she wasn't just rare—she was one of a kind. No wonder they were all so desperate to have her.

She turned her face to the wall, feeling the burn of humiliation creeping into her cheeks. And here she'd been thinking she might actually feel... Shit, all she had to do was *think* the L-word and people lined up to knock her on her ass. *Love.* Yeah, right.

"Why didn't you tell me?"

Dismayed by the tremor in her voice, she glanced at Kellen, only to find his eyes narrowed on her in the wavering blue light. Um, he was looking a little more pissed than he should have, considering he'd just ground his enemy under his heel. Literally.

"Empran, activate neural restraints." She sucked in a breath, then released it in a rush when Kellen finished. "Subject Ambassador Pret."

Pret relaxed at once, looking very much like a snakeskin rug on the bare stone, and Monica couldn't help the smile that twisted her lips.

"Nice to see somebody else getting a taste of that, for a change."

Kellen lift his foot off the rug and assumed an aggressive stance. Looking at her with fire in his eyes, he pointed to the floor in front of him.

Shit.

"Monica, come here. Now."

Her eyes skittered around, looking anywhere but at him as she stalked over and stood before him, her posture defiant despite the tattered state of her suit.

Sliding two fingers under her chin, Kellen tugged her face up until she met his gaze. And whatever he'd intended to say to her was momentarily lost in the shining depths of her eyes, swept away by the single tear that hovered on her lashes and then dropped to the stone floor. He heard its splat, felt its weight like a mace slammed hard into his chest.

"I don't think I care for the direction your thoughts are taking," he said roughly.

"You don't have a clue about my thoughts."

That, unfortunately, was quite true. But he knew self-doubt when he saw it.

"Your worth to me, Monica Teague, has nothing to do with your father."

She closed her eyes, sending another tear cascading downward. Leaning forward, she pressed her forehead against his breastbone and swallowed audibly, but Kellen wasn't about to let her get away with that. He urged her face up again, determined to make her look at him, but her eyes remained closed and the tears kept sliding down her cheeks, one after the other. He chased them with his lips and tongue, refusing to waste one more on the stone below.

"I'm sorry," she gulped. "It's just reaction —"

"Hush," he whispered, sucking at the corner of her mouth. "You've been very brave, *sziscala*, but you don't have to be strong every moment of every day. That's what your mates are for."

Her sob was more than Kellen could take. Drawing her into his arms, he kissed her unresponsive mouth as she wept, drinking in her gasping cries until she grew quiet and leaned into his embrace.

"If you imagine I only want you because you're Cecine's daughter, then it's you who has no clue about my thoughts," he told her, brushing her hair back from her eyes. They opened slowly, large, brilliant and filled with a pain he couldn't fathom. "I can't even begin to tell you all the reasons why I want you. But I do want you, Monica. *You*. Never doubt that."

"You want me," she repeated. The doubt still shadowing her tear-washed eyes made him tense with frustration. And just the slightest whisper of anxiety.

"I want you!" came a weak cry from the floor behind him. "I would treasure you —"

Kellen silenced Pret with a backward kick, but the moment was lost.

"Oh, you just had to talk about this stuff in front of him, didn't you?" Monica fussed, stepping out of his reach. She dashed the remaining wetness from her cheeks with her fingers and swiped the sleeve of her suit under her nose. "Fucking diplomats," she muttered. "They'll say anything to save their own asses."

"Nothing he could possibly say would save his ass," Kellen scowled.

"What are you going to do?"

He and Shauss drew their daggers simultaneously.

"Jesus!" Monica squeaked, jumping back. "What are you, the vigilante twins? Put those things away before you hurt someone."

"That is the point," Kellen drawled. "No pun intended."

"Forget it!"

"But what about your caption on alienassholes.com?" Shauss' smirk earned him an elbow in the ribs.

"I just said that to scare him. I didn't really intend for you to carve him up—unless he actually..." Her throat worked visibly. "Believe me, guys, there's nothing I'd like better than to watch this bastard writhe in agony, but I'm a doctor, for Christ's sake! I can't just stand here and let you torture him. This is a matter for the authorities now."

Kellen shook his head. "Not before we've extracted our own pound of flesh."

"Pound of flesh!" she shrieked. "You can't—wait a minute. Pound of flesh, huh?"

"What scheme is hatching in your delightful little head now?" Shauss demanded, obviously not trusting the calculating look in her eye any more than Kellen did.

"You want flesh?" she asked. "You got it." Her expression challenged him, but it was her seductive tone that made Kellen's eyes widen. "Can you get us all someplace with a little less atmosphere and a little more comfort?"

* * * * *

"Put him in tension restraints and prop him up in the corner," she commanded, trying not to smirk at the sight of her two mates frozen in place. Still blinking and disoriented from the unexpected flare into Kellen's quarters, she'd nonetheless stripped off her boots and suit and now stood defiantly naked, waiting for them to comply.

"What in Peserin's name are you up to?" Kellen asked. He looked so wary, it was almost funny.

But not really.

The feeling that she'd lost some vital component of herself in the last couple of days, some critical measure of personal power, made her desperate to reclaim it. There was only one way she could think of to do that.

"An eye for an eye. Sort of, anyway," she said, her tone deliberately breezy. God, was she insane? "If you really want to punish him, show him what he's going to miss when he goes into the Big House and becomes some bruiser's bony bitch."

"Monica—" both men said at once.

"C'mon, Shauss," she cut in. Planting her fists on her hips, she looked him right in the eye. "Unlike you, he can't stand to watch, so fuck me."

The growl that rattled in his throat was *so* empowering!

She crooked her finger at him. "I *dare* you. Get over here and fuck me now before some other yo-yo comes along with the bright idea of jumping your claim."

That got him.

"I'm not going to argue with you," he huffed as he dragged Pret to the wall and sat him up. "But you're taking my spur up the ass." Like magic, the little weasel remained upright and she wondered how in the—

"Hey, now! Maybe you're the one who needs to take it up the ass!"

"If you think you're man enough." He grinned as he approached her.

"Shauss, I'd watch my step, if I were you," Kellen advised.

Shauss glanced at him. "She doesn't scare me."

"Come on, Shauss," she taunted. "Let's play doctor. You whip that virgin ass out here and let me do a thorough exam, and I won't even bill your insurance company."

He was out of his uniform before she finished the challenge, and the battle of wills was on.

"Where would you like me?" he asked.

"You allow this female to talk to you in such—"

"Empran, neural gag, subject Pret," Kellen said in a weary voice.

Well, that was a neat trick. On someone else.

"Right where you are," Monica said to Shauss. "First things first, though. Kellen, you strip, too." The mix of hesitation and anticipation on his face made her smile grimly. He was going to suffer a little, too.

With the emotional walls he'd maintained for years in ruins around him, Kellen felt more naked fully clothed than he ever had wearing nothing. The idea of baring himself further in the presence of Pret was unsettling, but he couldn't resist Monica's invitation any more than he could resist the imperative to breathe. She stood there nude, hair flying around her in wild disarray, more beautiful and daring than he'd ever seen her, and all he could do was prepare himself to fuck the living hell out of her and hope he was able to walk out of the cabin under his own power instead of being carried out on a litter, a victim of her insatiable demands.

He propped an ankle on his knee and pulled off one boot. As it hit the floor, he commented, "This is a new side of you. I like it."

Her confidence flagged visibly before she shored up her defenses. "You don't have to sweet-talk me, Commander. We got that out of the way already, remember?"

"I don't know," he deliberated as he switched legs and pulled off the other boot. "I think we've established how much I want you. And despite his reticence, I have no doubt that Shauss feels the same way."

"I do," the lieutenant agreed gravely.

"You, on the other hand, remain something of a mystery." He straightened and looked at her expectantly. "Perhaps *we're* the ones who require sweet-talking."

"Oh baloney," she scoffed. "The only kind of encouragement you two require is a couple of well-placed holes to cram yourselves into."

Her assessment annoyed him, but deciding this wasn't the time to debate the issue, Kellen stepped out of his suit and tossed it into the growing pile on the floor. He stood facing her then, arms crossed over his chest, while Shauss closed in from the other side of her. When they were both within reach, she put her hands on their chests to hold them in place, breathing in nervous huffs as her eyes darted from his naked arousal to Shauss'. Her hesitation reminded him that, despite her bravado, the situation was as new to her as it was to them. To him, anyway. Shauss looked primed and ready to pounce. If he had any concerns, they didn't show on his face.

Kellen thought he couldn't be more startled when Monica shoved him, causing him to stumble backward and fall to a half-reclining position on the end of the bed. Then she dropped to her knees in front of Shauss.

His eyes widened. Surely she didn't intend…

The hope that she might have collapsed in a fit of exhaustion evaporated when the tip of her tongue flicked out to taste Shauss' straining cock. Surprised and dismayed by the seething tangle of emotions that threatened his self-control, Kellen turned his face to the bulkhead and counted to five.

And then to ten. But it wasn't working. He still wanted to kill Shauss. He wanted to drag Monica away from the man by her hair and make her taste *his* cock. Right before he fucked her brainless.

Every Power take him—he was *jealous*!

Logic immediately delivered a stinging lecture about the potential effects of such a destructive emotion on a three-way bond. There was no room for possessiveness in the new order of their society. But reasonable or not, Kellen was feeling decidedly aggravated. Worse, he was feeling usurped, a sensation that did not bode well for the future advancement of Shauss' military career.

Trying to school his features into a mask of lustful blandness, to reveal none of his inner turmoil, Kellen returned his gaze to the tableau before him.

The sight of her mouth closing around Shauss' fat purple glans rocked him hard, captured his imagination with cruel clarity, and the beast in him roared for release. It tested the boundaries of his self-control, requiring every ounce of determination he could muster to sit there, eyes slitted, and watch impassively as the thick bulb of flesh pushed repeatedly between her sweet lips. The knowledge that Monica had chosen to bestow her oral favors on Shauss first ate at him like the most potent of acids. She was *his*!

He nearly sagged in relief when she pulled away with a wet smacking sound.

"I don't know if I'm hungry enough to eat the whole thing," she quipped, eyeing Shauss' surging erection with unexpected humor.

Planting his hands in her hair, Shauss urged her forward. "Force yourself."

With his cock nudging her mouth once more, Monica ordered, "Spread your feet first."

His instant obedience was rewarded when she opened to allow him back into her mouth. She sucked at him with hungry mewling sounds that fueled Kellen's own raging libido even as they inflamed his urge to kill. She acted as if she and Shauss were alone in the cabin, as if he and Pret didn't even exist. Jaw clenched at the idea of being lumped in with Pret, he leaned forward, resting his elbows on his knees and staring at them with burning eyes, going quietly insane as Shauss lived *his* fantasy of fucking Monica's mouth.

Her throaty moan rang in his ears as she once again pulled off that thick stalk of flesh with a juicy smack of her lips.

"Wait a minute," she breathed. "We have a gauntlet down, I do believe."

The beast stilled at once, on the alert. There was no telling what the little Sparnite might do next. If his expression was anything to go by, her uncanny knack for torture affected Shauss just as badly as it did him. She sat back on her heels and sucked on her middle finger in a blatant imitation of what she'd just done to the panting lieutenant, thrusting it in and out of her mouth until they were all moaning. When she finally pulled it from between her lips, it was shiny and dripping with saliva.

Rising to her knees once more, she looked up at Shauss from beneath her lashes.

"Here it comes, big boy."

Shauss' grin was strained but indulgent as her hand disappeared between his long thighs. The man was obviously more comfortable with the intimate exploration than Kellen would have been, and the indulgence quickly gave way to arousal as Monica rose to her knees and took his cock into her mouth once more. She stroked his balls with her left hand, cupping and squeezing as she sucked and licked. And probed him. Kellen saw the muscles in her right forearm working as she manipulated Shauss' anus, saw his knees lock and his thighs grow taut and his hands twine into her hair as he began to grimace.

Eventually the rapt quiet was replaced by the sounds of harsh breathing, and not just Shauss'. Glancing at Pret, Kellen was brutally amused to see his erection bobbing between his thighs. The traitor looked utterly humiliated and Kellen marveled at how suitable a punishment Monica had devised for him.

"Fuck!"

The imprecation drew his gaze back to Shauss, who thrust deeply into Monica's mouth, twisting her hair in a manner that surely caused her pain. She didn't look as if she cared.

"She's fucking me!" The growl sounded stunned and not at all happy. "Monica, stop, you have to stop now. *Now*! Oh, sweet mother of—"

He watched in amazement as Shauss jerked hard, once, twice, and then roared out loud as he deposited his seed between Monica's glistening lips.

It was fully ten seconds before Kellen could close his jaw enough to whisper, "Holy shit."

Chapter Fifteen

ॐ

Still on her knees, Monica stared at the spot where Shauss had last been seen and gasped, "What? What did I do?"

He'd flared out without a word.

"Holy shit," Kellen murmured again. Then he burst into belly laughs the likes of which she'd never heard from any Garathani. He laughed until he had to hold his aching sides, until tears ran down his cheeks, until he slid to the floor and rolled in breathless agony. Kellen! The imposing commander, in stitches on the floor. Naked. And in front of a naked diplomat, no less!

Wait a minute… Where *was* the nasty old ambassador?

She glanced around the room, but there was no sign of him. Lurching to her feet, she snatched up her suit and clutched it to her chest. The rat couldn't have gone far, a fact that suddenly made Monica feel way too vulnerable. She glared at Kellen while she stepped into the shredded fabric and tried to arrange it over her breasts, though he obviously didn't notice, lost as he was in hysterics at her expense. He still hadn't recovered his composure by the time she got her boots on, which really pissed her off.

"Do you mind?" She nudged Kellen's bare ass with the toe of her boot. "Where's Pret?"

He took one look at her face and cracked up again. "Detention bay," he choked out.

"Quit laughing at me, asshole," she spat, reeling back to give him a good, sound kick this time. He caught her ankle and yanked her down on top of him.

"Peserin's delight, my *sziscala*," he wheezed as he squeezed. "I'm laughing at myself, not you."

"Sure you are," she grumbled. "Now put a sock in it and tell me what the big deal is."

"You tell me," he gasped, trying hard to catch his breath. "Come now, you're a physician. You should be able to figure this one out."

"What? I fellated Shauss, right? Something, I might add, that millions of American women do to millions of American men every day."

"And?" He finally managed to get a hold of himself and rolled them both to a sitting position.

"And what?" She stared at him. "I sucked him off and he came… Holy shit! He came in my mouth!"

"You begin to see the light," Kellen agreed, wiping his eyes. "To my knowledge, no other Garathani male in history has ejaculated anywhere but in a female's genitalia. We didn't think it possible, and believe me when I tell you we've all tried everything we could think of, not just for the last ten years but all our lives, to produce just such a result. What in Peserin's name did you do to him?"

"Nothing too startling," Monica said defensively. God, she didn't think she'd gone *that* far off the beaten path. She'd heard a lot of guys liked it, and Shauss had seemed open to almost anything. "I just massaged his prostate."

"Massaged his prostate," Kellen repeated blankly.

"You know, the prostate gland, that little donut-shaped —
"

"I know what a prostate is. I just can't believe something that simple could —"

"You mean you guys never tried that before?"

He winced. "Of course not. Why would we? That particular gland has no connection at all to our spurs, and it can only be accessed through our waste canals, for Peserin's sake!"

Shaking her head, she snorted. "Jesus, I can't believe you guys made it into space before we did. Talk about not thinking outside the box! You can't tell me that none of you, not even one out of the whole planet, is gay."

"Yes, as a matter of fact, I *can* tell you that," he assured her, sounding annoyed. "Our males don't share the same perversions as the males of your planet."

Monica gave him a cheeky grin. "Homophobic much?"

Kellen stiffened. "No, I'm simply stating a fact, and I'll state it again in language you can understand — we don't *swing* that way. Period."

"So that line you guys fed me about your females pleasuring each other was just—"

"We are not like our females," he ground out.

"Sure, you're not," she snorted.

"Monica…"

He looked like he could chew up a steel girder and spit out nails, so she strangled the laugh that hovered in her chest. Once he'd dressed, he gave her a stern glare and flared out without another word.

That was getting old fast.

* * * * *

The pizza had worn off and she was starved beyond belief, but that fucking computer still wouldn't do anything for her, like open the door or send her food, so she just sat there in the chair where she'd so recently had the living daylights spanked out of her and let her thoughts chase around like a dog after its tail.

Kellen had left nearly three hours ago and she hadn't seen or heard from him since. She wished she could figure out that damn flare technology and use it to get herself out of here. It was becoming apparent that he utilized some sort of nonverbal link with the computer—too much stuff seemed to happen without a hint of warning around him, like flaring and the restraints—but she was damned if she'd ask him. Assuming she ever had the chance.

The flare field drew her restless gaze. Darkness had fallen while she was showering off the cave grime and now she didn't even have the entertainment of watching the world go by. That was the bad thing about being in geosynchronous orbit—you couldn't see much when the sun passed beyond the Earth's rim. There was no television to watch, and she could only stare at that strange sculpture on the table—some sort of winged goddess with remarkably ugly features—for so long before it started to waver eerily in her vision.

She'd poked around in the built-in cabinets earlier, looking for something, *anything* to do—read a book, work a puzzle, play solitaire—and found only clothing. Which had its upside, since some of it appeared to be her size. Too bad Garathani textile designers had so little use for color. The three suits that looked like they'd fit her were gray, black, and white. No underwear, of course, so at least she didn't have to worry about panty lines. Unfortunately, there were also no socks. Her boots would no doubt be way beyond ripe before the week was out.

She had also found a silky white nightgown tucked in with the suits. She'd slipped it over her head after her shower, studiously ignoring the implications of the action, and been fascinated by her reflection in the flare field. The face was going to take some getting used to, more so now that one cheek was black and blue. But her hair, cut in shining layers of brown and blonde, bounced with healthy vigor every time she moved her head. And her body...

Settling deeper in the chair, she gave in to temptation and slid her hands over the tight mountains of her breasts, disconcerted and yet thrilled when her nipples hardened immediately. Yep, she was definitely built for sin and couldn't find it in her to regret it even a little.

Monica laid her head back and, shrugging aside a momentary qualm, allowed her hands to continue their exploration of her breasts through the silk. The rush of sensation when her fingers skimmed over her spiked nipples was damn amazing, and she did it again and again, 'til the areolas were drawn up tight and she was breathing hard. The hunger pangs she'd been feeling were suddenly displaced by a different longing, a little lower, a lot hotter.

Kellen.

Monica stirred on her chair, uncomfortable with the thick knot rising in her throat at the thought of him. He'd had her this morning. Boy, had he had her! Just the memory of how he'd subdued her was enough to elicit some big-time clenching in her nether regions, and she could still feel him forcing her legs open, scraping into her, grinding his seed into her...

Her groan was loud in the unrelenting emptiness of his quarters. Blushing furiously, she looked around to make sure she was still alone.

"Idiot," she huffed on a silent laugh. Like Kellen and Shauss hadn't already heard all kinds of caterwauling out of her. Good God, just this morning she'd ordered him, *begged* him to fuck her, and clung to him like Velcro while he did exactly that. It was almost impossible to get her head around the concept. She never asked for or expected anything from anyone. Saved a person a hell of a lot of disappointment.

Monica swallowed. She'd refused to beg for his kiss when he took her, and once again, he hadn't offered it. The action-packed hours afterward had left her little time to brood about it, which was all that had held the disappointment at bay. Then he'd kissed her, truly kissed her, and despite the lack of passion in the moment, she'd found it the sweetest, most satisfying experience of her life. She wanted more. Badly. She wanted to be kissed and petted and adored.

Shit. Wanting anything that badly was just asking to have it taken away. She needed to get over this now, get her mind on something else before he came back and caught her thinking about him, caught her touching herself...

Her pulse bounded into Mach territory at the image of Kellen catching her masturbating. What would he—what would *they* do to her?

Damn Shauss anyway! She'd gotten pretty worked up, doing that to him in front of Kellen, and it was telling on her now. What in the hell did he have to be pissed off about, anyway? For God's sake, she'd apparently given him the greatest blowjob in Garathani history and been hung out to dry for her trouble. *She* was the one who should be pissed.

Although she hadn't started this little journey of self-discovery with the intention of playing with herself, her heart raced as the idea bloomed. Could she do something so blatantly sexual, especially in this alien environment? The thought of getting to know her new body and how it functioned, and maybe getting a little relief out of the deal, was tempting in the extreme. *Especially in this alien environment...*

Chest heaving with excitement and no small amount of tension, Monica slid her hands down her ribs, over the newly concave plane of her stomach, inching her feet apart on the floor as she went. When her hands reached her thighs, her fingertips resting on the hem of the short nightgown, she stopped, waiting.

For what? Lightning to strike?

Taking a deep breath, she curled the fabric between her fingers and pulled it up until her lap was exposed. The sight of her thatch of brown pubic hair made her shudder with arousal. Shit, she was really a woman now. She held the gown against her stomach with her left hand while the right inched downward 'til her palm covered her silky mound. Spreading her knees wider opened her labia, allowed her fingertips to sink into the damp crevice. She stroked lightly, learning the intimate folds in a way she hadn't allowed herself in the shower.

When one fingertip found her spur nook, she trembled, circling the opening with avid curiosity. It wasn't hard to tell when she found her clitoris; her hips jumped and she moaned involuntarily as sparks shot up her belly. Reaching inside, she was surprised to realize her nook was deep enough to accommodate her middle finger all the way up to her palm. Pulling out raised quite a ruckus with her clitoris but, not quite ready to try for satisfaction just yet, she sent that questing finger farther south, adding another as she went. They slid at once into the slick recess of her vagina, which, in light of her line of work, shouldn't have been quite so new and fascinating. Did she come equipped with a g-spot?

Closing her eyes, she explored the ledge of flesh where it was supposed to be, rubbing in small circles, gradually applying more pressure. In a flash, tension wound tight in her belly and she choked back a moan at the force of it. *Oh, yeah, that's gotta be it.* She backed off the pressure and reached for her clitoris with her thumb. It had risen out of her nook and was very, very sensitive now. Feeling like an extremely bad girl, she sunk her thumb all the way into her nook, and when the knuckle fold scraped over her clitoris, she was shamed and thrilled by the stuttering moan that escaped her. God, she had her vagina full of fingers and her nook full of thumb, and oh, she wanted to come so bad…

* * * * *

"Look at her, Shauss," Kellen said harshly. "That's an order. Watch her fingers as she fucks herself and tell me you aren't wild to yank them out and take their place in her cunt."

"She's yours," Shauss insisted, keeping his eyes fixed on the bulkhead. He slouched in what Kellen was coming to think of as his accustomed seat in the corner, his uniform still pooled around his waist. The flare field concealed their presence, and because Monica hadn't spent enough time around flare technology to detect changes in the air currents when a field was nearby, she had no idea Shauss had been here watching her for most of the afternoon.

"She's *ours*, you moron!" Kellen growled. "I can't believe you would let pride keep you from claiming your own mate."

"Easy enough for you to say. She didn't just emasculate you in front of Pret."

"Nor did she you," Kellen insisted. "For Peserin's sake, she knelt at your feet and took your cock in her mouth, and I know for a fact she left it intact. How many Garathani men can lay claim to such a privilege? Pret was practically weeping with envy and *I* was so consumed with jealousy," he admitted reluctantly, "I could have removed your head with my bare hands. *We're* the ones she emasculated."

"She fucked my ass and made me come!"

"And Ketroc did the same to Pret in front of a dozen witnesses. He's the one who'll go down in history books as the pioneer of anal orgasm, and with the ignoble impetus of a rubber dildo in his ass instead of a lovely little mouth sucking his cock."

"*She* did it to *me* first," Shauss maintained stubbornly, "and we all know it."

Kellen shifted uncomfortably. As jealous as he'd been of Shauss before, it was true that he wouldn't trade places with him now. He'd realized the significance of Monica's accomplishment almost at once, and fast on the heels of that realization had come a shameful relief that he hadn't been her target. Then the irony of his sudden reversal had struck him and he'd ordered Pret to detention before hysteria overwhelmed him. Shauss was already the injured party—he didn't need Pret witnessing the reaction and relaying it to others. It could too easily be misinterpreted as humor at Shauss' expense rather than his own.

"Well, return the favor then, man," he prodded.

A whimpering sigh drew his eye back to Monica. She was dragging her thumb, wet from its foray into her nook, in lazy, luxurious circles around her clitoris. "Oh, Kellen…"

His whole body seized with lust. She was thinking about him while she stroked herself.

"Now tell me she's *ours*," Shauss said in a dampening tone.

"Damn you, Shauss," Monica groaned. "You were supposed to fuck me."

"You were saying?"

Shauss couldn't hide his wry grin, but didn't concede the point. "Even now she's sighing over you and ordering me around."

"I'm at a loss here, Shauss." Kellen raised his palms. "Monica can order you all she wants, but you are dominant to her, just as I am. And we both know that as much as she hates to admit it, even to herself, she enjoys it every bit as much as we do. What you need to do, for your sake more than hers, is reestablish your mastery of her."

Knowing the groan that rolled out of Monica then for the warning it was, Kellen ordered tension restraints to stave off her orgasm and grinned at the screech of outrage that followed. Shauss finally chuckled.

"My mastery of her," he repeated, scratching his chest. "We both know it's you who have her mastered and I am just along for the ride." He turned in the low seat and faced Monica. "All right then—you bring her to heel and I'll follow your lead."

* * * * *

Monica seethed at the neural restraint imposed on her out of the blue. And at such an inopportune moment!

"Kellen, you son of a bitch, where are you?"

A heartbeat later, he appeared out of thin air directly in front of her chair.

"No need to yell," he said mildly. "I'm right here."

"No need to—"

"While it's been fun watching you play with your cunt, and it's good to know you can keep yourself entertained when we're away," Kellen said, drawing his zipper downward, "I must insist that you not come without my permission."

"*Your* per—"

"When I release your restraints, you may use your fingers to fuck yourself to orgasm for us," he continued as if she hadn't spoken.

Monica's heart pounded at his words. One minute she'd been on the brink of getting herself off and the next Kellen was playing his domination games with her again.

At least they were back in familiar territory. It felt good to be angry with him. Safe.

He kicked his suit and boots into the corner and stood naked in front of her, his cock magnificently long and hard. Now that she'd looked, she couldn't take her eyes off it.

"I didn't quite hear you."

Shaking her head to dispel the fog of lust, she met his eyes. What was he talking about? She hadn't said anything.

"When I give you an order," he said patiently, "I expect you to acknowledge it, Monica. You may say, 'Yes, Commander' or 'Yes, Sir'—whichever you prefer."

Shit! He was deliberately provoking her again, but she needed to come so bad now, she didn't think she could argue with him.

"I'm waiting."

She closed her eyes and moaned, torn. God, he'd ordered her to make herself come…for *them*. "Shauss is here?"

"He's been here all along."

She whimpered. Oh, she was so close…

Kellen's fingers gripped her chin and shook lightly, forcing her eyes open. "What did I tell you to do?"

"Yes, Commander," she said blankly, shaking all over.

"What did I tell you to do?" he demanded again.

"Finger-fuck myself," she sobbed.

Her restraints eased at once.

"Then do it."

Monica rammed her fingers hard into her vagina, her thumb into her nook, and screamed as the orgasm slammed into her with the force of a tidal wave.

"Don't stop." Kellen's voice reached her before the contractions eased. "Fuck yourself to another so we can see just how you like it."

She couldn't obey. Boneless from the incredible release, she slumped in the chair and was dismayed to feel tears sliding down her cheeks once more. Jesus, she was so in love with him, he didn't even have to touch her. He broke her heart into a million aching little pieces every time he looked at her, and he apparently didn't even know what love was. She was just an object to him, a means to an end.

Get a grip! she scolded herself. Squaring her shoulders, she managed to stifle the waterworks and glare at him as she pulled her gown down to cover her lap and crossed her arms under her breasts.

"Go fuck yourself," she said deliberately. "In fact, why don't you and Shauss go fuck each other, now that we know you can."

"I wouldn't push him right now, Monica," Kellen warned.

"Where is he anyway? I haven't seen—"

Shauss materialized right beside Kellen, totally naked and looking so pissed, he actually took her breath away. He tossed something onto the bed and then leaned over and grabbed her wrists, grinding out, "I'll gag her. You fuck her. Now!" as he pulled her to her feet.

Genuinely alarmed, and perversely even more excited, Monica struggled as he lifted her still-crossed arms over her head. The action spun her to face the bed and he marched her forward while she kicked every inch of the way. Expecting to be shoved facedown and taken from behind, she was surprised when he picked her up by the wrists and flipped her over the big mattress like a sheet, depositing her on her back with her head at the foot of the bed.

"Here."

Kellen handed Shauss what looked like a rubber ball with straps attached to it. *What the hell?*

Shauss' grin made her blood run hot and cold. "It's a ball gag," he informed her. "Open wide."

She bit her lips mutinously.

"I think she wants you to spank her pussy again," Kellen murmured.

Damn it! She opened her mouth and took the gag, looking back and forth between the two men, her pulse pounding as Shauss fastened the straps behind her head.

"Why am I not surprised that you possess such a thing?"

"The internet is a wondrous thing," Shauss said, his tone dripping with satisfaction. "I could have used a neural gag, but this is so much more provocative."

Oh, she was liking this too much! It was just sick and wrong, and she *enjoyed* it... Shauss' hair brushed her face as he leaned over to pull her nightgown off, and she whimpered with need.

Then the mattress sagged by her hip.

"Hold her down," Kellen ordered.

Shauss immediately pinned her wrists to the bed and Monica jumped at the feel of Kellen's hot hands on the insides of her thighs, prying them wide. He climbed between them and knelt there, gazing down at her with a kingly expression that made her want to smack him. His sudden grin said he'd read her mind.

"Normally I prefer a good fight, but this is fun, too." He ran his palms up her rib cage and cupped her heaving breasts, squeezing and molding them and watching her face all the while. He pushed them together and made a low sound of regret. "They're not soft enough to fuck yet. That's something I'd really like to try."

"Wait a year or two," Shauss told him.

Monica's eyelids fluttered and closed as Kellen leaned down and took one stiff nipple into his mouth. They flew open again immediately when the light sucking was accompanied by a similar drawing at her other breast. It was a devastating double assault and she bucked wildly as it intensified, grunting and whining against Shauss' furry chest.

She screamed into the gag when, still suckling, Kellen bowed his back and shoved into her. She was wet, but still narrow and tender enough that his thick penis felt like a rough-hewn log. The scream faded to a whimper as he held there, jammed deep inside her body, murmuring words of praise and encouragement between long pulls at her breast.

Shauss' hands rubbed up and down the undersides of her arms, which now hung limply over the foot of the bed. Then the rough edges of his teeth scissored over her nipple. Her vaginal muscles clamped down hard as she screamed again. Oh shit—when had she become a masochist? He did it again and she stiffened, panicked. He was hurting her good enough to make her come.

"What *are* you doing to her?" Kellen moaned with a short laugh.

"Biting her."

"Hmm…" Then his teeth joined in the delicious torture of her nipples.

The raging orgasm fired every nerve in her body at once, and Kellen groaned and shuddered, pulling out and plowing back in through contractions so hard, they curled shoulders up off the bed. Both men drew away from her breasts, but she couldn't stop coming, couldn't stop screaming as he rode her roughly, and the muffled sound, the feel of saliva slipping down her cheeks from the gag, only drove her higher.

Monica thought she might pass out when his spur started slamming home. And then the weirdest thing happened—it was like she suddenly only existed on this isolated plane, bound to him, taken by him, *owned* by him. There was no touch but that of his body pounding hers, no sound but that of his broken groans, no sight but that of his face rising above her, hard and flushed and determined. His lips drew back in a grimace of need, and then he was shouting her name…

Oh yeah. She was liking the gag more every minute. She could say anything she wanted and not have to worry that he would actually hear it. *I love you so much, Kellen, oh God, I'm going to come again, please love me, Kellen, I love you so much…*

She was barely conscious when he climbed off her.

The rasp of a hard, furred chest lowering onto hers made her eyes snap open and suddenly she was looking into the black eyes of Lieutenant Shauss as his cock slid into her slick, aching vagina.

"*This* is how *I* like you," he rumbled. "Soft and wet and spent." He leaned down and nipped at her earlobe as he pulled out and eased back in. "Weak and helpless and unable to keep me from doing anything I like with your delectable body."

Feeling fuzzy and totally brainless, Monica sighed and slid her fingers into his hair, combing through it with immense pleasure. The disgruntlement she felt when he pulled out and propped himself up on one arm quickly vanished when he took his penis in hand and stroked the head over her sensitized pubis. Up and down he went, and up and down, and down, and down...

Chapter Sixteen

ဢ

"Mmfff!"

Monica's eyes were the size of Rimberian ice coins.

His might be, as well. He couldn't believe the man would actually…

Shauss, what are you about now?

"She fucked my ass, so I'm going to fuck hers."

With your spur.

"With my cock. I want to watch her face."

Kellen stiffened as Monica began to struggle. *I said master her, Shauss, not torture her.* When Shauss' mouth opened, he barked, "You're frightening her. Use the cerecom, and that's an order, Lieutenant."

Shauss reared back onto his heels and stared, his eyes slits in his stony face. Monica scrambled over the side of the bed and knelt beside it, plucking urgently at the straps behind her head.

So much for not commanding me in the mating chamber.

Monica is ours to protect, Shauss. Protect! *If I have to pull rank to protect her from you, then I will.*

I have no intention of hurting her, Commander! Terrans engage in anal —

Monica slammed the gag down on the mattress. "Goddamn it, you two! Quit talking about me when I can't hear you."

"My apologies," Kellen said at once. She fairly bristled with annoyance. "I was just making it clear to Lieutenant Shauss that —"

"His word is law in the mating chamber," Shauss finished angrily, pushing off the mattress. "He believes that I would harm you, which shows just how little he truly knows or respects me."

When had this bond spun so dangerously out of his control? "Shauss—"

"I knew sharing a mate would never work for me." He bent and grabbed his suit, then looked at Monica. "I wish you well, sweet one."

When he flared out, it felt as though an Aptormian ape had settled onto Kellen's chest. He blinked repeatedly, trying to make sense of Shauss' departure, of the pain that was swelling under his breastbone.

"Kellen, what just happened?"

She looked as stricken as he felt.

"I wish I knew." Unfortunately, he *did* know. He held out his hand and she took it, shaking her hair out of her face as she rose. The rightness of her delicate fingers in his stole the breath from him. It also made the loss of Shauss that much more wrenching. And loss, it was. He obviously intended to annul his claim to Monica, and the thought was almost unbearable. Peserin, but when had his heart gotten so entangled with these two who were his to protect?

At the touch of her hand on his jaw, Kellen focused on Monica. She was looking at him with concern. "He doesn't mean it, does he?"

"He doubtless does."

Her lips flattened. "I'm sorry. I didn't mean to come between you."

"Come between *us*?" Kellen's laugh was short and bitter. Life's ironies just got sharper with every passing day. He planted a kiss on her forehead and started pulling on his clothes. "I'd say we did a fine job of that without any help from you, little Terran. I'll have to find him and see what I can do to salvage something of our friendship."

aced. "I am going to
ugly piece of dirty
ch it fry him into a
he ran right into

bs!"

immediate
estigation."

tration,
bt her
d her
feet,
ded
ts
t

llen stepped
into her
ed her
d that
she was,
he moment.
a mate. Any
ntent in second

Which means I'll have
ature in my next second.
er."

* * *

ou fucking no-good piece of alien
hoarsely, "open this goddamned door

d."

She pounded her fists on the door yet again, as futile, but needing to work off more of her . She'd already tried to batter her way out with that culpture and been zapped with some sort of energy for her trouble. Her hair still stood on end from the ck, waving like a wheat field in the summer breeze. The ning lay where she'd dropped it, unbroken despite the rough treatment. Must be made of some tough stuff. "Connect me to Commander Kellen then, cyber-bitch, or I'll have your hard drive on a platter!"

"Unable to comply."

"Oh, for God's sake!" She stomped across the room, trying to smooth her hair once again. "Why can't you let me talk to him for just a few seconds?"

"Voice contact requires the authorization of Commander Kellen."

"He is *so* dead," Monica spat as she [...]
kill him myself. I'm going to take this [...]
marble and shove it right up his ass and wa[...]
fucking chicken nug— Ow!"

The white field sprang up so suddenly, s[...]
it with her forehead. *Oh, no way...*

"I was joking, you stupid bucket of doorkn[...]

"All threats to Garathani citizens result i[...]
confinement until Council security convenes an in[...]

"And how long will that be?"

"Unable to estimate."

"Well, hell." Monica gave one last growl of fru[...]
rubbing her forehead, which was still buzzing. No do[...]
hair looked even more special now. The bubble envelope[...]
completely. Not even the floor was visible beneath her[...]
which made her leery of sitting down. That was all she nee[...]
now—a mega-jolt to the ass. Thank God she'd dressed, bo[...]
and all, before pitching her fit. Sighing, she braced her fe[...]
apart and crossed her arms, prepared for a long wait. Kelle[...]
had to come back sooner or later.

*I'll have to be more careful to look for a submissive nature in my
next second.*

The man had no idea what kind of hell she wanted to put
him through for uttering those words. And that was nothing
compared to what she wanted to do to him for flaring out
before she could squeeze a single syllable from her frozen
vocal cords. *His next second, my ass!* Who the hell did he think
he was?

The field dissolved to reveal Minister Cecine, minus the
ceremonial robes. His stance mirrored hers.

"So you're the level four threat to our commander's
security?" Though he cocked an eyebrow, his expression was
forbidding.

"You'd better believe it." Monica scowled back. "And if you want to keep him alive, Sir, you'd better let me off this interstellar pimpmobile. *Now.*"

"That would be most unwise, daughter."

"Tough shit! I'm ready to be out of here." Then her eyes narrowed. "And don't you *daughter* me. You let them do this to me!"

"Do what to you?" He looked incredulous.

"Let them…" *Fuck me*? No way could she say that to him. "Let them…"

What could she point to? What *had* they done to her, after all, that she hadn't ultimately enjoyed? Except *this*, opened up this yawning chasm in her chest that she feared would never be filled again. "They made me—" Tears clogged her throat and she had to turn away before she broke down in front of him.

They made me love them, and it hurts so damn bad!

"They hurt me!" she finally managed to croak.

"I find that difficult to believe." He didn't sound so cocky now and Monica whirled to face him, let him see the tears streaming down her cheeks.

"Well, believe it." Her voice was unsteady and Cecine frowned.

"Daughter…" He took a step toward her and she backed up.

"My name is Monica."

Cecine held out his long hands in a gesture of supplication. "Monica, there is only one reason I can think of that Kellen and Shauss might have…acted in a manner you would consider distasteful. I'm certain they didn't intend to hurt you."

Her head tilted as she looked at him. What in the hell was he talking about? "I'm listening," she said brusquely.

"Will you sit?"

Since he'd phrased it as a question, she dropped into a chair and waited. She almost winced when he settled into her spanking chair.

"Has Kellen revealed anything of our pre-attack culture?"

"No. Was he supposed to?"

"No, he wasn't. Not until we leave Earth's orbit."

"Well, he's been a good little soldier, then."

His eyes narrowed at the sarcasm, but he let it pass. "Yes, he has, and probably much to his own detriment. Perhaps if you'd realized the kind of treatment he and Shauss received at the hands of our females, you might have been more receptive to their...demands."

Demands. Oh yeah, they'd made plenty of those, and she'd been way more than receptive.

"Treatment?" The word suddenly caught up with Monica and fear bubbled within her. "What kind of *treatment* are you talking about?"

"Our pre-attack society was matriarchal, Monica. Females ruled with iron fists and they used sex as a weapon to control their mates, indeed, all the males within the society. As if they needed another weapon," he added wearily.

Shock rippled through her, and disbelief along with it. Kellen and Shauss, ruled by females? The idea was almost ludicrous. She'd never known two males more alpha by nature.

Our females could, and quite often did, pleasure themselves and each other while we waited on them for relief... Kellen's words suddenly held ominous new meaning.

"I see you grasp the import of this truth, my dear," her father said. "And before you begin your diatribe about females being just as qualified to reign as males, let me assure you that our society functioned well for nearly a thousand years as a matriarchy. It wasn't until our leaders began taking their power for granted, and then abusing it more with each passing year, that the situation became untenable. Rebellion among the

"No. He won't agree, but I don't see how I can ever…" he couldn't finish, just sat there shaking her head while her heart crumbled into dust.

"Well, I suppose there's nothing I can do but set aside your bond," he said heavily. "I hope you'll still accompany us?"

"Of course." She leaned in and kissed his cheek. "I wouldn't miss it. Although I'd just as soon not run into Kellen or Shauss any more often than I have to."

"I'll see to it."

"Thank you…Father."

"Daughter." He set her down and stood. "I'd say I was happy to help you in this, but it would be a lie."

Monica cracked a small grin. "You'll get over it."

His response wiped it right off her face.

"Ah, but will you?"

* * * * *

"What do you mean, she's *gone*?"

Kellen swayed, overcome by the phenomenon Terrans called déjà vu. His voice sounded as if it came from very far away, perhaps even from some other mouth. Considering the question, he could only hope it did.

"I annulled my daughter's bond with you and Lieutenant Shauss," the minister repeated. He stood at the view field in one of the Council's conference chambers, staring down at the darkened surface with his arms crossed over his chest. "She was transported back to the compound an hour ago."

Kellen's ears were ringing now, and he wondered if he were about to have some sort of brain attack. *Monica is no longer my mate.* His mouth opened, working silently for several seconds before his vocal cords finally engaged. "I realize that Shauss wanted out of the bond. I've been trying to convince

males was growing, although to voice opposition to female leadership was to take one's life into one's own hands. Despite the fact that they relied on males to protect and serve them, the punishments they meted out for infractions of both recorded law and household rules were swift and severe."

Monica's head was spinning. "You've got to be kidding me."

"Hardly. If it had become known that I…" Cecine grinned ruefully. "Let me put it this way—I would have been executed if word of my liaison with your mother had reached Garathan."

Executed?

"And although our brief time together was more than worth dying for, your mother would probably have suffered the same fate if I'd tried to see her again. My mate still lived then, and while she no longer had any use for me in her bed, she would not have stood for my finding relief elsewhere. Vindictive doesn't begin to cover the nature of some of the females of that era. If I had known conception was possible…" He sighed and shook his head. "I would still have had to stay away, for your protection as well."

"You loved her."

"Yes, I did. Cecilia was lovely and kind and so very giving." He cleared his throat. "Of course, since I'd told her I could never return, I expected—hoped, even—to find her happily mated to another. Hearing of her death was painful."

"She named me after you, didn't she? Monica Sessienne. My grandparents pronounced it Sess-ee-EN."

His smile was nostalgic. "Obviously spelling didn't make our very short list of must-dos. She was amazing." He sobered. "As are you, daughter. Monica. You please me greatly."

There was no holding back the tears this time. Her face crumpled at his words, but she couldn't stop looking at him. "I do?" she choked out.

"You do. Like nothing else ever has."

"But you don't even know me."

"Oh, but I do. I've been watching you closely since the day Kellen claimed you."

"Oh yeah? How? I never saw you."

He smiled mysteriously. "We have our ways. There is much to love about you, Monica, but it's your compassionate heart that pleases me most. That and your courage." She had to look away at that. If only he knew. "You've spent your life turning adversity into opportunity, and despite being abandoned, you have devoted yourself to protecting and caring for others. These are the marks of a true leader."

Her nose prickled as tears threatened again and she sniffed. God, he made her sound like Gandhi, but she felt more like a snot-nosed kid. Where was a tissue when you needed one?

"I regret that you knew so little of love in your growing years, my child. May I?" He held out his arms and she hesitated only an instant before launching herself into them. Her father held her tightly while she cried, and the joy of it, chafing roughly against the pain of giving up Kellen and Shauss, only made her cry harder. *Oh, Kellen!*

"Kellen is a good man, Monica, wise and very controlled." He pulled back slightly and looked at her. "I selected him to administer Narthan's punishment because I knew I could trust him to exercise restraint in targeting only specified areas for destruction."

Monica's brow furrowed as she wiped her eyes with her fingers. "I thought he just toasted the whole planet."

"It suits our purposes for Terrans to believe that." He smiled grimly. "No, we sent out a planetary bulletin five days beforehand to allow for the evacuation of Narthan's three largest cities, as well as all their military installations and long-range spacecraft, before we destroyed them. We wanted to forestall any future attempts to finish us off."

Wow. Now she felt pretty smart for not bein[g] think of Kellen as a mass murderer.

"Part of the reason for our leniency—"

That was leniency?

"Was the suspicion that seditious Garathani male have been instrumental in delivering the virus."

"Holy shit, you've got to be kidding me! They wipe out half of their own population?"

"It's never been proven, but we haven't come up w[ith] other explanation for the simultaneous appearance of th[e] in eighteen of our major population centers."

"That's just heinous," Monica murmured.

"Indeed. But the point I'm making is that there is no trust more than Kellen. And Shauss is one of his most tr[usted] men." It dawned on Monica that she was still sitting on father's lap. Self-conscious, she tried to move away, bu[t] held her fast. "Will you tell me how they have hurt y[ou] Perhaps we could sort all this—"

"Minister..." His look said he would have preferre[d] different title, but she plowed ahead, "This isn't someth[ing] that can be sorted out. Honestly. Shauss himself has alrea[dy] decided to annul the bond."

Cecine practically dumped her onto the floor in h[is] surprise. He grabbed her hands just before her butt hit th[e] floor and hauled her back up. "You must be mistaken."

"I'm not. Ask him."

Monica waited, her heart in her throat, while he lost focus, concentrating on whatever was going on in his head. His frown told her Shauss was making it official, and it was all she could do not to break into fresh sobs. *Shauss!*

"I see." He looked at her intently. "And there's no way the bond with Kellen can be salvaged? Shall I contact him, as well?"

him to give it time. But may I ask why you..." He choked on the words.

"She wasn't happy with you."

"Wasn't..." Now he knew he was having a brain attack. Little starbursts of light were exploding at the edges of his vision and he was having difficulty drawing air into his lungs. He blinked to try to clear his sight, but the flashes remained and the ringing in his ears got worse. His stomach was pitching wildly, and for a second he flashed back to the moment when an inertial dampener had failed during his takeoff in one of the surface pods. This was exactly the same sickening sensation—twenty gs and a hefty dose of panic.

"Of course she was happy!" he declared unevenly, trying to get his bodily responses under control.

Cecine turned to him then.

"So tell me, Commander. If she was so happy, why was she crying in my arms as if her heart was breaking?"

"What did you say to her?" Kellen demanded.

"I?" Cecine looked affronted. "She said *you'd* hurt her."

"Hurt her!" His heart pounded. "On my oath, Minister, I would never hurt any female, much less one I—" Oh merciful Peserin, he'd fallen in love with her. Terrifyingly, painfully in love. With Monica, his little Terran—who was no longer his.

"One you...?"

Kellen blinked. "One I adore so completely," he said hoarsely. "I must speak with her, find out why she's done this."

"Ah, Kellen." Cecine shook his head. "As much as this grieves me, I must forbid it."

"No! Minister, I beg of you, please do not do this."

"I cannot do otherwise. She is my daughter." He turned back to the window. "I've already contacted marital liaisons on Garathan and arranged for your bond with a full-blood

Garathani maiden who will come of age in two point two years. I know this is poor compensation for your loss—"

"Compensation!" Kellen shouted. "I don't want compensation. I want Monica."

"Control yourself, Commander, or you will be relieved of duty until such time as you are able to."

Kellen automatically assumed a respectful posture, stiff and cold, and gave a short nod. Then he turned on his heel and left without another word.

Chapter Seventeen

֍

Standing in the darkness backstage, Monica wiped her clammy palms on her lab coat and drew a couple of deep, cleansing breaths. Jesus, she hadn't had stage fright like this since she played a little old lady in the second-grade pageant. Back then, the shaking hands and quivery voice had stood her in good stead, made her super-believable when facing the evil landlord who wanted to throw her out on her ear. Now it just made her look like a super-wimp.

She *was* a super-wimp. She'd hidden out in her room for the last three days, licking her wounds and drowning her sorrows in root beer floats that Shelley brought from the snack bar twice a day. Though she couldn't really take all the blame for that—Alliance leaders had decreed that she remain out of sight until they decided how to explain her existence to the Earth's populace. But now the matter had been taken out of their hands and she was being trotted out in front of the candidates in an effort to keep any more of them from jumping ship.

Project confidence, Monica! You are now the planet's foremost authority on the Garathani—act like it!

Her father was out there right now, finally laying it all on the line for the candidates. Although over a hundred of them had already left the compound, eight hundred and twenty sat in the cavernous auditorium, stirring restlessly as Cecine did some fast talking to counteract the anti-Garathani propaganda that had flooded the nation practically overnight. Whoever was behind the media blitz had woven just enough truth into the allegations for them to be dangerously effective.

197

For about three seconds, you could have heard a pin drop. Then excited feminine chatter erupted and a lone voice yelled, "No way!"

Monica stepped up to the microphone and nodded. "Way." She held up both hands and amazingly, the chatter ceased. "I stood up here just a couple of weeks ago and fumbled my way through the orientation, remember? Everyone called me Dr. Gothchild because of the hair and makeup and piercings? Well, I looked that way because I hadn't been exposed to enough Garathani pheromones to complete my physical maturation. I felt kind of like a freak. I mean, I was kind of a freak, but I always figured I must have just been standing in the wrong line when they handed out all the fun girl parts. So I tried to cover my flaws with all the Goth stuff."

She grimaced. "If I'd realized I was actually standing in the alien love child line, I probably would have done even more to hide the real me. No matter what the reason, it's hard being so different from everyone else, especially when you're young."

Several voices called out questions, but the only one Monica heard clearly was, "How could you have changed so much so fast?"

"That happened because I was exposed to a massive dose of male pheromones at a mating demonstration. It made me grow up practically overnight, though fortunately, I don't remember most of that. I'm told it was pretty ugly. Commander Kellen..." Monica's voice broke. *Kellen.* How she missed him!

She took a steadying breath before continuing.

"Commander Kellen and a Garathani doctor named Ketrok saved my life. But your daughters won't have to go through what I did," she hurried to reassure them. "Garathani males emit a constant residual stream of pheromones, and when exposed to them on a regular basis, females mature gradually, like human females."

"So what about the rumor that you were forced to take the commander and another officer as mates?" called a cynical male voice from the back of the room. "Or are you just doing your part to perpetuate the species?"

Monica's eyes narrowed against the glare of the stage lights. "I'm not mated to the commander or any other Garathani, Dr. McKay, not that it's any of your business. But I fully expect to be some day." She cocked her head to one side. "You know, it suddenly dawns on me that Mother Nature knew what she was doing by not letting me mature earlier. The thought of being bound for life to some puny, arrogant human male when I could have had a Garathani is enough to make me gag."

Encouraged by the low hum of laughter, she picked up steam. "In fact, I'm feeling pretty damn good about this whole thing. I mean, look at me! I may not have the face of an angel, but I've got measurements that would make a supermodel green with envy. Plus, I've got a whole planet full of impossibly hot men to pick from. What's not to like about being Monica Teague? Hell, they ought to put *me* on the cover of *Cosmo*—I bet that would pull in more recruits than that old *Uncle Sam Wants You* poster ever did. Women all over America would be signing on to produce the next generation of GaraTer children."

The applause and raucous shouts and whistles filling the air made Monica laugh out loud. Then she saw a flash off to the left and turned just as Kellen strode onstage without looking at her. Frowning, her father grabbed her upper arm, looking around as if he expected trouble. She was still blinking and trying to catch her breath around the sick pounding of her heart when he shoved her against Kellen. "Go. Now."

The auditorium disappeared instantly.

* * * * *

"What in the hell is going on?"

Kellen pushed her into an armchair. They'd appeared briefly in the transport bay and were redirected immediately to a room she'd never seen before. It looked like some kind of tactical room, and it was full of Garathani soldiers. Shauss was here, too, but he didn't look at her.

Kellen moved to stand beside one of the five flare fields overlooking the planet, his expression grim. "Empran, display surveillance sequence Terra two-nine-zero-four, image speed one-tenth."

The flare fields redistributed immediately into eight separate screens and showed what looked like satellite footage of cities. A few seconds later, a tiny dot of light appeared in the center of each image and spread outward until all the screens were blanked by an eerie yellow glow. Monica's skin chilled instantly.

"Seven minutes ago, eight major military installations in the United States, China and Russia were vaporized with what appear to be abbarint devices, killing millions of Terrans, the vast majority of them males. The detonations were perfectly synchronized, with less than one microsecond between the first and last explosions."

"Oh my God." Monica blinked in horror as the images replayed. Her exclamation rang in the silence that followed, and then all the men spoke at once.

"Abbarint devices!"

"Commander, are you certain?"

"There must be some other—"

"Silence." He slammed his hands on the table and all sound ceased. "Sensors indicate high levels of abbarane in the debris clouds, and although every element of that particular molecule occurs naturally on Earth, Terran scientists are centuries away from having the technology to synthesize it."

Monica sat there blinking back tears, her brain struggling to process what she was hearing. "Are you saying—"

"Extraterrestrial weapons destroyed those cities."

"Extraterrestrial…meaning Garathani?"

Growls of outrage rolled around her, but Kellen raised a hand. "That is what someone would like Terrans to believe, and at this point, it's what they're *likely* to believe."

"But—" Monica shut her mouth. Who else could it be? "Are there any other ETs in this neck of the woods?"

"None that we're aware of, but we must assume—" His head jerked to one side as he paused. "Empran, display major network satellite feeds."

The flare fields scrambled to display the networks, which all appeared to be airing breaking news. At Kellen's command, the squares scrambled again, forming a single large field that focused on a hard-looking woman in a black overcoat and furry cap. She was standing in front of the White House.

"The video footage we're about to show you was released to several major networks by an anonymous source just moments ago," she reported, obviously excited but trying to look grave. "The footage was accompanied by detailed schematics of the weapons used in the attacks and a comprehensive chemical analysis of abbarint, the highly unstable molecule used to fuel the deadly explosions. Our experts agree that the footage of the Garathani official planting several of the devices appears to be authentic."

The view changed to a crystal-clear full-color image of a man's back. He was dressed in what looked like a Garathani uniform and standing in a large office area. Setting an oblong box about the size of a small suitcase on one of the desks, he upended a round wastebasket and stepped onto it. After looking from side to side, he reached for the box, then pushed up one of the panels in the drop ceiling and shoved the box inside. Once the panel was back in place, he righted the wastebasket and turned from the desk before flaring out.

The room was deathly silent and Monica thought she was going to puke.

"There is no word from the White House regarding—"

Kellen's voice drowned out the reporter's. "Empran, flare Ambassador Pret to tactical two at once."

Pret looked startled to appear before them and then gave a smug smile as a new flare field formed around him.

"Empran!" Kellen shouted. "Deaden all—"

The field wavered, then began to arc. Monica had just an instant to realize that all the soldiers were hitting the deck and then Shauss and Kellen were barreling into her, knocking the wind out of her as they propelled her off the seat and under the table and covered her with their bodies. Pret's scream of terror was cut short by an eerie silence.

* * * * *

Squinting against the blindingly intense light, Kellen turned his head cautiously, keeping his chest and arms curved over Monica's face. His eyes widened slightly at the massive fireball hovering in the corner of the room and then he looked away quickly. There was no heat, just roiling, billowing light. He sat up slowly, pleased to find himself whole. This was the first true test of the ship's new flare-technology containment systems, and he'd half expected to be cooked alive by the blast—right before he was sucked into oblivion by the hull breach.

"Everyone into tactical three," he barked. Shauss rolled to his feet and together they pulled Monica, gasping and coughing, into the next chamber.

"Are you all right, sweet one?" Shauss asked Monica as they guided her to a chair. When she nodded, Kellen looked him in the eye for a long moment, and Shauss finally lowered his chin in assent. Kellen nearly sagged in relief. No matter what the minister had decreed, Monica was still theirs and Shauss would kill to protect her.

When all the men had gathered around the table and the door had closed on the harsh glow, he finally spoke. "Empran, ship's status."

"Condition Baya. Blast containment systems activated, currently drawing thirty-four percent of crunite power generation. All nonessential systems deactivated."

"What the fuck happened?" Shauss demanded.

"Empran, flare event analysis. Did the ambassador's field malfunction?"

"Negative, Commander. Scans indicate a convergence reaction resulting from polarity reversal of Ambassador Pret's activator."

A harsh laugh erupted from Shauss. "Someone blew his ass up."

Commander Kellen, explain the evacuation delay, Cecine demanded.

Minister, we have a situation on board. Evacuation will recommence momentarily. He hoped.

Empran, the minister ordered, *activate anti-aircraft field over the compound.*

Unable to comply. Insufficient power.

What is your situation, Minister? Kellen asked.

The US has scrambled stealth bombers for a retaliatory strike against the compound.

"Mother of Peserin!" He jumped to his feet. "Empran, dispatch Ayerra squadron to fly defensive maneuvers over the compound. Target Terran weapons systems only."

"Affirmative."

Monica stood up, too. "Kellen, what's going on?"

"Your government is taking the bait," he bit out. "Empran, estimate time to containment burndown."

"Three days, twenty-three minutes, nine seconds, Sol time."

"Establish communications with President Landon."

"There is no response."

By all the Powers! What else could go wrong?

"How many Garathani and Terrans are left at the compound?"

"Four hundred fifteen."

He closed his eyes for an instant, then looked around.

"I require options, men. We need to gather sufficient power for three wide-array flares. Now."

"Kellen, tell me what's going on! Is my father in danger?"

Jamming his hands through his hair, he looked at her. "They're going to try to bomb the compound, and we can't use the wide-array flares to finish the evacuation or maintain a defensive shield over the compound. Containing the reaction in that flare field next door is creating a severe drain on our power and the reaction won't burn itself out fast enough for us to assist those still at the compound."

She blinked at him. "Well, can't you just...beam it out into space?"

"As our power reserves stand, we couldn't flare it far enough from the ship. We'd still have to maintain the field to prevent the explosion from breaching our hull."

"Well, fuck!"

"Empran, estimate power savings if all personnel evacuated to Tarkan sector of the ship and all life support systems were taken off-line in the remaining sectors."

"Negligible."

"Goddamn it!" Monica looked furious. "I just found my father. I'm not going to lose him now. What else can we do?"

We. His heart warmed at the sound of it.

"I'm not hearing any ideas, gentlemen."

"Shutting down all propulsion systems might provide the necessary power," one of the men suggested.

"No." Shauss leaned back against the bulkhead and crossed his arms, shaking his head. "We're orbiting too low. We couldn't get them reinitialized in time to keep from hitting the atmosphere."

"Aaargh!" Monica dropped into the chair and banged her head on the table. "Let's think outside the box here, guys—there's got to be something we can do to get rid of that fireball. Don't you have a fire extinguisher you can squirt in there? Some kind of chemical foam or something?"

Kellen slipped his fingers into the hair at her nape and clasped her warm, slender neck. "No, my love, the reaction must burn itself—" He stood up straight. "Empran, flare Doctors Ketrok and Tysan to tactical three."

Ketrok appeared at once. Tysan arrived in the next instant. "Yes, Commander?"

Kellen walked up to the door and it slid open.

"There's a flare convergence reaction contained in that field, and it's critical that we reduce it quickly. Is there any substance on this ship we can flare into the field to absorb that amount of energy? An element or a chemical compound, anything at all?"

Tysan frowned thoughtfully. "Let me return to my station and research—"

"Tysan." Shauss took a page from Monica's book, rolling his eyes and letting his head fall back against the wall repeatedly, though it made no sound because of the biologic pad. "There's no time for research."

It made no sound…

"The biologic pad. Ketrok, would the pad absorb that energy?"

"Not without killing us all first."

"No, no! If we flared masses of the pad into the field, would it consume the energy? Could we get enough *in* there to consume the energy?"

Tysan held up one hand, his gaze unfocused for a few moments, and then excitement dawned on his face.

"This might work. No matter how small a sample of the pad we inject into the reaction, it will multiply exponentially, in direct proportion to the amount of energy it consumes. But the more we inject, the faster the products of reaction will be consumed."

Then he frowned. "Although the field will expand to accommodate an almost infinite amount of matter, the same cannot be said of this ship. Except for the command center, we should evacuate this level and the levels directly above and below it, and leave all doors and tranlifts between those levels open to allow for the expansion of the solid matter. We must also recalibrate the field to allow the escape of non-lethal gases and reconfigure venting systems for their forced expulsion to equalize the air pressure or risk a hull breach—and later, decompression and recompression issues."

Kellen nodded sharply as the door slid shut beside him. "Gather your best men and make it happen with all due haste."

When the herd of men had thundered out the door, presumably to make things happen, Kellen's midnight eyes focused on her and Monica felt her breath leave her like she'd taken a punch. Looking away, she reached up to tuck her hair behind her ear and was dismayed by the fine tremor in her fingers. She couldn't see him, but she knew Shauss still stood at her back.

She was alone with them. The knowledge sent thrills of awareness skittering down her spine.

"I must confess I am of two minds at the moment, my love."

She plastered her eyes to chest and kept them there as Kellen wandered toward her. "Oh, yeah? Which two?"

"The one that wants Shauss to escort you to the safest part of the ship until—"

"No fucking way."

"—this crisis has passed." He stopped directly in front of her. When she didn't look up, his fingers curled under her chin and tugged. Her instinctive resistance made him tug harder and Monica let her eyes slide shut as he forced her face upward. His thumb brushing her lower lip drew a gasp from her. "And the one that wants to take what's mine."

He waited until she opened her eyes to promise in a grating growl, "I'm not letting you go again, Monica."

Shit! He looked absolutely ruthless and she began to shake in earnest as his expression darkened even further.

"Kellen…"

"Your father may try to strip me of my commission and exile me to the Barren Quadrant for claiming you again." His eyes dropped briefly to her breasts and the sensuality of his smile was terrifying. Heat blasted through her, soaking her panties in one clenching pass. "He may even go so far as to have me assassinated. But do not think for a moment that the prospect is enough to make me give you up before I have drawn my last breath, before my heart has ceased to pump, before the last ounce of strength has drained from my fist."

He struck with blinding speed, yanking her up out of the chair, driving his mouth onto hers. Their teeth clashed for a split second and then she opened to his tongue with a high-pitched moan. Anxiety and arousal whipped her into a frenzy as she plunged her hands into the crackling fall of his hair and used it as an anchor for scaling his body. *I want. I need. I love. I hurt.* She returned Kellen's grunt with a cry of desperation as he grabbed her ass with both hands and ground her against his bulging cock.

And then he was prying her arms from around his neck.

"No!" she sobbed. "Kellen, please!"

Another set of strong arms closed around her, swinging her up like a child as Kellen stepped back, gasping for air, his face deep red with arousal.

"I can't let the need to claim you here, now, in front of a dozen men, take precedence over your safety."

Even as her pussy clenched in reaction to his imagery, Monica's eyes widened. Sure as shit, some of the men had returned and stood at attention in a half-circle around the table. Jesus, she hadn't noticed a thing! Heat poured into her face as she hid against Shauss' chest.

A heavy hand stroked down the back of her neck. "Keep her safe, my friend."

Chapter Eighteen

ॐ

"What the fuck is taking so long?"

She paced like a caged tigress in the ship's atrium, her white athletic shoes making annoying squishing squeaks on the biologic pad. All the pacing was probably wearing a rut in it.

"Monica, it's been seventeen minutes. What's the expression? Rome wasn't built in a day?"

Sighing, she took a breather, propping her hands on her hips. Although she'd shed her lab coat, she was sticky and hot.

Shauss stood there watching her, his arms crossed and his shoulders against the wall. The sympathy in his eyes made hers prickle. "Yeah, well, they're not trying to build Rome, are they? They're trying to keep it from being blown to smither—" A sob choked her for a second and she had to swipe away a tear with the heel of her hand. "Goddamn it! Why didn't he let me stay with him?"

"Because it's hard to save the day when you're fucking the heroine's brains out?"

Her startled laugh sounded more like another sob as she started pacing again. "Some heroine I am, stuck down here with my thumb up my ass. I should be doing something to help."

"Now there's something I'd like to see."

She stopped again. "What?"

"You with your thumb up your ass. Can you reach that far down with your thumb?" His tone was casual and, as usual, his expression gave nothing away.

"Shauss…" Monica stared at him. "I don't understand you. Are you trying to piss me off or are you trying to get in my pants?"

He stared back without moving. "I've already been in your pants, sweet thing. I just thought it would be interesting to see you in such a position."

"Bullshit." She braced her fists on her hips again. "You still want to fuck me."

"Monica, with the exception of the minister, there's not a Garathani soldier in this sector who doesn't want to fuck you."

"Yeah, well, you seem to be the only one pitching a tent in his uniform at the moment."

A tic appeared in his jaw. "Do not pick a fight with me. Drop it. Now."

"*Do not pick a fight with me*," she mimicked. His growl of annoyance made her laugh. "You started this, Shauss. What I want to know is *why*? If you're trying to distract me from Kellen and the big bang up there, you could have picked a hell of a lot better way to go about it."

Looking away, he said stiffly, "I apologize. Now drop this before you piss me off."

"Before *I* piss *you* off?" Her eyes bugged. "Shauss, I'm not the one who kicked you to the curb without so much as asking what you wanted, without giving you a chance to make things work. *You* left *me*, remember?"

Finally looking at her again, he opened his mouth.

"I'm not done yet," she barked, getting right in his face. "I'm not the one who acted like you weren't even worth the five minutes it would have taken to talk things out, and you know what, Shauss? That really pissed me off, because I *am* worth it, goddamn it!"

"I know you—"

"Still talking here!"

He narrowed his eyes but shut his mouth.

"Now, I don't have any idea why you wound up as my secondary mate when you obviously feel the need to be primary—is it your rank or your social status? I just don't know, and whatever it is, it's apparently not anything I can change. But the fact that you could bug out so easily over a misunderstanding really made me feel like shit. I was already feeling kind of like a booby prize..." Tears clogged her throat and she had to swallow before going on. "And like a total idiot because I'd managed to fall in love and it turned out you guys only wanted me because I was my father's daughter."

Jaw set, Shauss grabbed her and pulled her face against his chest, squeezing the back of her neck. "I'm sorry," he said roughly. "You must know that's not true, sweet one. I have...very intense feelings for you that have nothing to do with your bloodline."

"Then why? Why didn't you even *try*?"

"Monica..." His chin moved against her hair. "You love Kellen."

Monica drew back. "So? I love you, too, and I can't stand for things to be like this between us."

He smiled grimly. "You love me, *too*. I'm an afterthought, Monica." She opened her mouth to deny it, but he squeezed her tight. "It's Kellen who holds pride of place in your heart, Kellen whose name makes your pulse race, Kellen you would probably die for, and that's as it should be, since he feels the same for you. Now that I've seen it, I'm just not capable of settling for anything less than what he has with you."

Her eyes widened as she waited, letting his words sink in, and he shook his head, frowning. "Don't start feeling guilty for loving him more than you love me. That's not the only issue I'm dealing with here. Since coming to Earth, I've discovered certain things about myself that..." He bit his lip.

"What?"

His naughty grin took her by surprise. "Surely you've noticed I make...unusual demands."

Monica blinked. "And Kellen doesn't? Oh, you mean—" The burn started in her cheeks and she pulled out of his embrace, crossing her arms over her chest. Shit, just the thought of what he'd tried to do to her was enough to send her blood pressure skyrocketing. What it did between her legs didn't bear thinking about.

Swallowing hard, she forged ahead, "Well, if you'd waited around long enough for me to get that gag off, I'd have told you to go find some lubricant before you tried to…do that to me."

It was Shauss' turn to blink. Tipping his head to the side, he said in a disbelieving voice, "You'd have let me fuck your ass?" The words almost pulled a moan out of her. When she could only nod, he pressed on, "With my cock?"

Monica rolled her eyes. "What, do you want it notarized? Yes, Shauss, I'd have had anal sex with you—although there's no guarantee I would have liked it."

"You'd have loved it," he murmured with a grin.

"Oh, now don't start—"

An ear-piercing wail just about sent her through the roof, and a split-second later, a flash of yellow light dimmed the bank of flare fields. The shudder that rolled through the room made Monica's stomach drop sickly as all the blood rushed from her head.

"Kellen!"

* * * * *

Commander, if you're able, flare to the atrium at once. Your mate is hysterical.

Still dizzy, Kellen frowned, keeping pressure on the gash in his arm as he surveyed the trail of demolished furniture, the bulkheads and doors left scarred and misshapen by the expanding containment field. The pad had consumed the energy with explosive results, sweeping through four decks and crushing everything in its path. The mass had blasted into the command center without warning, nearly crushing him and several of his men before they could flare to safety.

Hastion, recommence surface evacuation and then recall Ayerra squadron. Notify me when all personnel are aboard. Empran, post an emergency meeting of all mission officers on transfer deck at fourteen hundred. I'll be unavailable until then.

He flared directly to the atrium, and the field had barely dissolved when Monica flew into him.

"Kellen! Oh my God, what happened?" Her arms were around his neck, her wet cheek rubbing against his, and her legs were around his waist. "I thought you were dead!" she sobbed.

He blinked, sliding his hands down over her ass and letting his fingers meet over the damp seam between her thighs. "You found the idea arousing?"

She leaned back and smacked his shoulder, glaring at him through her tears. "No, you moron! I was terrified."

"She was just winding up to give me a tongue-lashing when the alarm sounded," Shauss drawled.

"Monica, my love," Kellen murmured. "What am I going to do with you?" Her thighs wrapped around him and his fingers pressed against her fragrant heat made the answer patently obvious to his cock, but he was determined to set things right between the three of them before giving in to the desire scorching him. He released her bottom, letting her slide down to the floor, and her eyes widened as she saw him fully.

"Jesus, you're injured!" Blood was pouring freely from his wound again, dripping to the floor, and she grabbed his forearm and slapped a hand over the ragged flesh, applying considerably more pressure than he had. "What happened?"

"Our experiment was a bit more successful than we'd planned for. The pad consumed the products of reaction at such an accelerated rate, the mass tore up most of the command core before the reaction was reduced enough to flare it out."

"You flared it outside the ship?"

"Yes—you must have seen the explosion." He nodded toward the flare field.

"Yeah, well, it scared the shit out of me. I thought you'd blown yourself up." She frowned as she scanned his face. No doubt he looked battered. He'd been crushed face first into the bulkhead before his escape. "You need to get to one of the infirmaries and have this taken care of. I don't have my bag—hell, I don't even have a Band-Aid."

"Time enough for that, my love, after the evacuation is complete."

She bit her lip, looking uncertain, and all he wanted to do in that moment was kiss her.

"You keep calling me *my love*."

Brushing her bangs out of her eyes, he murmured, "Why do you suppose that is?"

Monica searched his face for a long moment. "Because you love me?"

"You don't sound very certain of it."

"You haven't said it."

"I love you."

She blinked rapidly and then a short laugh bubbled out of her. "Wow, that was pretty impassioned."

Though his heart pounded in his chest, he grinned back at her ruefully. "My self-control isn't legendary without cause."

But he pulled her to him just the same, holding her against his chest as he leaned in to claim her mouth. Their lips had barely touched when the minister spoke behind him.

"I distinctly remember forbidding you to pursue my daughter, Commander. Circumstances forced me to rely on you for her protection and now I find you assaulting her? Empran, send a security detail to escort Commander Kellen and Lieutenant Shauss to detention."

"No!" Monica's free arm went around his waist and squeezed tight. "Father, please don't send them away. This is my fault as much as anyone's."

"Then disentangle yourself from Commander Kellen and explain, daughter. It was my understanding that you wished no further contact with these two."

She stepped away from his body without letting go of his wound.

"Shauss, tear the sleeves off my lab coat, would you?"

Shrugging his confusion, Shauss obeyed, tearing both sleeves off the lab coat. Monica wiped her hands quickly on the ruined coat, then folded one of the sleeves into a rectangular pad and pressed it over the wound. Wrapping the other sleeve around his arm, she tied the pad tightly in place. "There, that ought to hold it until one of your doctors zaps it with whatever they used on Shauss when I stabbed him."

The minister crossed his arms over his chest, his robes swirling around him. "So tell me, daughter, what has caused this change of heart? You led me to believe you were afraid of both Kellen and Shauss, that they'd hurt you."

"I'm sorry. I just…" She shoved her hair back from her face with both hands, not looking at any of them. "God, it's hard to explain."

"Please try."

She sighed deeply. "I know it sounds really stupid now, but they just had so much power over me, it was…scary. And I don't mean brute strength," she added.

Her eyes finally met his and Kellen's chest squeezed tight at the tears hovering in them. "They made me feel things that I didn't want to, things that made me so damn vulnerable and helpless, and God, there's not much I hate more than feeling vulnerable and helpless. I'm supposed to be the strong one. I'm not supposed to need any—"

She spun around and walked over to the flare field, staring out at the endless night, her throat working convulsively. "It's generally been my experience that loving someone is the surest way to lose them, and I loved them so much already..." A tear trickled down her cheek and she dashed it away with the back of her hand. "And then sure enough, Shauss bailed and Kellen said something about his *next* second, and it just blew me away. I mean, what the hell was I supposed to do? I'm not a fucking computer—I can't just hit the delete button to dump my feelings for one guy and then load new feelings for the next one. I deserve better than that."

Kellen squeezed his eyes shut as regret at his own selfish carelessness washed over him. The thought of having to find another second had appalled him, but he'd had years to become accustomed to the idea of mandatory mate sharing. He hadn't even considered how she might feel about the situation.

When he looked at Monica once more, her eyes were filled with pain and longing. "You say you love me, Kellen, but what if one day you decide I'm not what you wanted after all? What if I'm too bitchy or I can't get pregnant or something and you decide to bail on me, too? Am I supposed to just let you hand me off to whoever's in the mood for a little hybrid nookie?"

Not what I wanted? His mind boggled.

"Daughter." Cecine's voice was gentle but firm. "I realize that you haven't had enough time with our people to understand the nature—"

"Minister, if I may be so bold as to interrupt."

"Yes, Commander?"

"I would like to request an emergency audience with the High Council."

The minister's head cocked to the side. "Now?"

"Yes, Minister. And I would request that all available senior officers be present."

Cecine looked at him for a long moment. "You do remember that you scheduled a meeting on transfer deck in less than an hour?"

"Yes, Minister. This will not take that long."

Sighing, the minister nodded. "Very well."

* * * * *

The Council chambers were a disappointment. She'd expected grandeur, pomp and circumstance, a red carpet at the very least, but the main room looked pretty much like every other room on the ship. Well, except for the massive silver and black mural painted on one wall, with six gold stars scattered haphazardly across it.

Kellen stood in the otherwise empty center of the chamber, his head bowed, feet apart and hands clasped behind his back as he waited. The wild tangle of hair trailing over his shoulders made her long for a brush. The shoulders themselves made her long for something else entirely.

Her father had taken his place at the center of a long curved table, sitting with four Garathani men she'd never seen before. From where she sat in the small gallery at the back, they looked old. Really old. *Dusty* old.

The main door to her right opened and Garathani officers filed in and filled every other gallery seat. The remaining officers took positions standing around the edges of the room. There had to be at least forty of them altogether.

When the door closed, her father spoke. "Commander, you have your audience. Speak."

Kellen's head went up.

"I request permission to perform the declaration ritual."

For a moment, no one said anything and Monica looked at Shauss, who sat beside her. He just shook his head as rumbles of male chatter erupted.

One of the old men leaned forward on the table, looking annoyed. "Why do you waste our time with foolishness, Comman—"

"I will decide what is a waste of time, Luide."

The old man hesitated before inclining his head. "Yes, Minister."

"Commander Kellen, you realize that you are no longer required to perform the declaration ritual as a prelude to taking a mate."

"Yes, Minister."

"Do you think your performance of this ritual will adversely affect your command?"

"No, Minister."

"Why not? There are many who might view such a gesture as a sign of weakness."

"They are welcome to challenge me in field tests, Minister. I know my own strength, and performing the declaration ritual does not change that."

Cecine watched him, nodding. "I agree. And the fact that you perform it willingly tells me your strength and wisdom have only increased with the passing years. You may proceed."

"Thank you, Minister." Kellen turned then and looked directly at her, his expression as inscrutable as ever. "Monica Teague, please come forward."

Monica started, her eyes going wide. What was he doing?

Shauss took her hand and stood, so she followed suit. Then he picked up her chair with his free hand and carried it across the floor, pulling her along with him. When he set it directly in front of her father, facing Kellen, and gestured, she sat, her heart in her throat. What in the hell was going on?

Shauss returned to his chair and the room was silent. Kellen just looked at her for a long moment, and then his eyes fell away as he balanced on one foot and pulled off his right boot.

What the fuck?

The left boot was next, and then he straightened and unwound the makeshift bandage from his arm, letting it fall to the floor. Her eyes narrowed in annoyance when a fresh trickle of blood snaked down the saturated fabric covering his forearm and dripped off his elbow as he reached for his zipper...

Her eyes jerked to his face. He was looking her right in the eye as he pulled the zipper down and peeled his uniform from his shoulders, shoving it all the way to his ankles before stepping out of it altogether. The breath froze in her throat as he resumed his earlier stance, feet planted apart, hands behind his back. She hadn't noticed anything before, but he was definitely working on an erection. All he did was stand there watching her, but his cock rose higher and higher with every pulse of blood through his body. Her blood pounded in sympathy, filling her cheeks, her breasts, the low places in her belly... She prayed all the men were too busy watching Kellen and his big bold cock to notice the arousal claiming her.

Using his uninjured arm, he grasped the swelling flesh of his scrotum, pushing it up like he had that first time in his quarters, offering it to her, and her throat went dry. She actually had to close her eyes for a second. Jesus, it was getting hard to breathe.

When she opened them again, he'd taken his cock in hand and was stroking it, squeezing it over and over like he was trying to get all the blood to the head. When it looked like it was as big as it could get, he suddenly walked forward until he stood just two or three feet in front of her and assumed his parade stance again, looking straight ahead instead of down at her.

"Daughter, you are free to inspect the commander in any manner you wish."

Monica's eyes bugged. Did he mean...

What the hell *did* he mean? With that great big gorgeous thing right in front of her face, it was hard to think about doing anything but tasting it.

Before the thought was complete, she'd scooted forward in her chair and reached out to grab his ass, pulling the head of his cock into her mouth and sucking it deep, instigating a chorus of masculine groans. She'd barely gotten a hint of his flavor when Kellen took a step back, breathing harshly and blinking repeatedly. His expression was far from neutral, but it was also far from reassuring, an odd combination of shock, arousal and consternation that made fire scorch her cheeks.

Shit. Talk about a total lack of self-control! *Cock yummy. Eat now!* No doubt she'd just committed some massive mating faux pas that would haunt her until *she* was dusty old. Biting her lips and slowly leaning back in her chair, she closed her eyes and prayed for a swift death.

A muffled snort sounded behind her, but no one said a word.

"Monica Teague, daughter of Cecine."

Steeling herself, she opened her eyes to find Kellen kneeling before her, his hands resting on his thighs, a river of blood trickling over his knee. His dark eyes were now bright with humor—in fact, there was a dimple indenting his left cheek and he looked like he was having a hell of a time not laughing out loud. She couldn't help smiling in return, her blush burning brighter than ever.

"Monica Teague," he said again, growing serious. "You are the most beautiful, most independent, most caring woman I have ever known, and I declare my humble desire to be your mate."

She put trembling fingers to her lips as joy and love and need all slammed her at once, making her face screw up against her tears as he continued, "I am fertile and have already fathered one child. I offer my skills for your pleasure in the mating chamber and my seed, if you wish it, for the planting of babes. I offer you my name, which carries some honor, and my possessions, which are many. I offer my protection, which is without equal among our men, and my fidelity, an oath that will bind me all my days. And above all these, Monica Teague, I offer you my love, which will not fade even after we are but vague memories of our children's children's children."

"Kellen," she whispered, holding out her hand. Instead of taking it, he put his hands on the floor and lowered himself until his forehead touched the biologic pad.

"I realize now, my love, that I made you feel like an object. Having experienced that sensation firsthand in my previous mating, I regret it more than you can possibly know and will do everything I can to make reparation for it." His voice was muffled by the pad. "I am unworthy of you, *sziscala*. My little fighter. But I beg you to consider restoring me as your primary mate."

Blown away, she opened her mouth but nothing came out.

"You need not answer now, daughter."

Was he kidding?

"Of course I need answer now!" She slid off her chair onto her knees and laid her hands gently on Kellen's hair, savoring the crispness of it. When he remained facedown, she grabbed two handfuls and pulled. "Please get up."

Her hands slid away as he rose slowly and looked at her, a question on his face. She leaned forward, her eyes on his, and kissed his lips softly before asking again, "Would you please get up?"

He frowned. "I am up."

She rolled her eyes.

"To your feet, Commander." He hesitated before standing, and when he got to his feet, blood hit the pad in audible splats before being absorbed like they were never there. "Goddamn it, you should have left that bandage on."

That got him smiling again.

Sinking back on her heels, she stared up at him. "Well, I'm nowhere near as poetic as you and Shauss, but here goes. I love you, too, Kellen. I think I always have. In fact, I think I must have been made for you."

"I know you were."

"Shhh—it's my turn, Commander." She laid her hands on her thighs, as he had done, only hers were relaxed, palms up. "I'm yours to do with whatever you will. I may bitch about it, but that's mostly just habit. I know you're fair and wise and determined to do what's best for everyone, including me. I'll try to be a little more agreeable in public, but I can't promise anything. I'll try to be a little more agreeable in the bedroom, too, but sometimes it's more fun to be a pill and take the punishment." She reddened as laughter rippled through the room. Kellen laughed, too, setting off explosions deep in her belly. "Jesus, I can't believe I said that. Oh well."

Then she focused on Shauss. "I love you, too, Shauss, and I wish you'd come back to us. If I have to, I'll learn to live with someone new, but I'd rather not. I know I'm not your dream girl and you're not thrilled about sharing, but if we all just talk a little more, we could probably make it work for you, at least until something better comes along."

He gave that self-deprecatory grin. "Like there's anyone who could top you, sweet one."

"Well, you never know." She craned her head around to look at her father. "We can do that, can't we? Let him go if he finds someone else? The bond doesn't have to be unbreakable, does it?"

"Not if you all agree to it."

"Kellen?" She looked up at him, pleading with her eyes, and he held out his hands and pulled her up. Then he cupped her face in his palms and leaned down slowly, oh-so slowly. He captured her bottom lip in a brief caress and then did the same to her upper lip while she sighed raggedly. When her knees began to tremble, he slid one arm around her waist and slanted his head, kissing her with all the carnal intent she'd longed for, and everyone else was forgotten.

Too soon, he raised his head and grinned at Shauss, holding her tight against him, his hard-on pressed to her belly. "Have you had enough of being alone again, Lieutenant? Think you can sacrifice a bit of your pride for the loving touch of a female?"

"If he won't, I will," someone said. A ripple of agreements followed and Monica frowned ferociously.

The two men looked at each other for a long, intense moment and she felt Kellen's cock give an interesting leap before his eyes narrowed on her. "I can live with it if she can."

Oh great. What the hell kind of deal had they worked out?

"Well, then," Shauss said, rising and crossing his arms over his chest. "It's a dirty job, but I guess somebody's got to do it."

"Hey, now." Monica let her frown deepen. "You'd better work on that attitude or there won't be any *loving touches* coming your way for a long time."

Laughter filled the chamber.

"Commander," her father interrupted. "Now that the matter has been settled to the satisfaction of all, we are due on the transfer deck. A thousand anxious Terrans await our guidance and I would rather not prolong the suspense any longer than I must."

Kellen pulled away at once and reached for his uniform.

"You will go directly to the infirmary and have that wound sealed." Kellen opened his mouth as if to argue, but her father held up that magical hand that stopped all conversation cold. "Ketrok, see that he does not leave the infirmary until he is fit for duty."

"Yes, Minister."

"Daughter, you may attend your mate."

"Yes, Father."

After Cecine had left the room and the men were piling out behind him, Kellen tugged on his boots, chuckling. "Now that wasn't so bad, was it? Showing a little respect at the right moments can have unforeseen benefits."

"Don't even talk to me until you've stopped dripping blood or you're going to macho yourself into an early grave."

"Monica, it's a flesh wound." He smiled patiently.

"Tell me that when it's developed a nasty, gangrenous infection and has to be amputated at the shoulder."

Shauss was one of the last to leave, touching his finger to his brow in a sardonic salute as he passed through the door, and a thought occurred to her.

"So what is it you can live with if I can?"

Kellen took her hand. "Walk with me to the infirmary, *sziscala*. It seems we have a few intimate details to iron out."

Chapter Nineteen

ജ

Monica lounged at the head of the bed, shivering with heat, unable to move a muscle. Although she wore a slim white nightgown, Kellen had pulled the neckline down to frame her naked breasts and posed her legs in a lewd sprawl, leaving her completely open to his view. But he didn't even look. Instead, he stripped out of his bloodstained uniform, tossing it into the corner, and dug through the cabinets while she watched. Pulling out a clean uniform, he laid it over the chair and dropped his boots into the sanitizer, then ducked into the shower without another word.

Asshole, she raged even as the fierce tingle in her bottom squeezed more slickness from her vagina. *Treat me like a piece of fucking furniture!*

That was how Shauss found her moments later, and the wicked curve of his smile sent chills down her spine.

"My, my," he drawled. "Kellen has a genuine flair for apology." He walked over and set a lumpy bag in one of the chairs and then turned. Eyes on her crotch, he asked, "Did he insert the penetab?"

An involuntary whimper broke from her as her back arched.

"Ah. Neural gag. I wondered why you were so quiet." Coming around the corner of the bed, he sat by her hip, facing her. "I'll just check…"

His right hand pushed her knee up and back even farther while the other skated down her thigh to her wide-open vulva, hesitating only a second before dipping into her moisture. Although he carefully avoided her hot points, she seized with

227

reaction anyway, and he smiled as he coated his fingers with her abundance of natural lube.

"I assume Kellen told you we'd reached an agreement," he murmured, stroking delicately around her nook, spreading her moisture, not quite making contact where she needed it so badly. "Never doubt that planting a seed in your womb would be an honor, sweet one, but if I'm not prepared to commit to this bond for life, I have no business fathering any of your children. Which is why I will spend only here," He reached up and pushed two slick fingers between her parted lips, stroking her tongue lightly. The salt tang of them made her moan.

"And, of course," his eyelids lowered when he pulled those fingers out and slid them down between her buttocks, "here." She squeaked as one of them eased inside her. "I brought lubricant, as ordered, and a few other surprises, as well."

Oh crap. Surprises were the last thing she needed right now. *Fuck me, already. I'm dying here!*

"Have all our guests settled in?"

Kellen ambled from the shower, toweling his hair, and Monica moaned with regret as Shauss withdrew from her and stood up.

"Yes, though several of them are less than thrilled with the accommodations and many are inquiring about their families. Most of the unrest quieted when the minister informed them that the compound had been obliterated. They all seemed quite relieved to hear that any family members who desired it would be flared aboard tomorrow."

"Any significant problems after I left?"

"Just one. He's spending the night in detention."

"Excellent." The towel dropped to the floor and Kellen stood there naked, fists propped on his hips, looking a lot like Tarzan. Though his cock was already standing tall, he watched her with amusement. "Your little nurse friend was surprisingly adamant about seeing her husband, so he was flared aboard this afternoon, as well. Miss King, on the other hand, had nothing to say to any of us."

Monica raised her brows. Poor Jasmine. Hadn't she been through enough already?

"I suppose I can't blame her, but she's going to have to get over her injured feelings. I suspect that life on Garathan will be a lot safer for her and for the others, at least until we have proven that we had no hand in the attacks."

This time she arched one eyebrow doubtfully.

"Yes, I know the video footage of Pret's page planting explosive devices has put our collective tit in a wringer..." She rolled her eyes at his sophomoric grin. "But we will get to the bottom of the matter eventually. Our tech science team has already determined that the images were captured by flare recording, which means that he was undoubtedly double-crossed by one or more accomplices." His expression darkened. "At least one of whom is probably aboard the *Heptoral* now. Pret was stripped to the skin before he was outfitted and placed in detention, so someone must have given him the polarized activator. Unfortunately, surveillance imaging has revealed nothing of value."

Shauss yawned. "Have you finished briefing her or shall I come back in the morning?"

Grinning once more, Kellen sat down beside her, stroking her still-sprawled thigh. *Thank God.* "I believe her briefing is complete, for the moment."

"Thank the Powers." Shauss went and picked up the lumpy bag. "I've been waiting all afternoon to try this."

"What is that?"

Kellen watched with furrowed brows as Shauss squirted clear gel all over the piece of plastic.

"It's an anal plug."

"Shauss…" He cocked his head to one side, ignoring the aroused whimper from beside him. "I thought you intended to plug that yourself."

"This will help to stretch her muscles so that she can accommodate me without too much pain." Shauss regarded him seriously. "I did take your concerns to heart, especially after she reacted with fear the last time I tried this. When she mentioned lube this afternoon, I decided it would be wise to read up and dig a little deeper into my treasure trove of Terran toys."

Kellen shook his head as Shauss crawled up between Monica's legs, holding the glistening plug high. "Sometimes I wonder about you, Lieutenant."

Shauss separated her buttocks with his fingers and carefully began pushing the plastic into Monica's anal sphincter. Her breathing grew harsh and her nipples stood at sharp attention. "One of our mission objectives was to observe and participate in as many of the Terrans' customs as we could."

Kellen laughed outright. "I doubt the Council had *this* in mind." Although if they could see this little tableau, they'd probably have it in mind quite often in the future.

"How does that feel, Monica?"

At her throaty groan, Kellen ordered the gag released. She immediately sobbed, "Oh my God, Shauss. Just put that thing away and fuck me. Please, *please*! I need to come, damn it. Now."

"So amenable tonight," Shauss murmured without looking away from his task. "Patience, sweet one."

She let out a short scream. "Goddamn it, I didn't take you guys back so you could torture me!"

"Are you certain of that?" Kellen asked, leaning over her face. "I distinctly remember you enjoying every bit of torture we administered last week."

"There we are." Shauss sat back and surveyed his handiwork with satisfaction. "We'll leave that in for a bit. Was there something you wanted to do while I wait?"

Kellen's cock jerked as the memory surfaced. "As a matter of fact... Empran, release restraints, subject Monica Teague."

Her fingers flew to the juncture of her legs and he burst out laughing as he grabbed her wrists. "Oh, no you don't."

"You bastard!" she screeched, kicking out with her feet.

"Monica, I'm doing this for your own good. The more desperate you are for release, the less likely you are to feel any pain when his cock slides up your ass."

"A likely story," she spat, glaring at him.

"All right, then." He grinned. "I'm doing this because I want you to finish what you started in the Council Chamber this afternoon and I don't intend to let you have an orgasm until you do."

She stilled instantly, blinking. "Well, you could have just said so."

"What would have been the fun of that?"

Rolling her eyes, she tugged against his hold. "So you want me to blow you, huh?"

"Sucking was more what I had in mind." When he released her, Monica sat up and then immediately shifted her weight to one side with a slight wince.

"Does that mean you want the whole nine yards?"

He looked down at her for a moment and then nodded. "The whole nine yards."

Her smile made his stomach flip. "I thought you'd never ask."

* * * * *

"You have no idea how often I have imagined this," Kellen rumbled after the two of them had arranged her to their liking, on her hands and knees and utterly naked. He stood at the side of the bed, feet braced apart, his hands caressing her shoulders while Shauss stripped and climbed up behind her. "Shauss is lucky not to be studying the mating habits of penguins on Terra's polar ice cap for the next ten years. I had intended to be the first to fuck your mouth. Fortunately for him, I could think of no suitable punishment for you, and since you were the one who instigated it, I had to let him off the hook, too."

Monica looked away, a stubborn thorn of remembered pain pricking her. "Paybacks suck, don't they?"

"Paybacks for what?"

"Nothing. It doesn't matter anyway."

"I think it does." He squatted down 'til he was eye-level with her. "Paybacks for what?"

"Kellen, it's just a stupid human girl thing, okay? Just forget it."

"No orgasm until you tell me."

She started to flop back but Shauss was there to hold her in place. Sighing, face burning, she looked down at the mattress and mumbled, "I wanted you to be my first kiss, okay? No offense, Shauss, but I just—"

"None taken." His hands smoothed over her hips. "I've always known you were his."

Kellen leaned forward and peered up into her face. "I'm sorry, my love. I had no idea a kiss would mean anything to you. Dendriin never let me near her mouth with any portion of my anatomy. Of course, I'd seen Terrans kissing, but they do it so casually, I just assumed it was…no big deal." He pulled her face to his, exploring her mouth with his tongue until she was breathless and groaning. "I wish I'd known. I enjoy kissing you."

"That's okay." She smiled. "Shauss did a bang-up job of it and I figured I owed him anyway for carving him up like a Christmas goose."

"You did, indeed," Shauss declared with a slap to her ass that stung like hell.

She ignored him. "But I didn't tell you that to guilt-trip you, Kellen—I just wanted you to understand that I know where you're coming from."

"Not quite," he said dryly. "You had your feelings hurt, whereas I was foaming at the mouth with jealousy and ready to flare Shauss to the planet's molten core."

"I appreciate your restraint," Shauss murmured, sliding a hot hand over her mons. "Weren't you about to experience her mouth for yourself?"

"Indeed I was." After one last, lingering kiss, Kellen rose once more. "And speaking of appreciation, Monica," he said, cupping her chin and smiling down at her. "Thank you for taking me into your mouth in front of my men." She groaned in embarrassment. God, was he serious? "Honestly, my love, nothing could have increased their respect for me more."

"Well, I'm glad it was good for you," she muttered, cheeks burning. "I'm never going to live that down, am I?"

Still holding her chin, he took his hardening cock in hand and brushed it against her lips. "I sincerely hope not."

* * * * *

The shaking of his thighs was almost as gratifying as the guttural moans rolling out of him one after another, almost as delicious as the taste of his pre-come on the back of her tongue. Slipping her hand down between her thighs, Monica liberally coated her fingers with her own slickness, bumping into Shauss' fingers in the process. He was too damn good at keeping her on the edge.

Scooting her knees forward slightly, she rose up, bracing her other hand on Kellen's hip, then reached between his thighs. Intolerable excitement hammered her as she spread her lube against his anus and then began working a finger into him. In a heartbeat, his hands were wound tight in her hair.

"Monica!" he wheezed, pushing hard against the back of her throat, nudging her cheek with his spur. The sensation was electrifying, but she couldn't completely suppress her gag reflex and Kellen backed off at once, squeezing out, "My apologies."

So polite.

Smiling on the inside, since her lips were too stretched to do the job, she sucked him back in, determined to swallow him down. Then her fingertip reached its destination and began a slow pulsing. Seconds later, he swelled in her mouth, growing impossibly hard, and then he was shouting out loud as he spewed in her mouth. Monica swallowed until there wasn't a drop left to get before releasing him.

Kellen fell to his knees and she collapsed onto her elbows, almost tipping face first off the bed. He was all over her before that could happen, knocking her to her side, holding her against his chest, and kissing her until little sparks of light appeared around the edges of her vision.

Monica gasped as Shauss removed the plug from her bottom and rolled her to her back.

"I can't wait any longer." He pushed her knees up and then his thighs pressed against the backs of hers. "Hold these."

Kellen took her ankles and pulled until she was practically folded in half. Eyes wide, she slapped her hands against the mattress and then grabbed the thin sheet when Shauss pushed the head of his cock into her ass with an animal grunt. He didn't stop there, just pushed and pushed, slowly, inexorably filling her. Not wanting to worry Kellen, she tried not to make too much noise, but Jesus, it was...weird. It burned... Oh God, she was stretching too far.

"Uh!" Shauss went deeper. "Oh shit. Shauss...Kellen!" Tears streaked into her temples.

"Monica?"

"I'm fine! Sorry, Kellen, I'm fine." She gulped in air as fast as she could. This was too much.

234

"Monica, look at me." Obeying blindly, she took in Shauss' concerned expression. "Do you want me to stop?"

"How much more?"

"No more. Just lie there and get used to it while I sit here and go insane."

"Okay, lying here." She closed her eyes and made a concentrated effort to relax. Now that the worst was past, she could hear both men breathing harshly. Then they leaned over at the same time, tugging at her nipples with their mouths, and she heard nothing but her own desperate screeches. Sensation was everywhere at once, slick, cool hair clutched in one hand, warm, crackling hair in the other, hot, wet suction at her breasts, strong hands sliding down her legs, over her torso...

When she opened her eyes, Kellen's nipple was right in front of her face, so she seized it, returning tug for tug, and his groan sounded in her ear. Then Shauss pushed up, bracing himself on his arms, and began to move inside her. The thick, intrusive ache made her doubt she would be able to climax, but once Kellen covered her mouth with his and let go of her ankles so that he could play in her nook with his fingers, all hell broke loose. She was too busy shrieking and shuddering to notice when Shauss' spur got in on the action, but the sudden realization that it was sliding heavily against the back of her vagina, that her every orifice was being stimulated at once, drove her right over the edge of sanity.

When she surfaced, Kellen was still plumbing her mouth and Shauss was still going strong. His hair brushing her sweat-dampened breasts as he drove in and out gave her an incredible chill and she locked her feet behind his waist, doing her best to give back thrust for thrust.

That was apparently all he needed.

"Mother of Peserin!" His shout squeezed her heart tight while the feel of his hot ejaculate rushing into her backside squeezed another squeal of delight from her throat. He collapsed onto her with a heavy groan, panting and nuzzling her throat. "Now *that* was truly inspiring."

Kellen settled on the mattress next to them. "My friend, you have no idea."

* * * * *

Her shouts had turned to hoarse squeaks by the time Kellen curled his hands under her shoulders and drove home one last time, shuddering as he came inside her again. The aftershocks were intense and Monica kept her arms wrapped tight around his shoulders, gasping against his neck until they had ceased completely.

"Wow." She relaxed into a boneless puddle on the mattress. "You guys are amazing."

Kellen rolled off to her side and propped himself on his elbow, stroking her hair away from her face. "Trust me, my love, you are the amazing one. I am humbled."

Disconcerted by his serious expression, she laughed unsteadily. "That'll be the day, right, Shauss?"

There was no answer. When she propped up on her elbow and looked around, he was nowhere in sight. "Where did he go? *When* did he go?"

"I believe he slipped out while we were experimenting with position sixty-nine."

"It's just sixty-nine, not *position* sixty-nine," she said, trying not to giggle. Then she frowned. "Well, the rat. He could have at least given me a kiss goodbye." Her eyes widened and she sat up. "Kellen, I never kissed him. Oh my God, do you think—"

"He's fine, Monica." He pulled her down until she snuggled against his chest. "Now that we both know the significance of kissing, I don't think he's inclined to kiss you anyway."

"But I love him, too, and no matter how tough he acts, he's only human. He needs kisses like everybody else."

"As you were so quick to point out once upon a time, my love, we are not, in fact, human — we are Garathani."

"I know, but —"

"For now, all Shauss needs is sex, which you freely give him. Don't push him for anything more when he can never be first in your heart." He squeezed her shoulder. "Can he?"

"You shouldn't even have to ask that." She slid her palm over his ribs, then farther down. Despite the fact that he'd come twice in the last hour or so, he stirred immediately beneath her questing hand. Smiling, she sat up and urged him onto his back for a thorough once-over, marveling at the ripples her touch provoked in his six-pack abs.

"Did she really treat you like an object?"

When he didn't answer, she took Kellen's face between her palms and kissed him gently, mouth open, inviting him in to play, and when he accepted the invitation she closed her eyes with a sigh. After a long while, after they'd gotten to know each other's mouths a whole lot better, she raised her head and draped her body completely over his, squeezing his full-blown erection between her thighs. "She was a fool."

He smiled. "Perhaps. But at least I was well cared for. I have a feeling that Shauss may not have been so fortunate. Whatever the case, he feels the need to maintain some distance, and you would be wise to respect that."

The idea that Shauss might have been seriously abused brought her every protective instinct roaring to life, but she gritted her teeth and held her tongue. The time for protecting him had long since passed. He was an adult and would have to work things out his own way.

"You're probably right," she finally said, combing her hands through his hair. "I just hope he finds someone of his own someday. He's really special and deserves the kind of happiness we've found." Then she grabbed two handfuls and tugged. "But we're going to have to do something about this *next second* thing. I don't think I'll ever be ready for that."

Kellen rolled her to her back and looked into her eyes. "Nor will I, my love, but we'll just have to wait and see what the future holds. Until then, I intend to enjoy every moment that you're mine."

The tenderness of his look made her heart beat funny, but she didn't look away. She was his. And he was hers. *Hers.* The reality still hadn't quite sunk in.

"Well, don't get too excited." She couldn't help grinning. "I won't turn into a model alien overnight. It'll probably take you years to whip me into shape."

Chest shaking with laughter, he dropped a kiss on her lips. "I look forward to it."

Why an electronic book?

We live in the Information Age—an exciting time in the history of human civilization, in which technology rules supreme and continues to progress in leaps and bounds every minute of every day. For a multitude of reasons, more and more avid literary fans are opting to purchase e-books instead of paper books. The question from those not yet initiated into the world of electronic reading is simply: *Why?*

1. *Price.* An electronic title at Ellora's Cave Publishing and Cerridwen Press runs anywhere from 40% to 75% less than the cover price of the exact same title in paperback format. Why? Basic mathematics and cost. It is less expensive to publish an e-book (no paper and printing, no warehousing and shipping) than it is to publish a paperback, so the savings are passed along to the consumer.

2. *Space.* Running out of room in your house for your books? That is one worry you will never have with electronic books. For a low one-time cost, you can purchase a handheld device specifically designed for e-reading. Many e-readers have large, convenient screens for viewing. Better yet, hundreds of titles can be stored within your new library—on a single microchip. There are a variety of e-readers from different manufacturers. You can also read e-books on your PC or laptop computer. (Please note that Ellora's Cave does not endorse any specific brands.

You can check our websites at www.ellorascave.com or www.cerridwenpress.com for information we make available to new consumers.)

3. *Mobility.* Because your new e-library consists of only a microchip within a small, easily transportable e-reader, your entire cache of books can be taken with you wherever you go.

4. *Personal Viewing Preferences.* Are the words you are currently reading too small? Too large? Too… ANNOYING? Paperback books cannot be modified according to personal preferences, but e-books can.

5. *Instant Gratification.* Is it the middle of the night and all the bookstores near you are closed? Are you tired of waiting days, sometimes weeks, for bookstores to ship the novels you bought? Ellora's Cave Publishing sells instantaneous downloads twenty-four hours a day, seven days a week, every day of the year. Our webstore is never closed. Our e-book delivery system is 100% automated, meaning your order is filled as soon as you pay for it.

Those are a few of the top reasons why electronic books are replacing paperbacks for many avid readers.

As always, Ellora's Cave and Cerridwen Press welcome your questions and comments. We invite you to email us at Comments@ellorascave.com or write to us directly at Ellora's Cave Publishing Inc., 1056 Home Avenue, Akron, OH 44310-3502.